D1197075

HAT CHECK

A Troy Bodean Tropical Thriller #1

DAVID BERENS

Get FREE Books!

As a thank you for buying this book, I'd like to invite you to join my BeachBum Brigade Reader Group. You'll be up-to-date with all the latest from David Berens and you get FREE BOOKS for joining.

To join, click TropicalThrillers.com and your free download link will be sent immediately. It will never cost you anything, ever!

For Laura, Olivia Grace, and Jacob.
Everything I do, I do it for you.

Hat Check

A TROY BODEAN TROPICAL THRILLER #1

Part I

Hat Check

"Put one person's hat on another person's head."
-Chinese Proverb

1

Non-Discretionary Spending

RICK HAIRRE HAD NOT KNOWN before today that the barrel of a gun tasted like pennies. He wasn't sure how he would have known that anyway, but he did have a distant memory of sucking on a penny trying to fake a fever back when he was a boy. He'd skipped more than a dozen days of the third grade and had, to his bewilderment, been told he would have to repeat it. That was his first duel with karma. There would be more, but tonight was likely to be the biggest.

More likely, the taste he was experiencing was the coppery tang of his own blood pooling in the crevices of his ever-swelling mouth. Though he'd held many a firearm in his day, and still kept a small Glock in his glove compartment, he had not known the butt of a gun felt so heavy and cold when used as a hammer on one's head. It hit him like a ten pound sledgehammer when his attacker had come around again, smashing it into his jaw. He guessed he would probably lose most of the teeth he'd spent so much money on veneering prior to the last election cycle, and wondered if he'd ever get a chance to see his dentist again—an odd longing—to see the dentist. He imagined grinning at Doc Sanders with a bloody jack-o'-lantern smile. "Guess I went a bit overboard on the flossing, eh doc?" He would've chuckled if he could've, but it hurt too bad to even breathe.

As the current Vice-Chairman of the 2012 Murrell's Inlet's Board of Directors, he counted his *acquisition* of funding in excess of seven million dollars for the Tourism Conservation & Wetland Education Project as his crowning achievement. It was a private deal, with several *under-the-table* understandings. All parties to the deal would remain anonymous, and a small fee of a half million dollars would be deposited directly into another account of his choosing for managing the deal with ... *discretion*.

But beyond his selfish interests, the money would provide the local community with informational pamphlets, catchy bumper stickers, kids coloring books, and rental home refrigerator magnets discussing and educating tourists about the delicate ecosystem at work in his precious inlet home. And with a few fun tidbits he'd learned about a particularly powerful and influential member of congress, he just might be able to lobby his way into some federal funds. That kind of money would not only educate the masses, but would actually go a long way into making real reforms. He could kiss these kinds of slimy deals goodbye.

Sure, it turned his stomach to know that the money was dirty. But it was a lot of money—no that wasn't quite right—it was the kind of money that rich people use to buy a new boat when they get their old one wet.

Counting the zeroes on the freshly-issued, cashier's check helped him stomach the fact the money had come from the nearby Consolidated Paper Mill. Naturally, it had come with a catch— Rick would bury any mention of the pollution a recent team of independent environmental scientists had discovered traveling—or rather gushing— downstream from the mill. A toxic mass of chemical muck that killed everything unfortunate enough to swim through it, drink from it, or even, depending on the hardiness of the creature, poison those that ignorantly waded through it. He mentally snapped his fingers. He had meant to call on the Baker family this week to see how their youngest was doing. Thirteen year old who'd trolled upstream toward the mill, no knowing anything of the rottenness of the water, had taken seriously ill. The rumor mill around town had started to give credence to the notion that the boy had suddenly developed leukemia. Rick tried to shake the notion away, but a sharp pain ran up and down his spine. He wondered if the guy had hit him so hard with the gun, he'd gotten whiplash. If the boy did turn out to have leukemia, they'd all be in court so fast, it would feel much the same. But that would never happen.

To protect the parties involved, namely Rick and the mill's owner, the money had been channeled through a governmental sounding company. The mill owner encouraged Rick to get the federal grant and sneak all of the money into the bank account together. No one would question a few extra million if the grant was large enough. With this cover story, Rick felt sure he would soon be rising above Vice-Chairman.

As the blood trickled from his nose, he vaguely wondered if the two hooded men *interrogating* him suspected that a completely untraceable cashier's check with a seven and six zeroes was tucked away in his Outback Tea Stained straw cowboy hat. Another thought occurred to him through his throbbing haze of pain; what if these two men had been sent by the mill owner to collect the check and get rid of any evidence of the deal—namely Rick. But that didn't make any sense. The deal had just been made, and everyone was happy to go along with the stipulations of said deal. Then again, what if they'd heard about the Baker boy and had begun to work their way through tying up all the loose ends.

When Rick had chosen the life of a politician, he'd been too green to know the lower tier guys in local governments made little if any in the way of salaries. Some were even volunteer posts. Most were only in it for the power. He smiled wanly at that last thought ... what power did the Vice-Chairman of the 2012 Murrell's Inlet's Board of Directors actually have? Not much. Yet, now, here he was, his bleeding cheek pressed onto the cold, hard ground, thinking he was the linchpin to this whole dirty deal. They could get the money back from Rick, settle with the Bakers, clean up the water, and everyone would forget about it, just like they had at the end of *Erin Brockovich*.

But if he hadn't been jumped by these two gun-wielding brutes, the acquisition of these funds—however ill-gotten—would've gone a long way to further his ambitions. His power and influence would grow for sure. And even if that seemed like a selfish pursuit, he'd long since grown past that. He was in it for his daughter. She was in reality, his stepdaughter, but they shared a bond that erased the fact that she was not biologically his. He thanked God he'd had the foresight to wire his half a million straight into her account. He smiled at the thought of her shock the next time she checked her balance. His heart ached at the likelihood he wouldn't be around to explain the huge addition of funds to her. She might never know that he was her secret benefactor.

The Outback Tea Stained straw cowboy hat he wore—the one sitting a few feet away from him, hidden just under a steel, folding chair—had been a gift from her long ago. It was one of those Father's Day gifts that some might have equated to a pink and purple paisley tie, or a pair of socks with fire-breathing dragons and unicorns on them. But not Rick. Even though it was somewhat out of character for a short, pudgy bald man to wear such a thing, he wore it proudly. It had, in some ways, become a part of his brand. And it helped keep his hair in place when the wind picked up off the ocean. As he struggled to maintain consciousness, he couldn't remember why he'd folded the check and slipped it into the band of his hat behind the colorful peacock feather perched there. It was one of those odd moments in which one hides the a key or an important note as a way to ensure you'll know where it is only to forget its location the next day. He'd forgone his wallet or the inside pocket of his suit jacket, and carefully folded the check in half three times and slipped it into the inner band of his hat. And there it remained.

A kick to his gut brought him back to his current, grim situation. Why was this happening? Rick retraced his steps back to the covert meeting in the back of the long, black, heavily tinted car and sorted through what he could remember of the conversation. Nothing struck him as odd or sinister —aside from the fact that he was making a deal with the devil for some serious cash. He'd climbed out of the car after shaking hands with the mill's owner and there had been smiles all around. His last text to his daughter—a newly acquired skill for him—had said he'd be stopping by for dinner. He'd planned to let her in on the secret of the rather large deposit in her bank account.

For the life of him, he couldn't figure out what had prompted his sudden kidnapping outside Lee's Inlet Kitchen and was even more unsure why they had smashed the butt of what appeared to be an AK-47 against his face and sending his beloved hat skidding across the floor. He would've handed over the check had they just asked! He'd tried to tell them that, but his efforts to speak were hampered by his crushed jaw. He tried to point toward the black chair straddling over the hat, but when he moved his arm, the bigger of the two men stomped on it as if he meant to make wine.

His dinner—Lee's homemade clam chowder—exploded violently from his stomach with the pain from the next wicked kick to his belly, and he was still retching as they hovered around him whispering to each other.

"Where is it, mate?" one of the hooded men growled in a strange accent—maybe Australian, or South African?

Rick opened his mouth to answer, but all that came out was more of his favorite from the appetizer menu at Lee's.

Apparently, that was an unacceptable answer, as the man's fist slammed into the top of Rick's head, dislodging his expensive European hairpiece.

Guaranteed to stay on in a hurricane, my ass, he thought as the toupee flopped to the ground.

His baldpate glistened brightly as warm blood began flowing down into his eyes. His thoughts began to jumble wildly through his life and he saw himself in his high school senior pictures with already thinning hair. After a few unsuccessful attempts at a comb-over, he just clipped it closer and closer to his head. By the summer of his senior year, he was a nineteen-year-old bald guy. It'd been bad enough that he was born with a build like that of Danny DeVito and not as good-looking as most of the guys he'd played with on the football team, but his last name was *Hairre*. *Hairre*, for God's sake. With a name like that, and a chance to re-invent himself upon starting college, he'd sought out remedies to his ever-expanding baldness. Since the summer between high school and his freshman year at Clemson University, he'd been a closet member of the *Hairre* Club for Men.

Before the chocolate-brown head of hair— woven strand-by-strand—had become part of him, his high-school classmates often asked if he'd shaved it because of sickness or cancer treatments; sometimes he said yes. Years later, Susan, his wife of fourteen anniversaries, had succumbed to the pancreatic version of his lie. When he visited her in the hospital, he would remove his hairpiece and be bald with her as she suffered. He wondered if his current hair-jarring episode was karma circling back around for another go at him. He prayed the Baker kid would be spared from the dreaded disease.

As the images faded from his mind, he wasn't sure if he was losing consciousness, the blood was clouding his eyes, or his thick-rimmed glasses had finally shattered away, but his vision began to swim and go dark. His head lolled down to touch his chest and he thought with sadness that he would never get the blossoming red stains out of his seersucker sport coat. God, he loved that jacket, another part of his burgeoning brand, just like Matlock.

As if he'd read Rick's mind, thug number one ripped the front of the jacket open, sending a silver button ricocheting across the floor, and shoved his hands down into the inside pockets.

"No," Rick moaned, but no one was paying him any attention anymore—just like no one paid attention to him at the city council board meetings. But all that would change when he delivered the seven million dollar check.

His view of the world was dimming rapidly when the man tore into his pants pockets, scattering the assorted contents on the concrete floor of...wherever they had taken him. A crumpled toddler photo of his now grown stepdaughter slipped out of the hooded man's grasp and hit the floor. A spatter of blood from Rick's forehead dripped down onto the picture. Everything was in slow motion now. He knew his end was near.

He wanted to cry out, *take my wallet, take my '56 Dodge Royal convertible ... take anything you want ... take the check, for God's sake, just let me live to tell my sweet girl I still love her*! But his wrecked jaw could only mumble and spew blood.

The check! In his final thoughts, he wondered how they'd missed it. His eyes flitted to the forgotten cowboy hat lazily tilting to and fro mere steps away under that black chair.

And that's when the darkness took him and ended Rick Hairre's tenure as the 2012 Vice Chairman of the Murrell's Inlet's Board of Directors.

2

Troy's Crick

TROY CLINT BODEAN stood motionless on the rickety wooden dock. The smell of low tide wafted around him like the smoke of a good cigar: saltwater, mud, fish guts, and sunscreen. He breathed it in, closing his eyes to experience it in all its low country glory.

The sun had risen slowly above him and the heat of the day was just beginning to warm his skin. He had his brand new and ridiculously expensive Loki Lightning Redfish Rod propped against his left thigh, and his right hand gently tested the silvery web of line for any sign of resistance. He dabbed a trickle of sweat from his eyes with the light blue bandana around his neck and pushed his salt-stained LSU cap back on his head. It felt a little tight on his thick, black hair that was at least two months overdue for a trim. It almost touched his sunburnt shoulders. He grinned at what his former CO might've done upon seeing such an unkempt soldier.

The two hours of near daylight had brought him absolutely nothing; not a tremble, not a bite, not even a nibble. *Damn you, Debby*, he thought while rolling a toothpick back and forth between his teeth.

The tropical storm that grew only slightly above the hurricane designation—dubbed Debby, by the World Meteorological Organization —had plowed through Northern Florida and churned up the East Coast, leaving Pawleys Island with nothing to catch but a sunburn. But no one else was out, so he thought the few fish that may have been left in the storm's wake might be hungry and food might be scarce. It was looking more and more as if he really was the only one out today ... including fish.

Hurricane Debby, he thought, was a perfect name for the storm, just like his ex-girlfriend, Debby Robinson, in Vegas. She too had crashed into (and out of) his life and left nothing but baggage and debris in her wake. *Good riddance*, he thought as he chewed a little harder on the toothpick.

Troy had seen a great many things in his life.

He'd had a relatively incident-free tour as an Apache AH-64 pilot in Afghanistan that ended abruptly with a shrapnel-ruined right ACL. Upon rehabilitation and return to the states, he'd learned his only surviving relative, his youngest brother Ryan, had been honorably discharged (reason unknown) and disappeared. Troy had been shot at all over kingdom come, took a hit to the knee that almost cost him his leg, and survived hell on earth ... only to find that he had no one to come home to—no friends, no family, no nothing.

Down and out and alone, he'd grabbed one of the few vocational opportunities offered to an injured war vet—bartending in a shady Las Vegas strip joint, The Peppermint Hippo. More than a few of his war buddies were patrons of such establishments, drinking and laughing loudly to drown out the sound of gunfire in their heads. His own tour had been short enough that he never heard those phantom screams.

After a few desperate months of searching for work, he'd taken the job of D.J./bouncer. Lucky for him, the gig included the apartment above the club that was little more than a one-room loft with a bug-ridden bed, a futon, a dorm-room refrigerator, and a hot plate. After the thumping stripper tunes finally fell quiet around five in the morning, he often ate lukewarm SpaghettiO's out of the can then slept on the futon. More than once, a strung-out stripper or two had crashed in his bed—without him. A hero's welcome indeed.

But Debby had been different, or so he thought. She wasn't called *Cinnamon* or *Candy* or *Porsche* on stage, but *Gidget* ... a name he fondly attached to the movie starring Sandra Dee. Her music had always been rather tame as well, leaning more toward Bon Jovi than Marilyn Manson.

He'd never seen her touch alcohol, or any other mind candy handed out in the alley back behind the club. She always made the customer happy without crossing whatever professional line there could be between a stripper and her mark. When she'd asked to stay with him, it'd been because her Mercedes had refused to start after her shift, and she wasn't going to let Slick Mick's Quick Towing screw it up like she'd seen done to so many abandoned cars in the club's gravel lot. Even if it was only a C-class, it deserved better than that.

He'd offered her a beer and they'd finished what was left of a *Longboard* twelve-pack by seven-thirty. They hadn't even slept when the Mercedes dealer's flatbed truck came to rescue her ride. In the glow of their buzz, she'd grabbed his cellphone and typed in her number.

"You'd look good with a beard," she'd said, and brushed her hand on his then only stubbly cheek and climbed into the tow truck sporting a pair of his gym shorts and an old LSU hoody.

When he finally worked up the nerve to call her, he hadn't known she'd stepped out on the balcony of her extravagant condo atop the MGM to take his call and set up their first date. He also hadn't known her husband had been in the living room of said condo watching the races and checking his numbers.

A couple of dates later, a sudden, unexpected, and oddly quiet, not to mention awkward meeting outside her condo's bathroom door with her *Mafioso-looking* husband, had led to an embarrassing towel-only run through the casino floor of the MGM.

Teddy (the Mafioso husband) had come to The Peppermint Hippo escorted by Vinnie and Louie—apparently, those names really *did* exist for Italian bodyguards—and politely asked him to leave Las Vegas if he knew what was good for him. Which was exactly what Troy had been planning to do anyway. His bag was already packed.

He took the 93 down to Kingman and hopped on I-40 and traveled east as far as he could hitchhike. When he got to Memphis two weeks later, he turned south on 55 and headed back home to Louisiana. He had learned to drink to pass the time during that long and crazy trip and spent the next ten alcohol-dazed years on and off shrimping boats off the coast of Louisiana. He made a lot of money and drank most of it up. Bought a boat of his own and became a bona fide businessman ... with a bona fide drinking problem. An alcohol-induced near-death experience in an overturned boat shook him out of that daze and he sold his boat. It made him enough money to set him up nicely for a while and keep him from hitchhiking to his new destination, wherever that would turn out to be.

He took the first Greyhound bus out of town and left the New Orleans Union Passenger Terminal in his rearview.

Hours later, when he stepped off the bus into the hot sun, he was in Litchfield Beach, South Carolina. He spent the last of his money on an old, dilapidated beach house on Pawleys Island, and had just enough left over to get a very nice fishing rod and reel.

Watching the lazy creek water swim past his wooden dock, he thought he'd just about seen it all. As he watched the abandoned twelve-foot aluminum Jon boat drift in, he knew he'd been wrong.

The boat itself was quite unremarkable. Hurricane Debby was probably responsible for the un-piloted craft's lonely drift down the creek. It was rusted and salty, but only looked to be four or five years old. It was bluish gray aluminum with only a trolling motor attached on the back. Behind the black identification numbers SC-1971-LD on the side, it had large, sun-peeled green letters, saying: RENT ME.

It bumped against the dock he was fishing from and he put his right foot out to push it back out into the current. Given his past with bad juju floating into his life, he was going to let this one drift into someone else's path. That's when his eye landed on the hat: a beautiful, straw cowboy hat, its owner nowhere to be seen. He looked slowly up and down the creek.

When he was certain he was alone, Troy reached down into the boat and picked up the hat. It was worn, but in good shape; no holes, pretty clean, and expensive looking. It had a brightly colored plume of some kind stuck into the band on the back. *Peacock maybe*, he thought. He sniffed the inside of the hat. *Is that ... Old Spice?* It looked well taken care of and smelled clean, so he felt assured there were no bugs in it.

He gently laid the Loki rod down on the dock, removed his ragged LSU cap, and folded it into his back pocket. The cowboy hat fit perfectly and rested neatly above his Costa Del Mar Pescador sunglasses. With his eyes so well shaded, he saw the immense shadow of what had to be a thirty-pound red drum swim out from under the dock.

That's a dang big fish, he thought as he saw it jerk his line and yank his ridiculously expensive rod and reel flying into the creek. Suddenly, the realization hit him, and he leaped into action.

"Hey," he shouted and jumped into the water after it. The silver barrel of the reel glinted and he lunged after it, but the fish had other plans and took off. Unfortunately, the line was not reeling itself out, but holding fast and dragging his beautiful Loki away from him. He cursed himself for leaving the tension so high. He half-swam, half-crawled forward in the shallow water knowing he must look like he was drowning—or attempting a very awkward butterfly stroke.

He plunged his head under and squinted into the distance as the glint of chrome winked and rushed away from him into the dark water. He planted his feet on the bottom and lunged. His bad knee caught what could only be described as a blade of rock jutting out of the creek bottom and pain knifed into his leg. He ignored what he felt sure must be another tear to his ACL, and plunged forward.

He stuck his head up, and with a gasp of air and a quick scan downstream, he again leaped toward the rapidly escaping rod and felt the end of it tickle his fingertips. But then it was gone. He lurched again, blindly flailing after it, but his bad knee jerked him back in a shock of pain. He limped to a standing position, now harder to hold with one good leg, and peered into the current. There was no sign of the fish, the rod or the reel.

"Dangit!" He slapped the surface of the water.

He lifted his leg to examine the damage to his knee ... no cuts, just a few minor abrasions. His knee was starting to turn purple, but it didn't look like he'd done anything more than bruise both it and his pride. He sat back down in the cool water; it felt good on his aching joints.

As he massaged his throbbing tendons and watched the hypnotic current drift slowly down the creek, he wondered how he was going to eat tonight. He'd spent the last of his shrimping money on the

Loki Lightning Redfish Rod—and two sixers of *Coronas*. It was a greenhorn mistake, laying down his fishing pole unsecured. His shrimp boat first mate Harley would've given him hell if he'd—

His thought was interrupted as the escaped Jon boat thumped him hard in the back of the head. He tumbled forward and swallowed what must've been at least a quart of salt water. Scrambling out of the path of the boat sent a new shock wave into his knee, and he coughed harshly, expelling the briny water. He gingerly stood up and the boat nudged him like a lost dog.

"Double dangit," he cursed as he shoved the boat past him down the creek, "stop followin' me!"

It finally drifted away but seemed to look back plaintively. Troy flipped his hand toward it like he would if it'd been a stray dog. "G'on, now, git!"

Troy waded painfully to the creek bank and began limping his way back upstream. Assessing himself, he was sure his ACL was re-torn, and an egg-sized knot had risen on the back of his head. But all in all, he was ok. He reached up to check the knot and was flabbergasted to realize the straw cowboy hat was somehow still perched on top of his head. And there it would remain.

His fingertips came away from the bump on his

head with a splotch of blood on each. Dang boat had split his skin, though probably not bad enough for stitches. *Salt water's supposed to be good for that stuff anyway*, he thought.

As he took stock, he was relieved to find his Leatherman tool still strapped to his belt and his Costas still on their croaky strap, though the LSU cap was long gone from his back pocket.

Dang, he thought, *lost my favorite hat.*

3

Spotted Dick

DEPUTY CHESNEY R. Biggins was the first on the scene after the tip had been phoned into the Garden City Police Department. His CB radio had squelched out the call, and he'd been only too happy to leave the *Keep Georgetown Beautiful* rally and head out to Midway Inlet.

"Dick, we got a hard one for ya out there!" snickered the voice from his crackly CB.

Chesney (whose middle name was Richard) was the constant butt of jokes at the Georgetown PD. His very mature colleagues had discovered that when used together, his middle name, shortened to Dick, and his last name, Biggins, were far more entertaining than any of their old fart jokes. Chesney had heard it all before ... in middle school.

"I'm on it, Todd," he replied with no hint of emotion in his voice.

"Thank you, Deputy Dick Biggins!" Todd's boisterous reply was backed by howls of laughter. Chesney reached over and turned the volume down on his radio. *Idiots*, he thought.

He already had a full front and back page of scribbled notes with key details from the tip called into the station that morning. Holding the yellow pad in his lap he reviewed the facts as he drove:

1) Two hikers—maybe joggers—had phoned in the tip at 7:02am.

2) Both are medical professionals on vacation from Tennessee.

3) Discovered dead body of a man while jogging out by Old Beach Road.

4) Body was bloated and had apparently washed up on the beach (Their medical opinion given the state of rigor was that the man had been dead less than twenty-four hours).

5) Being vacationers, they didn't recognize the discovered man.

6) Man was dressed in a light-colored suit with some stains around the chest and neck ... blood?

As Chesney read the last word, his cruiser

slammed into something and jolted him out of his thoughts.

"What in God's name!" he blurted as coffee sloshed sideways out of his thermos and burned his right hand. "Great."

It only took a second for him to register what had happened. With his eyes down, his cruiser had swerved onto the sidewalk and run into a parked ice cream truck. Several startled children were staring in wide-eyed wonder at the police car now jammed into the crumpled mess of the truck.

"You've got to be kidding me," Chesney muttered, throwing his car into park and wiping the coffee from his hands as well as he could with the yellow pad.

He sighed as he opened his door and stepped out of the cruiser. He immediately recognized the *old-timey* round ice cream truck that belonged to *old-timey* Willie.

One-eyed Willie—as the local adolescent crowd called him behind his back while making a dirty joke that they probably weren't old enough to really understand—was a bent up old black man from down in the deep south of Alabama; Chickasaw, he thought the old guy had told him once. Said he'd been the on-call cook for events at the J.C. Davis

Auditorium and the Charles E. McConnell Civic Center. Said he'd learned to make ice cream down there that *no one, not no one, could resist.*

He reminded Chesney of Dick Hallorann, the chef of the Overlook Hotel, as played by Scatman Crothers in the Stephen King movie, *The Shining.* He had that odd way of being the grandfatherly comfortable type, and creepy as hell, at the same time. He only had one eye for God's sake ...

Willie's truck was a completely round vehicle with a pointed roof that was designed to look like some sort of circus tent. Bright blue and red diamond shapes attracted children from blocks away while hidden speakers warbled out such favorites as *Pop Goes The Weasel* and *Twinkle Twinkle Little Star.*

The impact on the police car was minimal; a basketball-sized dent in the bumper was the extent of the damage. The ice cream truck, however, was not so lucky. The back end was caved in, making the formerly round truck look more like a horseshoe or a crescent moon.

Willie had apparently scrambled up on the coolers in the front of the truck to avoid the crash. He was still sitting there shaking, half in rage and half in fear, and a nutty buddy ice cream cone in one hand and an orange crush flavored push up in the other. Both were halfway melted lumps of streaming, dripping goop sliding down on Willie's recently spotless white *ice cream man* coveralls.

"My truck!" he yelled, coming to his senses. "Look whatchu gone 'n done to my truck!"

It wasn't easy to look Willie in the eye; his only good eye, anyway. The other was covered with an oddly painted patch that was supposed to look like a clown's eye. The pupil didn't quite point in the right direction, giving him not only a crazy looking eye but a lazy one as well.

"Calm down, Willie," said Chesney, who held his hands up. "Don't worry, the city will pay for the damages."

"Pay fuh the dam-a-ges?" The one-eyed ice cream man slid down off the coolers and slopped the two melted treats to the floor. "Do you know what kind a truck dis is?"

"No, sir ... I don't."

"Issa fully ree-stored Merry Mobile ice cream truck!!" He said *Merry Mobile* as one word; *murraymobeel*.

Willie lurched toward Chesney and the officer swore he could see the eye painted on the patch reddening with anger. *Creepy*, he thought and shuddered back a step.

"Look, Willie ... " he raised both hands and eased toward his own car door. "Just go down to the station and file a report. The city will make sure you're compensated for any repairs."

"Ree-pairs??" the ice cream man croaked. "Who you know dat ree-pairs nineteen-fifties ice cream trucks, huh?!?"

Chesney said nothing but inched closer to his cruiser. Willie took his *ice cream man* cap—the kind that looked like an old white sailor's cap with a black glossy patent leather bill—off his head and smacked it to the ground.

"And here it is, Satuhday ... biggest day'a da week fo an ice cream truck. Dagnabbit!"

Chesney didn't bother to reply. He quickly opened his car door, slid in, and shifted it into reverse. The metal squealed as his bumper pulled torn pieces of the ice cream truck away as he backed up. Willie screamed again as frightened children, who would surely have therapy-requiring nightmares about this day, scattered in all directions. Clumps of ice cream splattered against Chesney's back window as he pulled away.

Cruiser number 47 was back on track, heading south on Ocean Highway—though now it was dragging a sparkling piece of red, white and blue metal under its front end.

————

OCEAN BEACH ROAD ended in a mix of sand and gravel and Chesney's tires crunched as he stopped his car. A man and woman were standing beside the road. *The unlucky body discoverers*, he thought.

The man looked to be in his late fifties with sandy-brown thinning hair and was marathon-runner rail lean. He wore almost distastefully small blue running shorts and a faded brown *Life is Good* t-shirt with a picture of a jogger on the front. Chesney noted that the man's socks were pulled up high on his calves and wondered if he was aware that style had gone out with the seventies.

The woman appeared to be around the same age, but more appropriately dressed in a blue road-race t-shirt emblazoned with the bright orange words: *Knoxville Track Club Expo*. Chesney couldn't help notice that while the man's hair looked windblown and unkempt as if he'd been on a long beach run. The woman's blonde hair appeared to look the same way it might have when she first stepped out the door to go jogging. She was wringing her hands in worry and looked to be on the verge of tears.

As he approached them, the man put out his hand and opened his mouth to speak, but the woman spoke before he could say anything.

"You must be the officer we were told to wait for," she said quickly and rubbed her arms as if she were cold. "We've been waiting for over an hour and it's really starting to get windy. Well, at least it *feels* like it's windier than when we got here, don't you think so, Jack?"

"I—"

Jack had hardly opened his mouth when she interrupted and spoke—or rather tittered—rapidly and turned to back to Chesney. "But it could just be my imagination, what with all this excitement over the ... well, over the ... "

"The body, ma'am?" Chesney helped her.

Once again Jack opened his mouth, and once again she butted in. "It really took us by surprise—" she thumbed toward Jack— "and he didn't even see it. I'm the one who spotted it out here, which is really odd, considering I didn't have my glasses and my eyes, ugh, they really are getting worse. I don't know what I'll do about it ... just keep buying stronger reading glasses I suppose."

"I'm sure the nice officer doesn't want to hear about your reading glasses, Dianne" Jack said with a grunt.

"Jack and Dianne ... ?" Chesney pointed his pen back and forth from the man to the woman.

"Oh yes, Jack and Dianne Smith," the woman said, "from Knoxville, Tennessee. We've been coming to Pawleys for over twenty years now."

She considered this for a moment and launched into it again. "Gosh, almost thirty years, I guess. We used to stay at the Dolphin House on the North end of the Island, but then we moved further south to a new place. It was okay, but I didn't like the layout of that one. This year, we're staying in a beautiful place ..."

Chesney scribbled a new note on his yellow pad as she continued to ramble on:

7) Joggers are Jack and Dianne Smith

It was all but inevitable that the song lyrics entered his mind ... *somethin' somethin' somethin' bout Jack and Diane, somethin' somethin' somethin' doin' best they can.*

When Chesney looked up, he realized she was still talking about their various rental homes on Pawleys Island. Jack rolled his eyes and put his hand on her arm.

"I don't think this is what the officer wants to know."

"Well, of course, it isn't, but I was just being polite."

"It's okay, really," Chesney said and looked around them. "I'd actually like to have you show me the body."

Jack opened his mouth again, and of course, she started speaking before he could get a word out.

"Oh yes, oh yes," she said excitedly—as if about a new baby in the family or an exciting new restaurant she'd discovered—and laughed uncomfortably. "It's really incredible to find such a thing. I mean, we are medical professionals, well, he's in the NICU and I'm ... well, we have seen bodies, but ... it's not a normal thing for us to ... And naturally, that's why you drove all the way out here."

"Yes ma'am, it is." Chesney snuck a glance at Dianne's husband who said nothing but rolled his eyes yet again. He had the feeling that he'd have to wade through the woman's never-ending details for at least an hour when he might've gotten the same information (sans asides) from the man in two or three minutes.

She pointed to the other side of the road and walked toward the cruiser. As she passed by, she noticed a scrap of metal hanging beneath the front bumper and raised her eyebrows.

"Did you have an accident on the way?"

"Something like that, ma'am." Chesney tried to brush off the story casually. "A bit of a tangle with an ice cream truck."

As soon as he'd said the words, he wished he could take them back.

"Oh gosh, that reminds me of the ice cream truck we used to have in Louisville when I was a little girl," she said, off again. "It was round and had a tent on top and the man would stand in the middle. I used to sit out by the end of the driveway with a nickel ... can you believe it was only a nickel back then? But, anyway, it's true, I'd sit out there at the end of the driveway and wait on the ice cream man for hours!"

She laughed and kept telling her story, but Chesney's attention had shifted to the two bare feet sticking out of the scruffy brush.

He couldn't help hearing more lyrics in his head:

Somethin' somethin' somethin' life goes on,

long after the somethin' somethin' somethin' of living is gone.

4

Another Hat Trick

KARAH CAMPOBELLO, whose mother couldn't decide between the names Kelly and Sarah for her firstborn daughter and simply combined the two, had just finished reading page one of her new beach novel—*Ocean Blue Murder* by Carrie R. Hughes—when she heard the commotion a few docks north of her. Her head was a little fuzzy from a Drunken Jack's hangover, but she was suddenly alert with the prospect of something exciting happening today.

She was alone in a hammock and guessed the man she spotted hadn't noticed her lying there. It was something she was used to—not being noticed —but her sophomore year of college was going to change all of that, she was sure of it.

Her dad had just bought her a glittering silver

Land Rover that perfectly matched her Ray Ban Wayfarers. Surely the guys at Auburn would notice her cruising the campus in her sexy new ride ... if she went back.

She had come to Pawleys claiming to be in for the week on Spring Break visiting her cousin, Laura-Kate. But back in Auburn, her grades had been slipping and her performance on the volleyball team had been less than stellar. The partying life of a sorority debutante was taking its toll on her and as a result, both her academic and athletic scholarships were in danger of slipping away.

With school having been paid for (or so he thought), her dad had taken the money out of her college fund and bought the new Land Rover; a wonderful and terrible surprise. Karah was now in what she'd call a pickle! Without that money, her dad wouldn't be able to send her back ... but God that Land Rover was a nice ride. *Oh, well, I'll figure that out before next semester*, she thought.

She laid the open paperback book on her stomach and watched the man a few docks away.

He was a good-looking guy, maybe forty, a little lanky but in decent shape. His ruddy tan was the kind she'd seen on fisherman and construction workers. Jet-black almost shoulder length hair crept out from underneath what looked like an LSU baseball cap. His hair matched his jet-black, exquisitely manicured beard. He had sunglasses on, but she thought he must surely have blue eyes ... piercing, navy blue eyes, like the last scream of the ocean before a storm, as her beach novel might call them. She grabbed her phone to snap a pic for Instagram: #springbreak #vaca #bestever.

Karah watched intently as the scene with the boat played out. Man picks up cowboy hat out of boat, exchanges it for his own cap. *Eww, bugs*, she thinks but continues to watch. Man pushes boat away from dock, but then leaps into water for no apparent reason—she hadn't seen his rod and reel fall in—and proceeds to splash and gargle his way downstream doing ... a butterfly stroke? The noise—and the man—continued to move closer, splashing crazily down the creek.

Goosebumps formed on her sun-warmed skin as she watched. This was way more exhilarating than her novel. She bit her lip as the man finally stopped *swimming* and stood up. He rubbed his knee and peered down into the water ... looking for something, she guessed. His gaze was disappointed and never moved in her direction, though now they were only ten or fifteen feet apart from each other.

He eased back down in the water and she straightened to snap a photo with her phone. At exactly that moment a streak of silver flew toward him from behind.

She gasped but soon realized the boat had caught up with him. Thankfully, it hadn't appeared to hit him hard enough to do much real damage. Even sprawled out in the creek she could see he was more handsome at this distance than she'd realized. *This vaca is going to be amazing*, she thought. She added the #hottie #headboat and #ouch hashtags to her Instagram photo.

She almost giggled out loud when he sent the loose boat downstream, waving it off like a ... well, kinda like a stray dog. He was muttering to himself as he limped out of the water and hiked back toward his own dock. *The cowboy hat did suit him much better*, she thought.

Sitting up she watched as the boat he'd been wrestling with drifted past. She considered swimming out after it and hauling it back up to the man. *I found your boat*, she would say while batting her eyelashes furiously. But no, she had just washed her hair and didn't want to get it wet. Besides, he hadn't seemed too concerned about the drifting boat anyway.

Putting her book aside, the first page now splotched and smeared with the sweat and suntan oil from her stomach, she rose from the hammock and stretched. She thought about pulling on her gorgeous new Trina Turk cover-up pants over her bikini; it was early yet, but the summer heat was starting to creep up in the rusty, red Coca-Cola thermometer hanging on one of the gazebo posts nearby, so she left the pants folded on the hammock.

She looked back upstream and watched as the mysterious—and crazy hot—stranger limped into a beach house a few homes up from her rental. She sat down on the edge of her dock and dipped her feet into the cool water. She pulled her hair out of its ponytail and ran her fingers through it.

She would eventually have to knock on his door, of course, but she needed some excuse, a ruse to explain why she'd come calling.

"Come on, Karah," she said, and kicked her legs slowly in the water and spoke to her reflection. "What's it gonna be?" *Can I borrow a cup of sugar?* No ... that was too obvious. She needed a hook, something he'd remember. *So, I see you're a fisherman. Can you teach me to fish?* Ugh, that was awful.

As she pondered this something brushed against

her leg. She jerked her feet out of the water, expecting to see a fish or a snake ... maybe even a jellyfish. But no, it was a small lump-shaped thing, dark and purple in color. She leaned over to study it and when she was sure it wasn't alive, she reached down and picked it out of the water with two fingers.

The object quickly shed the water and she flipped it over. A smile crept onto her face.

"Sorry to bother you," she said recognizing the LSU logo," but I found your hat."

She grabbed her book and her pants and rushed inside grinning with excitement. She felt like she was *in* a beach novel!

Shower ... gonna need a shower.

5

Hairre Today, Gone Tomorrow

DEPUTY CHESNEY BIGGINS recognized the bloated face of Rick Hairre immediately. The vice-chairman —ex-vice-chairman, to be exact—was puffed up and slightly blue. His hairpiece was missing, but that wasn't a surprise. Everyone that had known Rick when he was younger knew he'd been wearing a hideous chocolate brown toupee for the last fifteen years or so.

What did take Chesney a few minutes to deal with was the fact that the man's eyelids and lips were half gone, eaten by various marine creatures. It gave him an odd look of surprise.

"Hey Sarah, I'm gonna need a wagon out here," he said into his walkie-talkie. "We're gonna need to call Winchester in on this one too."

"Winchester?" came the crackled reply at the other end. "What's up?"

Winchester Boonesborough was the local District Attorney and would surely want to be in on this ... since Rick was an elected official, however trivial his office might be.

"It's Rick Hairre," Chesney said.

"Oh." Sarah seemed at a loss for words. "I'll make the call."

"Thanks."

Rick was wearing a light blue seersucker suit that made him look like Mayor Larry Vaughn from the movie *Jaws*.

Very Martha's Vineyard, Chesney thought.

Around the collar of the suit were black-maroon stains that were probably blood. Even in his bloated, chewed-up state, he had the marks from what looked like a severe beating on his head, face and neck. Chesney was no crime scene tech, but he knew Rick had been tortured, and torture requires motivation ... usually motivation to get information.

"Oh my God!" came a shocked voice from behind him. "That poor, poor man!"

Chesney jumped and suddenly felt like a twitchy audience member who had screamed in a horror movie when a black cat jumped onto the screen. He had visions of a Zombiefied Rick Hairre sitting up and strangling him.

The sudden outburst had come from Dianne Smith, the woman who'd discovered Rick's body with her husband. Chesney stood and quickly regained his composure.

"Ma'am, sir, I have everything I need from both of you." He ushered them away from the body. "If you will, I'm gonna need you to go down to the station and fill out a statement. Just a formality, of course."

He handed a business card to Jack Smith and watched as the couple walked back to the beach. Within a few minutes the ambulance pulled up. By then, Chesney had done a full circuit around the body, careful to give it a wide berth but looking for anything unusual that might give him some clue as to the nature of the councilman's demise. So far, he'd found nothing.

Paul D'Antaglia, the township's paramedic who also served as the Medical Examiner, nodded as he stepped out of the ambulance. "Yo, Chesney. Got somethin' big, eh?"

Chesney pointed toward Rick's prone figure. Paul

snapped on his gloves and carefully knelt beside the body as his assistant (and wife) Carol stepped out of the ambulance carrying a medical kit. Paul was a native of Maine who'd married Bostonian Carol during med school, and after successful careers up north they'd semi-retired to Pawleys Island. Both were in their late fifties and had seen hundreds of crime scenes. Chesney had worked with Paul on several cases and thought the man made a great investigator. Not only was he obviously more medically savvy than a cop, but also more legally savvy than most paramedics, and more *street-savvy* than the actual Coroner. His insight was invaluable.

"Alas, poor Rick. Guess we can forgo checking for a pulse," Paul said to Carol. "Thermometer."

She handed him what Chesney thought looked like a meat thermometer with a dial on the top and a long skewer on the end. Without much ceremony, Paul plunged it into Rick's side. After a minute or so, he looked up at Chesney. "Given his state of rigor and liver temp, I'd say we're looking at forty-eight hours."

Chesney scribbled a few notes on his yellow pad. "Ideas on cause of death?"

"Well, he's got some obvious signs of animal gnawing, but I don't see any tracks to or from his body. With the bloating, I'm inclined to think he was nibbled on in the water."

"I'm sure they'll be able to see more when he's on the table, but it's obvious he was beat up pretty badly." Paul pointed toward Rick's head. "This one here looks like it could be our culprit."

At the top of the man's wispy-haired head was a deep gash. The wound was semi-circular and looked to be severe enough to crush the skull, though there was no blood. *Probably washed off in the water,* Chesney thought.

"Looks like a pistol-whip," Chesney mumbled. "Somebody beat the crap out of him, maybe beat him to death."

"Oh Jeezus, Ches. Who the hell would treat old Ricky like that?" Carol asked in a Kennedy-esque Bostonian twang.

"I have no idea." Chesney paused upon seeing a van of crime scene techs pull up and start unloading cameras and number cards and q-tips. "Hey, make sure they get everything, clothes, shoes, pocket contents, all that ... might be something there to help us find out who did this."

"We'll get you everything you need to get this bastard," Paul said and slapped Chesney on the shoulder.

For the next hour, more than two hundred HD photographs were taken of Rick's body and the surrounding area.

As the techs were snapping their last photos and cleaning up their number cards, Winchester Boonesborough pulled up in his black '89 Lincoln Towncar. He didn't get out of his vehicle, but waved Chesney over impatiently. *Oh, shit*, he thought, *not now*.

"Deputy Biggins, what have we got here?" Winchester demanded from his partially rolled down window. "Have you got this thing under control?"

He sighed heavily. He knew the D.A. wouldn't get out of the car, effectively staying as far away from the scene as he could and still be *at the scene*.

Winchester Boonesborough, the son of a billionaire lawyer from Dallas, Texas, had a reputation for taking all the credit for successful cases and denying responsibility for unsuccessful ones. He was well known for pointing fingers at the shoddy work of those at the crime scene for failures. In short, nobody liked him.

Chesney started toward the Towncar and opened his mouth, but was interrupted before he could speak.

"Hey, Ches," Paul called, saving him from a run-in with the D.A., "I found something you might want to see."

Chesney held up a finger indicating *wait just a second* to Winchester and headed back to where Paul and Carol were finally loading Rick's body for delivery to the coroner.

Paul reached into the ambulance and held up two Ziploc evidence bags.

"When we picked him up, we found his wallet beneath him. Contents seem intact but spilling out a bit ... and this thing." He held up a bag with what appeared to be a small black USB drive.

Chesney took the bags. "Thanks, Paul."

"You betcha," the paramedic said and shook hands with him. "Letcha know when we've got more for ya."

He closed the back of the ambulance and they drove away, leaving the crime scene in eerie silence.

Chesney was baffled by the USB drive. He'd have someone in the lab get all the data from that and log that into evidence later. He held up the bag with the wallet in it. Protruding out of the wallet's cash pocket, he saw a piece of paper, waterlogged and almost transparent. The ink was faint, but still legible. He held it up in the sunlight and could read most of what was printed on it.

LEE'S INLET Kitchen
  Clam Chowder Ap-Bowl $5.95
  Iced Tea $2.50
  Pch Cobbler – A la Mode $6.95

Sub $15.40
  Tax $ .93
  Amount $16.33
  Gratuity $25.00
  Total $41.33

RICK HAD SCRAWLED in what appeared to be a twenty-five-dollar tip and scribbled his name at the bottom. *Seems a bit excessive*, Chesney thought. Under the signature, it had the restaurant's address, phone number, date, time and server's name, a Georgiana S.

Ah, I see. Chesney knew Georgiana Starlington; anyone who had been to Lee's knew Georgiana. It seemed everyone in town was infatuated with the restaurant's young waitress. In a town where the female wait staff tended to be transient at best, she'd been there for quite a while now. Not one of the typical "blonde bimbo" types either; more "girl-next-door", and that was indeed rare around here.

Georgiana did have mildly curly, dirty blonde hair, but usually she had it pulled back in a messy braid or ponytail. Not too flashy, not too plain. She was probably five or six years out of college and had come to Pawleys with some kind of typical university degree that had led to ... yup, you guessed it: bartending. She was definitely a cute girl; Chesney felt his eyebrows rise. Would definitely have to question her about— His thought was interrupted by the sound of an '89 Lincoln Towncar door opening.

"Please tell me I haven't wasted two hours of my life sittin' in my car out here watchin' the Pawleys Island C.S.I. poke around," the D.A. said, his voice contentious at best, snotty at worst. "I'm leavin' today for a week in the Hamptons and I don't want to be late."

"You have anything at all for me, Deputy?" Winchester spread his ill-fitting suit jacket apart and put his hands on his expansive waistline.

Chesney opened the door to his cruiser and

without skipping a beat, reached into his shirt pocket and flipped open his sunglasses.

In his best David Caruso voice, he said, "Hairre today ... " Pausing for effect, he put his sunglasses on. "Gone tomorrow."

6

Guts for Garters

DARREN "THE BODY" McGlashen slumped down into a crusty, duct-taped recliner in the back of a dark, mostly empty storage unit in a dark, mostly empty parking lot behind a cheesy tourist trap store called Balls—as in beach balls.

He was a scrawny guy; thus, the nickname must've been one of those obvious "opposite" nicknames, like calling the biggest guy *Tiny* or calling a really slow guy *Flash*. The recliner squalled and creaked under even his emaciated frame and noticeably sagged to one side.

Another man, giant and heavily tattooed, stood by the steel door peering out into the night. He chewed nervously on a McDonald's drink straw. His arms were sleeves of skulls and flames and tribal markings ... no smiley faces or peace signs anywhere to be seen. In his back pocket, he'd stuffed two knit toboggans with eye and mouth holes roughly cut into them. Under his belt buckle, he'd stuffed a small .38 caliber pistol. The pearl handle had dark gelatinous blood in the grooves.

"Well, that didn't go well at all now, did it, mate?" Darren asked the nervous man by the door.

"Nah."

"Boss ain't gonna like it none."

"Nah."

Darren rubbed his thumbs into his temples. "Will ya shut up and lemme think, mate?"

The other man said nothing.

Darren stood up and kicked his boot against the side of the recliner. It cracked and groaned and one leg apparently rocked its last. The heavy chair lurched forward and fell on his right foot.

"Aw, shit!!" he cried.

"Will you bloody well keep it down?" the tattooed man shushed him.

"Christ, the damn things broken my toe!" Darren tugged at his ankle. "Get it off me, mate!"

The tattooed man shrugged, and mumbled, "Stupid as a two-bob watch."

He reached down and lifted the front of the recliner, and Darren shrieked.

"Shit, shit, shit, stop!"

"What the hell?"

"Put it down!!"

The big man dropped the recliner and Darren screamed again.

"If you don't shut your trap, mate, I'm gonna shut it for you!"

"Damn, it's cuttin' me, it's cuttin' me," Darren whimpered.

"Oh, for shit's sake." he spat, and grabbed the front end of the recliner and heaved it backward against the storage unit wall. The metal clang almost drowned out the sound of *The Body's* scream.

In what appeared to him as slow motion, Darren saw the chair fly up and off his foot, followed by ripped pieces of shoe and his grossly severed first three toes. Blood spurted from the stubs and he screamed again before fainting.

WHEN HE CAME TO, he was back in the recliner and the tattooed man was back at the door. He was relieved to see that the man had apparently removed what was left of his shoe and tied a makeshift tourniquet around the ball of his foot with his own sock and remnants of the duct tape from the recliner.

"Toes?" Darren croaked. "Gotta get to a hospital, mate. They can stitch 'em up good."

The huge man nodded out into the night. "Tossed 'em."

"Shit."

Darren could see the blood oozing through the sock and thought he might need to put some Neosporin or antiseptic or something on the ... wounds. He reached down and gently massaged the upper part of his foot above what was left of his toes. It ached like hell and he could feel his pulse throbbing in and out of the arch of his foot.

"They were smashed and useless anyhow."

"S'truth," Darren mumbled. "But shit, mate, shoulda at least lemme toss 'em."

"Boss ain't gonna care about them toes, he's gonna cut the rest off anyhow if we don't get that check back." The tattooed man looked back at Darren.

"You dumped him?"

Nod.

"Can't be found?"

Nod.

"Good. Then we gotta retrace our steps and find that damn check or the boss'll have our guts for garters.

Nod.

7

Geaux Tigers!

TROY WALKED INTO HIS BUNGALOW, dropped his keys and his knife onto the dining room table, and collapsed on his futon couch. His head ached and his knee was a knot of pain. He took the straw hat off his head and tossed it onto the arm of the futon. Water from his shorts dripped onto the well-worn wooden floor.

"Shit," he muttered, looking at the growing puddle of saltwater.

He limped into the bathroom and grabbed a towel. His cheekbones were a little red and the sun had given him a raccoon tan line around his Costas. He gingerly touched the bump on the back of his head, and felt a tiny gash, but no blood came off on his fingertips. So, no stitches necessary. He stripped off the khaki shorts and threw them over the shower rod to dry and wrapped a white towel around his waist.

Beer, he thought, *and a nap ... and some ice on this dang knee.* As he popped the top off a Corona, a timid knock came at his beachside door.

"Oh, for Pete's sake," he muttered, "What now?"

He tossed the cap in the sink and slid the bottle opener onto the counter. He took a long gulp and thought; *damn a lime would be terrific right now.*

He set the beer down on the dining room table next to his keys and knife and tucked the towel around his waist a little tighter. It was a dollar store towel; white, scratchy and just a bit smaller than it needed to be.

He glanced through the blinds on the door, but the sun was dazzling and he couldn't really tell who was standing there. He opened the door and suddenly realized his state of undress. Standing on his porch, mouth agape, was a young girl holding a wet LSU baseball cap—his LSU baseball cap.

She was pretty, probably college age, brown hair with a tasteful amount of auburn red highlights, big green eyes, slim, but with an athletic build. She was wearing a two-piece bikini with a coral bottom and a teal ... no, a sea foam top. Her skin was tan and slightly red as if she'd come straight from the beach, but she was dry and clean and smelled like Herbal Essence shampoo ... something with coconut in it. A sheer wrap was draped around her hips.

The girl's eyes flitted from his chest to his towel and back up to his eyes.

"Yes, can I help you, darlin'?" Troy asked.

"I um ... I ... well ... uh ... "

The girl was visibly trembling and her pupils were dilated. *Dang college girl all hopped up on pills.* He'd seen enough of that back in Vegas to know the telltale signs.

He nodded toward her hand. "My hat?"

"Uh huh," she grunted and held out the cap.

"Yeah ... cool," he said, reaching for it.

Her grip didn't quite let go when he grabbed it. His thumb briefly brushed her hand and he thought she might faint. Her eyelashes fluttered wildly and she seemed to snap out of a daze. She let go of the hat and smiled.

"You're welcome," she cooed sweetly.

All in all, quite an attractive picture; too bad she was all hopped up on some new *club candy* she'd probably picked up on South Beach.

"Well ... um ... thanks."

"You're welcome," she said in exactly the same tone she'd used before.

He shrugged his shoulders and closed the door in her face. He shook the dampness out of his LSU hat and slipped it over his drying hair. He looked back at the door. Through the blinds over the front door window he could see the girl was still standing outside. Poor thing was probably stoned out of her gourd.

He wondered idly if he should call the police, but then another thought crossed his mind; how had she known it was his hat? He replayed the morning's events and came to the conclusion that she must've seen the whole boat incident. Had she seen him steal the cowboy hat? *That settles that*, he thought, *no police*.

He squinted at the girl's blank face through the partially closed slats on his front door ... *but what if she goes to the police? And does what? Reports a stolen cowboy hat?*

He glanced over his shoulder to see the straw hat precariously balanced on one of the futon's wooden armrests. The cool ocean breeze drifting through his open windows teetered it back and forth ... beckoning him.

———

WELL that certainly didn't go anything like I had planned, thought Karah Campobello as the door politely closed in her face. She stood on his front porch in a daze.

God, he'd been so stunningly good-looking she'd frozen up when he opened the door. It was probably the fact that his tan chest was still dripping with salty water and his waist was barely wrapped in a beach towel.

He'd taken off the cowboy hat and sunglasses (and his khaki shorts) and put on a towel that exposed a fresh tan line ... and a glimpse of a script tattoo on his waist that read, *Geaux Tigers!* She'd been right; his eyes (framed by a slight raccoon tan line) were an amazingly deep ocean blue. She caught herself starting to drool and snapped out of her trance.

She tried to think of an excuse to knock and start again, but nothing came to mind.

"Dammit, Karah," she muttered, "think!"

As she stood there, she realized she could see him through the blinds on the door's square window. Suddenly, she felt very much like a Peeping Tom, or Peeping Sally, as it were. Instantly, she crouched down to hide herself from the window ... and immediately regretted it.

She wondered how many people strolling up and down the beach had witnessed her odd behavior. So, she turned toward the ocean, sat down, stretched out her legs and pretended to belong on the porch.

She cringed when she heard the door open behind her. Surprisingly, the man (now wearing the LSU cap) sat down beside her. He had his hat tipped back and his sunglasses hanging from green Vineyard Vines Croakies around his neck again. He held two open Coronas.

"Beer?" he asked and held one out for her. "I'd offer you a lime," he said with a smile, "but they went bad last week."

Karah took the beer and took a long drink. It was ice cold. A few grains of sand bit her lip in a way that made it taste like the best beer she'd ever had.

"I guess you're wondering what I'm doing sitting on your porch?"

"Yeah, somethin' like that." He sipped his beer. "Kinda strange, really."

She grimaced. "I know it's a little creepy (he nodded) but I just saw you lose your hat and it washed up to my dock and I thought it'd be a good way to get to meet you and—"

"So," he interrupted her, "you're not all jacked up on pills or speed or somethin' are ya?"

She crinkled her nose. "Huh? What? Ha! No!"

He visibly relaxed and laughed, and Karah smiled her best million-megawatt smile. "I guess I did sound a little crazy, huh?"

"That ya did, that ya did."

She slapped her hand to her forehead and laughed. "Ugh ... I'm sorry."

"Next time," he said, flashing his own Tom Cruise-esque grin, "just knock on my door."

They sat in silence for a moment with the waning sunlight and the briny breeze blowing across the porch.

"Troy," he said simply and held out his palm.

"Karah," she said shaking his hand.

"Nice to meet you, Karah." He stood up and wagged his empty beer bottle. "Another?"

She nodded and handed him her dead soldier.

"Cool." He tilted his head upward. "Let's have these on the roof and catch a killer sunset."

Now this, she thought, *is a little more like it.*

8

Georgiana On My Mind

GEORGIANA STARLINGTON WAS MORE than a little tired when she walked into Lee's Inlet Kitchen this morning. It'd been a long night of bartending at Drunken Jack's and after work she'd been coerced into having a few more fruity-umbrella drinks with her cousin.

"Just one more!" her college aged cousin had yelled. "Woooohooooo!!"

And *one more* had inevitably turned into four— or maybe it'd been five more—before they crashed for the night.

The breakfast crowd was shuffling in, booths and tables filling with old salty dog fisherman types getting ready to hit the sea up for its daily bounty. Some smoked while they ate and Georgiana thought hazily that she might've even smoked a cigarette last night.

She shook her head to clear the cobwebs. *Not as young as you used to be, girl*, she thought.

She dropped her things into a locker in the back, pulled on her apron, grabbed two plates and hurried out to the dining room.

As she put the breakfast specials in front of two white-haired men, she found her smile and tried to brighten her voice to match. "Good morning, boys," she said and winked at one of them. Neither replied, and just nodded thanks and started to eat.

Yikes, she thought, *I must look worse than I thought*. The two men, who she knew as Whitey and Felton, were usually quite chatty. Whitey just stared at his newspaper and Felton smiled a little, but she could see it was just to be polite.

She was about to ask what was wrong, but as she did the bell on the front screen door dinged and a police officer walked in ... they often ate here before their morning shifts.

Grabbing a menu, she ushered the officer toward a seat at the bar. As he sat, Martha, behind the counter, shoved a cup of steaming black coffee in front of him.

'I—" he started, but Martha interrupted.

"Two plates up, Laura-honey."

"Martha!" Georgiana snapped back at the older lady behind the bar. "Who's going to get the plates?"

Martha silently mouthed the word *sorry* and spoke louder. "Two plates up, GEORGIANA."

"Yes, ma'am," she said and headed back to the kitchen.

Georgiana Starlington was actually not her real name. After years of experience with stalkers and crazy guys, she'd learned never to use her real name when she was serving, daytime or night. Laura-Kate was the name given by her mother when she was born, but there were very few people who knew her by that name.

She'd chosen Georgiana to remind her of the last few years she spent with her mom in the Tanner Hospital in Carrollton, Georgia before the cancer took her away. After she graduated from the University of West Georgia with a bachelor's in Environmental Science, she packed a suitcase with her most prized possessions (some clothes and a couple of books) and drove east, all the way to the coast. She'd thought finding work in her field would be an easy thing to do, given the current administration's fervor over the environment, but apparently, everyone else had thought that too. So, bartending and serving paid the bills ... for now.

It was a crazy morning at the Inlet Kitchen that never let up. Through lunch until two-thirty, Georgiana never got a break and never had anything to eat herself. Her hangover had become a throbbing headache, and threatened to sideline her for her dinner shift and late night bartending at Drunken Jack's if she didn't get something in her stomach. She pulled her apron off, put in an order for some clam chowder, and poured herself a sweet iced tea.

She slid into a seat at the bar next to the police officer that had come in earlier.

"You still here?" she asked, smiling.

"Ha, no, made a couple of stops and came back," he said and smiled over his own iced tea. "I actually didn't come in for breakfast earlier. I came to see you."

Georgiana's mind raced. What had happened last night? *Oh God, did we drive? No, we took a cab, I remember that much ... What could it be?*

He must've seen the trepidation leap into her face, because he immediately held up his hands, and said, "You haven't done anything wrong, miss. I just needed to talk with you about something."

Her mind leaped to another unacceptable

conclusion; *oh geez*, he was here to ask her out.

"Look, Officer ... ?"

"Biggins."

"Officer Biggins, I'm flattered. I truly am, but I'm really ... unavailable at the moment." She couldn't remember how many times she'd waved off potential suitors and wannabe daters at the bar with one line or another like this.

He picked up his napkin and wiped his smiling mouth. She was having trouble reading this guy.

"No ma'am." He blushed. "I'm not here to ... well, never mind that. I'm here because we've had a piece of evidence come up in a case that ... "

He paused and stepped off his barstool. He reached into his pocket and produced what looked like a Ziploc bag. It said EVIDENCE on the side and contained a rumpled piece of paper.

It was her turn to be a little flustered. She'd basically just accused him of hitting on her, which in his case might not have been all that bad. She guessed most people would say he was plain. He wasn't particularly tall, not ridiculously handsome, but good-looking enough. His hair was cut short, but not quite a cop *buzz* cut. He did have a nice smile though.

"Tell me what you can about this," he said,

handing it to her.

Georgiana flinched ... *Oops, was I staring*? She felt the warmth in her cheeks and hoped they weren't too red.

"It's a receipt."

"Yes, I can see that. But we found this receipt on someone that was apparently tortured ... and ultimately murdered."

"Murdered?" she asked, looking closer at the receipt.

Chesney nodded, pinching his lips together.

She checked the date and time stamp. Couple of days back, lunch rush ... her mind searched back through the faces she had seen, but there were too many such days and they all ran together.

The signature line was a scribble, no help there either. The tip line was written in a curvy scrawl too, kind of familiar, kind of like ... Georgiana felt her hands go numb.

"Twenty-five dollars," she whimpered and felt tears sting her eyes. "Oh my God."

Apparently not noticing her sudden surge of emotion, the officer said, "Yes, quite a lot, we thought, but hey, you are the town's best ... "

That was the last thing Georgiana (Laura-Kate) heard before she fainted.

9

Ev'rybody Jus' Be Cool

DARREN "THE BODY" McGlashen was sweating something fierce. He could tell his foot was swelling in his shoe, but he was afraid to unwrap the tourniquet. His tattooed accomplice, Man'ti, was driving, but the New Zealander kept trying to drive on the wrong side of the road. He'd nearly killed them both heading straight into the headlights of a UPS truck. They swerved just in time to leave a brown scrape where the driver's side mirror had once been ... not that he cared.

It was a stolen van that the previous owners had apparently *stolen* from the seventies. Bronze, with white pin striping around each and every panel, the van's look couldn't be considered complete without the airbrushed sunset on the back doors. Two crescent-moon shaped windows in each side near the back let light into a bed built for two. Orange shag carpet on the walls carried the musty odor of long past parties with beer, wine, cigarettes and cigars. Under the dash, clearly bolted on aftermarket, was an 8-track tape player, currently housing *The Best of The Doors*. Darren had insisted on fast-forwarding and flipping, fast-forwarding and flipping, again and again in an attempt to find his favorite Doors song, *Been Down So Long*. After several of Darren's failed search attempts, Man'ti grabbed the whole 8-track player, jerked it out from its loosely screwed in perch, and flung it out his window.

"What the f—" Darren cried, incredulous, but upon seeing his companion's dark eyes, he let it go.

Man'ti swerved again, jerking Darren so hard to the right he hit his head on the passenger side window.

"I dunno which is worse, mate," Darren said through his fevered haze, "the pain in m' foot, or your drivin'."

Man'ti said nothing.

A muffled ding sounded from Darren's pocket and he murmured something incoherent about a *big trouble* and flipped open his prepaid anonymous cell phone. He squinted into the blue light of the phone, trying desperately to make out the last message. He held the phone closer, then farther, then closer. The haze of pain in his head blurred the image, making it completely unreadable. Frustrated, he snapped the phone shut and shoved it back into his pocket.

"Gotta stop, mate ... " Darren's head lolled from side to side, " ... find me a chemist, mate. Amcal, Saugatuck, somethin'."

"You're delirious," Man'ti growled, "ain't none o' them places here."

Darren gritted his teeth and screeched, "DRUG STORE!! Find a damn drug store—"

His scream was abruptly interrupted when Man'ti's fist slammed into his jaw. The darkness that closed in around him was comforting. So, so comforting.

————

MAN'TI HAD HAD ENOUGH of the scrawny guy's wailin', so he knocked him out. He thought he might be right about needing meds though, so he pulled into the CVS just a few blocks away from Crazy Sam's Mini Warehouse where they'd been camped out.

He wasn't sure what to get, but he thought the Pharmacy bloke ought to be able to point him in the right direction. He parked the stolen van, but left it running. When he walked in, he could feel the stares of the workers inside, but he was used to it.

He stood almost two-hundred centimeters and weighed one-hundred-fifteen kilograms, average for most inmates at Rimutaka Prison in New Zealand, but way above average for CVS #2736 in Murrell's Inlet, South Carolina. Picture an American Football linebacker, but meaner.

The girl at the register in the front of the store just stared and pointed when he asked for the druggist. He walked slowly to the back of the store, picking up duct tape, diapers and petroleum jelly on the way.

The pharmacist's eyes went wide at the site of the hulking man at the counter. Man'ti calmly put his things down in one of the chairs near the pharmacy window, pulled the .38 from his belt, and pointed it at the man in the white coat.

"Larry," he said, finding the man's name on his CVS nametag, "I need somethin' fa pain and somethin' fa infection."

Larry didn't move. Instead, he peed. Man'ti

smacked the man on the side of his head, not to kill him, just to put him out.

He walked behind the counter and two female pharmacists cowered behind the medicine shelves. One was crying, the other was shaking and moaning.

"Ev'rybody jus' be cool," he said as tucked the gun back into his belt. "Jus' gotta get some drugs for m' friend."

Friend was a stretch, he thought, but he needed Darren alive to get what he was after.

He pointed to the pharmacist who was crying. "You, get the pain pills."

She grabbed a prescription bag from the counter and began shoveling medicines in and sobbing.

"And you," he said, turning to the pharmacist who was now rocking back and forth, but seemed to have it together somewhat, "antibodies."

"Well, what's the infection? I can't just give you anything ... "

Man'ti lurched forward, jutting his jaw an inch away from her nose. She yelped like a hurt animal.

"Toes," he growled, "ripped right awf."

She nodded and grabbed a bottle of pills. She shoved them into Man'ti's hand and sputtered, "This will help fight infection, but if there are bone splinters or jagged edges, it could become re-infected at any—"

"Got it." He grabbed the bag of pain pills and shoved the antibiotics in with them. "G'night, ladies."

He stepped over Larry, the pharmacist, and gathered his things from the chair in front of the counter. As he walked by the candy aisle, he grabbed a giant bag of orange circus peanuts, some peanut M&M's, and three bags of Haribo brand gummi bears.

It was tough to carry all that he'd picked up and things kept slipping and falling from his arms. At the front door, he dumped all his stuff into one of the shopping baskets.

"May I?" He raised his eyebrows at the girl standing at the front register. She turned and ran toward the back of the store.

"I take that as a yes."

10

#Hottie #Headboat #Ouch

TROY WOKE in the hammock hanging from the pilings under his beach house. He had come here to sleep so that Karah could have the bed to herself. She'd protested, saying that she would take the futon and he could have the bed, but the futon was *unsleepable* for more than a nap, so he'd insisted she take the bed and he would make do. And so, here he lay. He didn't mind at all, as he'd spent more than a few nights under the house in the hammock; sometimes it was planned, sometimes it was due to the fact he couldn't find his keys.

Warm air breezed over him, and he stretched. He could hear the comforting whoosh of the waves rolling in and racing out along the sand. The cowboy hat was tilted down over his eyes and sunlight peeked in through the straw.

Fighting the urge to catch another hour of shut-eye, he sat up, rolled out of the hammock and creaked his way up the back steps. He wasn't sure if it was the decades-old wood groaning, or his body protesting the beating he'd given it chasing his rod and reel down the creek yesterday.

Guessing from the tide and the hazy early sun, it must've been about nine in the morning. He thought wistfully that it would've been a perfect morning to break out his rod and catch a few dozen fish from the creek ... if some blasted fish hadn't decided to take it for a ride out to sea.

He opened the door, more than half expecting Karah to have vacated the premises (he was used to this sort of thing happening as well.) However, he was surprised to be hit by a surge of breakfast smells emanating from the kitchen. She was pushing a spatula through what appeared to be a skillet of scrambled eggs while a plate full of bacon sat nearby, dripping and drying on a paper towel. He didn't remember having bacon in the house, or eggs ... or paper towels for that matter. The smell of the food was intoxicating.

She beamed at him from behind the kitchen counter as he came in. "Coffee or juice?"

"Coffee," he said, scratching his head, "So ... where did all this—"

"Relax," she said, stopping him mid-sentence. "I needed my *venti iced chai tea with soy and espresso* from Starbucks, so I hit up the Farmer's Market on the way back."

"You needed a what?"

She laughed. It was an infectious sound.

"Never mind, silly." She grinned and handed him a large Starbuck's cup with a pink wrapper saying *Now Proudly Serving Pastries from La Boulange Bakery in San Francisco*. "I got you a white chocolate mocha. It's definitely not truck stop coffee, but I think you'll like it."

She watched and waited expectantly as he took a sip. He was pleasantly surprised. It wasn't merely good ... it was *damn* good! It wasn't really coffee in the technical sense, but more like hot chocolate, but he supposed that's what the *granolas* were serving down at Starbucks anyway. He nodded his approval and slurped more of the warm, sweet coffee-esque beverage.

"Yayyy!" She clapped her hands together and

smiled an even bigger smile. "I hope you like bacon too."

"You're kidding, right?" He slid onto a stool and pulled himself up to the bar that looked into the kitchen. "Who doesn't like bacon?"

"Good," she said, scooping some of the scrambled eggs onto a plate and piling bacon on top.

"Hats off at the breakfast table, mister," she said, filling her own plate and coming around to perch on a stool beside him. He took the hat off and flung it over to the futon.

"Better?" He grinned.

She nodded, smiling around another bite of bacon.

Apparently, she had raided his closet to find an old Pawleys Island Fourth of July t-shirt and a pair of his boxers. Suddenly, she bit her bottom lip.

"I hope it's okay I borrowed some of your clothes," she asked, and nodded to the t-shirt. "More comfy than a bikini to sleep in."

"Mi casa es tu casa." He chewed a piece of bacon and sipped more coffee.

"I can put 'em back if you want ... " She started to raise the t-shirt.

Troy could see the tan skin of her stomach

underneath and nearly choked on his bacon. "NO, no ... just keep it. Or you can bring it back later, or whatever."

She looked puzzled, but then grinned and maybe blushed a little.

"Troy!" she playfully, pushing his shoulder and raising an eyebrow. "I have my bikini on underneath!"

"Ah ... oh ... um ... " he stammered. It was his turn to blush.

She winked at him and picked up her cell phone from the counter. She tapped the screen with her thumbs in a flurry of what he thought must be a text message. Pause, set phone down, pick up phone, more tapping.

"I need to check in with my cousin in a bit anyway," she said and looked up from the screen with a tinge of worry creasing her eyes. "I've been texting her since last night, but she hasn't texted me back."

Troy caught a glimpse of the phone's screen. "Hey, what is that?"

"What is what?" she said guiltily, and thumped the phone to her chest, hiding the screen.

"Let me see it," he said and arched an eyebrow.

She sighed heavily and handed the phone to him. He slid his finger on the screen and was somewhat surprised to see an image of himself kneeling in the creek water, hands on the back of his head, silver jon boat floating past.

"You saw that?" He wasn't sure if he was *creeped* out or not.

She nodded but said nothing.

"How much did you see?"

She shrugged her shoulders. "Um ... everything?"

His eyebrow arched even further and he looked back at the screen. Under his photo were the words: *KarahC1989: #springbreak #vaca #bestever #pawleys.* Then another line: *KarahC1989: #hottie #headboat #ouch.* Apparently, a friend had seen the photo and commented as well: *LaKatLit: OMG total babe! Please tell me u talked to him!*

Troy handed the phone back to Karah and said nothing.

"I'm so sorry," she said sheepishly. "I'll delete it right now!"

He shrugged his shoulders and a smile tugged at the corner of his mouth. "Hashtag hottie, eh?"

She bit her lip again and the blush returned fiercely.

After breakfast, he made her leave the dishes for

him to do and she made him promise he'd *hang out* with her after she checked on her cousin. He wasn't sure what a college girl would think of as *hanging out*, but he presently didn't have much else to do, so he'd agreed.

11

Balancing Act

LAURA KATE STARLINGTON (known to most Pawleys patrons as Georgiana) sat in a booth at Lee's Inlet Kitchen crying, clutching the evidence bag containing Rick Hairre's last lunch receipt.

"He's my ... was my stepdad," she said and choked out a sob. "Are you sure he's ... "

Deputy Chesney Biggins sat across the booth from her. "Georgiana, I'm afraid—"

"Please, call me Laura."

He started again. "Okay, Laura, I'm afraid it's definitely him."

More tears burned her eyes.

"I found his body ... well, I found him myself," Chesney said, obviously trying to soften the blow.

"Why? I don't understand." Laura looked up at him. "Everyone loved him."

The deputy shifted nervously in his seat, erupting one of those squeaky-farty vinyl seat booth noises that would've been funny under any other circumstances but now just heightened the anxiety.

"We really don't know much yet," he said, and lifted a hand and rubbed the back of his neck. "That's why I came to you."

He shifted in his seat again. "I only thought you were the last person we could confirm to have seen him. I had no idea you were his daughter."

"Step daughter, yes," she said, "but he's the only dad I've ever known."

"So, you're a Starlington?" Chesney raised an eyebrow. "Of the Starlington Stables Starlingtons?"

Laura took a sip of coffee that had long since gone cold, but she was numb from shock anyway.

"My mother's family," she added. "Pretty distant relations though. I haven't kept up with any of them since she died."

He nodded, but didn't say anything. She knew what he was probably thinking. The Starlingtons were ridiculously rich. To *not keep up with them* would seem strange to most people. But her mother had been the black sheep of the Starlingtons, preferring a simpler life, not carrying on the family's legendary horse breeding tradition. They hadn't exiled her mother, but preference definitely went to her siblings. Laura was pretty sure she wouldn't be in the will.

An awkward silence stretched between them before Chesney spoke again. "So, how did you know it was his receipt?"

She smiled, and tears welled up in her eyes again. Wiping them away, she said, "My bank account had gotten low and I accidently bounced a check. I told Mrs. Reedy, my landlord, to hold it, but she must've forgotten."

Another sip of cold coffee. "Anyway, the bank charged me a twenty-five-dollar overdraft fee, basically putting me in the negative."

Chesney nodded, looking a little confused.

"So, dad was gonna give me the money, but I refused. Heck, I was gonna get paid in a week and I'd have it then."

A look of sudden understanding jumped into the deputy's eyes. "Ahhh, the tip. He gave you the big tip to cover it."

She nodded. He scribbled a note on a yellow

pad. Laura thought it looked as if he was trying to be discreet about being an officer and collecting clues. He kept the yellow pad on the seat beside him and only looked at it through a sideways glance. *Sweet*, she thought.

"Laura," he said and glanced up from his notes, "did Rick have any enemies?"

"God, no." She let out a sigh. "I think everyone loved him, didn't they?"

"As far as I know, yes," he said, "but you just never know." He paused, looking pained about discussing the details of the case. "But, it's obvious he was ... well, he was beaten," the deputy glanced at his notes again. "and his wallet was intact, credit cards, a little bit of cash, receipts, et cetera." He touched the bag containing the receipt on the table between them. "So I've pretty much ruled out any kind of mugging or robbery."

Laura could tell he was trying so hard to be delicate. She brushed her hair back over her ear.

"He was clearly ... tortured." Chesney breathed out heavily. He used his hand to draw a semi-circle on the back of his head. "We think the final blow was here. And it looks like he was hit with a gun." He paused again, then, "God, I'm sorry, Laura." He put both his hands on the table in front of him, clearly unnerved to be telling her these details.

She laid her hands on top of his. "It's okay, go on."

His hands were hot and starting to sweat. She could tell he was nervous. But he was a cop ... *he should be used to this kind of thing, right*?

He took a deep breath, steadying himself, and continued. "From what little evidence we have so far," he said, sounding more officer-like, "it's clear that Rick was tortured at gun point and ultimately beaten so badly that he died from the wounds."

Laura could find no words ... everything went numb. She guessed she might be in shock.

The deputy exhaled loudly and pulled his hands out from under hers and began to wring them together. "I'll know more once the autopsy is complete."

"Hey." Laura took his hands again. "It's okay. I'm the one who's supposed to be all torn up here, right?"

"Yes, yeah, you're right," he stammered. "It's just that this sort of thing never happens here and I've never had to deliver news of murder to next of kin. Sure, people have died, but it's always natural causes."

"Can I see him?" Laura asked.

Chesney clearly balked at this idea. "I don't know Ms. Starlington—"

"It's Laura." She let her lips form into the slightest of smiles. "And I'm a big girl. I'd like to see him."

He nodded, "Well, he'll be in a state of ... well, post autopsy. He'll have a few new scars."

She felt a lump rise up in her throat and said nothing, afraid that if she started to cry now, she'd be overcome and never stop. First her mom with cancer, now this ...

A crackle of static suddenly erupted from Chesney's radio. "Ches, we've got a 211 at the CVS. Can you get over there?"

"I'm sorry," he said to Laura.

He pulled a card out from his shirt pocket and handed it to her. "My cell number's on there. Call me later and I'll take you to see him."

He stood up and clicked his mic. "I'm on it, over. ETA five minutes."

"Give it some thought," he said as he shuffled out of the booth. "Who'd want to hurt your dad? It could be a political rival or someone he voted against or ... heck, I don't know."

She shrugged. She truly didn't know either. As

he half-jogged out the door, he held up his hand in the universal *call me* sign. She sat in the booth, numb, overwhelmed and aching, and staring at his card ... *what to do now*?

"Honey?" Martha startled her so badly that she jerked and knocked over her coffee mug. The last trickles of coffee in her cup splashed on the table.

"Oh, baby, I'm so sorry." The older lady took a rag from her apron and wiped the table. Then she looked up at Laura who now had tears running down her cheeks. "Go home, honey. I'll take care of this."

Laura nodded, afraid to speak. She handed her apron to Martha and ran out the door. Jerking open her forest green Jetta's door, she threw herself into the driver's seat and slumped forward on the steering wheel. And that's when she finally cried for her dad.

About thirty minutes had passed when she finally felt herself calming. She pulled the visor down to look in the mirror. Her cell phone dropped in her lap and she wiped her eyes as she clicked it on.

Fourteen text messages, all from Karah.

She replied: *on my way, gotta stop by bank first.*

She took a deep breath, and checked to make

sure she'd gotten most of the mascara out from under her eyes. Zipping open her beer-stained Coach wallet, she double-checked to make sure the twenty-five dollars was still there from her dad's tip, and headed to the Georgetown Kraft Credit Union.

12

I'm Gon' Flick 'Em Off

THE 1973 COACHMEN Trailer bounced along U.S. Route 521 at a whopping 37 miles-per-hour. The sides of the trailer, in between the rusted sheet metal, were off-white with two four-inch wide stripes of what might've at one time been adventurous yellow and outdoorsy orange. Amazingly, the two propane tanks hopping up and down at the front of the trailer hadn't flown off on the bumpy corn-farm road. Empty as they were, they wouldn't have caused more than a fender bender, but they hung on anyway.

In front of the trailer, in similar rusted-through condition and pulling mightily with its motor constantly redlining, was a 1977 bumblebee yellow-on-black-on-rust Chevy Camaro. Half of its once majestic chrome bumper was gone and the other half was pitted like a moldy cucumber. Sitting on the very front edge of the long bench seat, hands at two and ten, Winston No-Filter cigarette threatening to drop ash at any twitch, was Ellie Mae Gallop ... oldest (by a minute or so) of the Gallop twins.

She scrolled through the ancient FM/AM dial on the radio until the familiar strains of a classic rock station fought through the static.

She threw her head back and sang with the tune. "Dussstttt in da weendddd, all we are is dosstt in da weeeeeenddd."

"Hell yeah fer some original Kansas," she yelled to no one in particular.

"Hey, Ellie Mae, cain't ya go no faster?" crackled a voice from the trailer through a toy army walkie-talkie.

Ellie Mae glared down at the green speaker. *It's a gall-dang Camaro haulin' a gall-dang trailer; do ya think it'll go any faster?* Without clicking the *talk* button, she said, "I cain't hear y'uns!"

Without skipping so much as a beat came the reply. "I knows ya can hear me up 'ar!" the walkie-talkie screeched.

Ellie Mae snatched up the toy and clicked the button. "If y'uns think ya can drive this heap a she-it better 'n me, Daisy Mae, why don't ya jus come up 'ere an have at it."

With that she held down the *squelch* button, which emitted a loud squelching sound. She threw the walkie-talkie into the back seat and cursed as the ashes from her cigarette—Winstons, *because they taste good, like a cigarette should*—finally gave way and flopped down into her lap.

"Hey!" the voice erupted again from the speaker in the back seat, "pull over. I gotta pee."

"Gad o' mighty," Ellie Mae muttered. "Ever' ten miles, dammit."

She tapped the brakes, adding another squeal to the cacophony of sounds coming from the two vehicles, and drifted off the road onto the shoulder. Glaring into the rear-view mirror, she ran her fingers through her hair. Fine and limp like corn-silk and stuck to the side of her head like strands of wet albino kelp, her white blonde hair looked as frazzled as her nerves. *T'aint easy drivin' this heap*, she thought. Splotchy sun freckles dotted her nose, threatening to be cute under icy blue eyes. Crow's feet—from hard living, not from age—were deeper than she remembered. Being in the daylight hadn't been much of a luxury she'd been able to enjoy the past few years.

She pulled out a greasy old Chapstick she'd found at the last gas station and wiped the top off on the seat next to her. Her thin little lips were cracked and dry. *Not my best look*, she mused, and winked at herself in the mirror.

"Always did look bett'r under blacklights in the dark, half nekid," she muttered and then shouted, "Hey! What're you doin back 'ar?"

In the mirror, she saw an exact replica of herself stepping down from the rust-bucket trailer. Well, almost exact, except the version of herself coming out of the Coachmen had her hand on her belly— her swollen, eight-and-a-half months pregnant belly.

"Hold yer damn horses!" yelled Daisy Mae Gallop as she let the screen door slam shut on the trailer and stepped carefully down the metal steps.

Without much ceremony, the pregnant girl waddled into the high grass on the side of the road and squatted down, pulling up her short denim skirt. "Quit yer lookin'," she called to her sister in the driver's seat of the Camaro, "yer makin' me pee-shy."

Sliding into the front bench seat of the car, she yelped and squirmed. "Damn leather's hot as tar'!"

"Saves gas ta keep the AC off," Ellie Mae said while tapping the fuel gauge. "Don't like it, get back in the trailer."

Without asking, Daisy Mae reached up and cranked the air conditioning up to high.

"Gimme just a couple minutes to cool the seat, then."

"Two minutes," Ellie Mae snapped, looking down at the 2.5 gallon container between her legs. "We ain't got enough cash for anymo' gas and we got a long way to go if we gon' git to yer baby daddy before dark."

"Hey, this was yer idear to go after'im."

"Yeah, he's gon' pay fer what he done to you." Ellie Mae nodded down at her sister's bulging stomach.

Daisy Mae looked absently out the window and nodded.

Ellie Mae pushed the accelerator deep to the floorboard and the old car grunted in protest. As the motor squealed, it lurched slowly onto the road. A loud bang sent the car into motion and the trailer acted like it didn't want to go either. Finally, they were rolling.

No sooner than they had gotten up to speed—a brisk forty-two miles-per-hour—a bright red Miata with two younger versions of themselves raced up behind them. The two girls were blonde, tan and skinny, and wearing bikini tops and pony-tails. Justin

Bieber blared from the radio and both girls were screaming along.

"Well, looky here," said Ellie Mae, jerking her thumb back to the oncoming car.

The Miata suddenly started honking its horn and revving its engine. The girls were laughing and pointing at the junkyard wreck driving in front of them.

Ellie Mae threw her arm out the side window. "Go around, dammit!"

"I miss those days," Daisy Mae said through tears, mascara running down her cheeks.

"Oh, hell no. Don't be cryin' over these bitches. Yer just hormonal."

"My baby needs her daddy," she heaved in between sobs.

"Don't worry little sister," Ellie Mae said, grinning, "when they pass us, you hold the wheel; I'm gon' moon 'em!"

Daisy Mae wiped her nose on her sleeve and sniffled through a smile. "Yeah, do it! And I'm gon' flick 'em off!"

The two ex-stripper twins laughed as the two younger, blonder girls edged around the trailer.

"Git a load of 'is!" Ellie Mae shouted, jerking down her skirt, panties and all.

She stood up and shoved what she could of her naked backside through the driver's side window.

"Yeah, bitches!!!" screamed Daisy Mae, flipping double middle fingers at the young girls.

In the first of an unbelievable turn of events, one of the girls in the Miata was also smoking a Winston cigarette. Upon seeing Ellie Mae's butt sticking through the window of the rusted-out Chevy Camaro, she flicked her cigarette at it, still lit. In the second of the unbelievable turn of events, the lit cigarette flew through Ellie Mae's legs and landed in the crotch of her panties—panties that had been absorbing the fumes from the 2.5 gallon gas container between her legs for the entire trip. In the third of the unbelievable turn of events, the fireball did little more than singe the hair from her legs, but Ellie Mae screamed and pushed herself backward over the bench seat in an effort to escape the fire.

She landed in a heap, tearing at her skirt and panties that were smoldering and threatening her backside. Ripping them off, she flung them out the window.

"Dammit, dammit, dammit!!" she howled. "Those skinny-ass whores!!"

"Omigawd, omigawd, omigawd," Daisy Mae was crying, "we're gon' die!"

The pregnant girl was holding the steering wheel, but the car was careening from side to side, threatening to leave the road.

In the fourth and most unbelievable of the wild turn of events, the gas can had slid forward, kicked by the escaping Ellie Mae, and wedged itself between the bottom of the dashboard and the gas pedal. The car was racing along at nearly seventy-five miles an hour and wobbling badly. Daisy Mae was holding her belly with one hand and the steering wheel with the other.

"My baby!!" she screamed, "my poor baby's gon' die!"

"No, he ain't!" Ellie Mae said regaining her composure and getting madder by the second. "Gimme one more second, I'm climbin' back up 'ar."

In one of the least graceful returns to a front seat of all time, Ellie Mae rolled back over the bench seat and plopped down into the driver's side behind the wheel.

"Give it to me," she said, jerking Daisy Mae's hand from the steering wheel. "Them ho's don't know who they're dealing with."

She reached down between her legs and pried the gas can out from in front of the accelerator.

Handing it to Daisy Mae, she said, "Let's go get us some young blood."

She slammed the gas pedal back to the floor and whooped out the open window.

"Hell yeah!" Daisy Mae said, still holding onto her belly.

The two young blonde girls couldn't have looked more surprised to see the rambling wreck come flying up behind them ... and then pass them by. Daisy Mae held up her double birds and screamed ... no words, just a scream.

Her scream died in her throat as she realized they were leaving the red Miata in the dust.

"Hey, why didn't you slow down, 'er stop 'er sumpin'?" she asked, looking over at Ellie Mae.

Ellie Mae's eyes were wide and she looked as pale as a ghost. She nodded her head down between her legs. "No brakes. We got no brakes."

"Shit!" Daisy Mae clutched her stomach. "Hey, whar's yer pants at?"

13

Venus Fly Trap

"THAT FOOT'S gotta come off, mate," Man'ti said, grimacing as he unwound the crusty makeshift bandage wrapped around Darren's toes, or stubs. "Infected as hell."

The lanky man was sweating profusely. "Screw that! Just put the damn medicine on and get 'em bandaged back up, ya prick."

With that, Man'ti stopped being gentle and ripped the remaining dressing off his companion's foot.

"Owwww, shit!!!"

"Wrap it up ya bloody self." Man'ti threw the drug store bag at him.

Darren looked down at his ruined foot. The

stubs of his missing three toes were black and green. It looked like frostbite, but it burned like they'd been dipped in lava. He tried to brush off the black with a cotton ball dipped in alcohol, but if the fire hadn't been hot enough before that, it was blistering now.

"Damn it all," he moaned.

Man'ti had shoved his way back up to the driver's seat of the bronze van they'd procured. He clicked on his iPhone and mumbled. "Take the meds too, mate. Doubtful, but ya might save that leg."

After a few minutes of exquisite pain, Darren had cleaned and bandaged his toes with a piece of diaper wrapped in duct tape. He gingerly pulled his sock onto his foot, but his shoe was not an option. The sharp pain subsided to a dull burn after his CVS medicine kicked in and he was able to limp up to the passenger's seat.

"Done in by a bloody recliner," he grunted as he slumped back into the seat.

"I'll put it on ya tombstone," Man'ti mumbled, clicking out a text on his iPhone.

"Who the hell ya chattin' with this time o' night?"

"Ya mum, that's who."

Darren lunged for the phone and Man'ti

slammed his elbow into his nose, which promptly exploded into a gush of blood.

"Are you frickin' kidding me, mate!?" The skinny man's hands were side by side on his nose, but blood still poured out between his fingers.

"Don't touch m'phone," Man'ti said with a darker menace in his tone than Darren expected.

"Shit, mate, all ya hadda do was say so. I think ya broke m'fookin' nose!"

"Touch it again and I'll put me fist through ya face."

Man'ti grabbed a dingy towel from under his seat. It looked like it had been used to check the oil in the van. He threw it at Darren, hitting him in the face.

"Wipe that shit off, we're goin' fer a beeyah."

Darren mopped up the blood pooling in his lap. "What the hell'm I supposed ta wear, mate?"

Man'ti's jaw tensed. He looked like he might elbow Darren again, but he un-gritted his teeth.

"Check in me bag," he said, thumbing toward the back of the van, "think I gotta 'notha shirt."

Darren quickly crawled to the back as Man'ti fired up the van. He swallowed two more pain pills and dug into the big man's black bag and found a black t-shirt.

It was an XXL ... and sleeveless ... a combination that looked absolutely comical when he slipped it on.

"This place betta 'ave whiskey," he called to the giant driving the van, then mumbled, "I could use a damn whiskey!"

"Drunken Jack's has whiskey galore, mate."

That was the last thing Darren "The Body" McGlashen heard before he passed out.

———

TAMMY-ANNE TIDMORE HAD BEEN a teller at the Georgetown Kraft Credit Union since it opened back in 1952, and at eighty-four years-of-age was the longest tenured employee in the company (and maybe in the country). With 48 employees at different branches, the credit union today still boasts a ratio of 297 members per employee—which is relatively small for a credit union. Of the over 13,000 members, Tammy-Anne knew almost all of them by first name.

It was no surprise that she looked up when *Georgiana* walked in to the Jetty Drive branch and exclaimed, "Good mornin', Miss Laura Kate."

"Hi, Mrs. Tidmore."

The grandmotherly lady slipped her hand below the old-school casino style cage and took Laura's hand. "I heard about your daddy. Fine, fine man. I'm so sorry for your loss."

Laura nodded and said nothing, afraid the tears would start again. Tammy-Anne squeezed her hand knowingly.

"What business you doin' this fine day?"

Laura took the twenty-five dollars her stepfather, Rick Hairre, had tipped her, and slid it under the bars toward Tammy-Anne. "Taking care of my late fee."

The pepper-haired woman looked down at the money and then back up at Laura. She had a smile on her face and a raised eyebrow, as if she was being had by some private joke.

"Uh huh," she said and winked. "This should put a dent on your balance."

The teller clicked a few keys, put the money into her drawer, and handed Laura the receipt. "Now don't be spendin' all that at once, hun."

Laura had no idea what she meant, but she shoved the paper in her purse and nodded, not sure how she would manage to spend zero dollars at all.

"See ya later, Mrs. Tidmore."

A ding from her phone startled her as she got into her Jetta; a text from Karah.

-SRSLY WHERE R U? U will not believe what I've been up 2!

-Sry can't talk now. Work at DJ's tonight. 2 much happening to text.

-What's going on? I'll be there. What time u work til?

-Close.

-Ugh, ok, save me a seat at the bar.

-RT

RT–*ROGER That*—was Karah's signature sign-off and it just so happened it was what her dad liked to say too. The tears threatened to spill out again ... *Stop it, Laura, you can cry later, but right now you gotta go sling the whiskey.*

She hadn't shared the news of her father's murder with anyone at Drunken Jack's yet; she just didn't want to deal with the whole scene of, "*Are you okay? Do you need anything? Who would murder your dad?*"

She didn't want her co-workers to look at her any differently. For starters, they had no idea that her father was the semi-famous local politician, Rick Hairre, and beyond that she didn't want to attract any attention from whoever might have killed him.

The last thought stopped her in her tracks. Her Jetta idled at a traffic light, the cars behind her honking and pulling around. *What if they come after me too?*

———

MAN'TI LEFT Darren passed out in the van. He was a bloody mess anyway, with his rotten foot and broken nose. He figured he'd arouse less attention and get more drinking done alone. On the drive up to Drunken Jack's, Man'ti had thought once or twice about dumping the scrawny man into a hole and covering him up. But the boss had hired him to come on this job for a reason; somebody had to take a fall.

During the day, Drunken Jack's was a family restaurant boasting almost fresh crab, shrimp, grouper, clams, oysters and calamari. After sunset, the long wooden bar attracted a rowdier, saltier crowd. Most nights (in season), there was a guitar-playing singer crooning out Jimmy Buffet, Bob Marley, and the occasional Grateful Dead song.

Man'ti didn't want any seafood and he didn't want any pseudo-beach tunes blaring in his ears. He parked himself on a barstool way down at the end of the bar, away from the tourist crowd and closer to the ruddy tanned crowd that stared into the bottoms of their glasses.

Most of the people at that end of the bar didn't even look up when he sat down, and that's the way he liked it.

"What'll it be?"

Man'ti was startled. He was looking into the eyes of the prettiest girl he'd ever seen. *Georgiana* (it said on her name tag) was tan and slender, but not anorexic like a college bimbo. Her blonde hair hung in loose ringlets down around her elfish face, and her eyes were deep brown with an auburn and gold glow in the center of her irises. The huge man of few words was struck even more speechless.

"Well?" she said, holding her arm outstretched at the yards and yards of bottles behind her.

"I um, I'll have a ... " he stammered.

The bartender almost rolled her eyes, but was

clearly used to this reaction. "Whiskey? You look like a whiskey drinker."

Man'ti nodded.

She walked away and his eyes followed her down the bar. He watched her every move as she poured a cheap, generic brand of whiskey into a tiny rocks glass.

Get a hold of ya self, mate. Man'ti mentally slapped himself in the face. He shook his head and some of his senses returned as she set the glass down in front of him.

"Six bucks," she said, sliding a napkin under his glass.

The glass of liquor didn't touch the bar for more than a second. Man'ti picked it up and chugged the whiskey down in one gulp.

"Right, let's start a tab," he said, and pulled his wallet from his pocket and handed her an American Express Black Centurion Credit Card, "but don't be bringin' me any more 'a that shit you just poured me. Let's go top shelf tonight, honey," he said and winked at her.

She grabbed the card and he held it for just a beat. He saw her eyes flick to the Tag Heuer Monaco V4 on his wrist. She didn't need to know whose wrist he'd borrowed it from; poor chap hadn't needed it anymore, as his time had run out. Man'ti grinned at his own pun.

"You're the boss."

"At's right." Man'ti leaned back and crossed his arms. "Let's 'av a bigga glass, hun. I don't want no tiny shot 'o whiskey."

She looked down at the card and read the strange name printed on it. "Is that Swedish or German?"

"It's thirsty." He didn't smile. "And don't be slo—" He was interrupted before he finished his sentence.

"Let's make that two 'o them, sweet tits," a voice said as a scrawny man slid onto the next barstool and slapped Man'ti on the back.

Oh, fa fook's sake, Man'ti thought, *shoulda dropped 'im in that hole after all.*

The waitress turned her eyes back to the big man questioningly.

He nodded and sighed. "Why not."

———

KARAH CAMPOBELLO, you look soooooo cute tonight! At least that's what she told herself when she checked out the beautiful aqua dress she had ordered from Venus just for this trip. A veritable trap for any man who witnessed its beauty! It had a self-tie halter showing off her sun-kissed tan shoulders from her hammock time and a multi-colored skirt of purple, yellow and pink that blended into a print of leopard and flowers at the bottom. It was jeweled on the top and sparkled like a rainbow. *Cute! So damn cute!* She thought of Troy and wondered what he'd think about the dress. *Hold up,* she thought to herself, *lemme take a selfie!*

She snapped a quick pic with a slightly sly smile and texted it to him.

-"*What ya think?*"

-"Nice."

-"*You like?*"

-"I like."

-"*I'll be showin' it off at Drunken Jack's in a few.*"

There was a long pause before the next message chimed.

-"Not my scene."

-"*Your loss. ;-P*"

-"Catch up with you after?"

She couldn't help but feel a few butterflies in her stomach.

-"*We'll see.*"

She clicked out of the text messenger. She knew

she would go see him after a few margaritas at DJ's, and wondered what an evening with Troy might be like on a Tequila buzz. Her background was now set to a pic she took surreptitiously of Troy fishing this morning. Same khaki shorts, same tan skin, new straw cowboy hat.

Her phone pinged again.

-"Ok, you got me. On my way."

Karah sighed as she slid her phone back into her purse. *A man of few words, a very sexy man of few words.*

She walked up to the front door of Drunken Jack's, winked at the cheesy pirate on the entrance sign, and brushed the creases from the drive out of her new dress. It felt like it was going to be a great night.

LAURA DUG THROUGH HER PURSE, spilling lipstick and sunscreen and keys out onto the table in the break room. *What the hell? It's gotta be in here somewhere.* In one hand, she held the black Amex card as she rifled through her belongings. As she was stuffing her scattered things back into her purse, inspiration hit her and she reached into her back pocket. There it was; the card the cop had given her. *Okay, Deputy Chesney Biggins, let's see what you can find out about misterrrr ... she looked back at the American Express Card and raised an eyebrow ... Victor Böhring.*

14

Hard Drive

THE CURSOR BLINKED WAITING for another entry. Username: _____PIN: ____

Chesney Biggins tapped his hospital style latex-gloved finger on the ENTER key a few more times, hoping something magical might happen. The small zip drive he'd found on Rick Hairre's body had proven to be password protected and encrypted beyond his limited hacking skills. With his sketchy knowledge of Rick, he'd tried several dozen possible passwords, none of which had opened the drive's contents. He'd even called in to the local Game Stop to see if any of the pimply-faced employees could work it out.

Dusting for prints had also been a bust; the only

partials they found belonged to Rick. Picking up the second evidence bag on his desk that contained Rick Hairre's wallet for the one-hundredth time seemed like a lost cause, but something new occurred to him as he pulled out its contents. Could there be a password clue in these things?

One at a time, he laid the cards and scraps of paper out on his desk. Studying them carefully, again, he made notes on his yellow pad bought solely for this investigation.

1. Georgetown Kraft Credit Union Debit Card
2. BankAmericard Rewards Visa – Expired
3. Driver's License – Issued to one Rickard Bertram Hairre. *Rickard? Must be a family name.*
4. Hair Club of Georgetown membership card, ID #4747
5. Humana Medical Insurance Card issued by city council of Murrell's Inlet.
6. Five city council business cards
7. Post-It Note with address: 700 S. Kawasaki – googled for SC, no match. Closest match JFK Auto in NC.
8. Receipt from Lee's Inlet Kitchen

Nothing here, Chesney thought to himself. *No thoughtful password scrawled on the back of anything.*

"Wait a sec ... " he mumbled to no one while picking up his phone. Flipping over the GKCU Debit Card, he dialed the number of the main office.

"Georgetown Kraft Credit Union, this is Tammy-Anne speaking, how may I direct your call?"

"Tammy-Anne, this is Deputy Biggins, could I—"

"Oh, just terrible isn't it, Ches? I just can't get over what happened to that poor man. Why, Laura Kate was in here just a few minutes ago and she looks devastated."

Interesting, Chesney thought. "Well, Tammy-Anne, that's kind of what I'm calling about. I need to get some information from Rick Hairre's account." The line went quiet. He could tell she was still there from the background bank noise of teller drawers opening and microphone chatter from the drive-through. "Tammy-Anne?"

"Now, you know I can't give you any personal information over the phone."

"You realize I can get a warrant for what I need, but Boonesborough is gone to the Hampton's for a week and I really need to—"

"Mmhhmm," she interrupted him, "over the phone would be big trouble for everyone."

Over the phone? Huh? Ohhhh, probably a recorded line.

"Understood, Tammy-Anne," he said and felt himself nodding. "10-98, 10-17."

Tammy-Anne had once been married to a police officer many years ago, and he hoped she'd know the code as his indication that he understood and was en route. He shut his laptop and slid it and his yellow pad of notes into a duffle bag. He slid the evidence bag in with them, careful not to put his prints on anything inside.

"10-4," she answered.

Fifteen minutes later, he pulled up to the drive-through at the Georgetown Kraft Credit Union. Tammy-Anne came to the window and pulled over the Burger King style microphone.

"Well, helloooo, Deputy Biggins," she gushed as if they hadn't spoken in ages, "what can I do for you today?"

"Hi Tammy-Anne," he said and touched the bill of his hat, "workin' late tonight I see."

It was nearing 7 o'clock; closing time for the credit union was 5.

"End of the month," she said, smiling, "and folks need extra time to get their checks in before the weekend."

He slid Rick Hairre's debit card into the drawer, and said, "I need to make a withdrawal."

"Certainly." She took the card and walked away from the window.

He wasn't sure exactly what he was looking for, but he guessed there was enough information in Rick's bank file to get him farther along than he was currently.

"Here ya go, darlin'." She placed a manila folder in the drawer along with the debit card. "Be sure to deposit that back soon."

"10-4."

He put his cruiser in drive and flopped the folder down into the passenger seat. Suddenly, his personal cell blared out the scream and guitar riff from *Won't Get Fooled Again* by The Who.

Random number, someone who wasn't in his contacts. *Voicemail can get that one*, he thought while clicking the reject button.

————

"REALLY?" Laura Kate said into her phone as she listened to the voicemail message.

"This is Chesney Biggins. I can't answer your call

right now, but if you'll leave your name and number, I'll get back to you as soon as possible."

"Chesney, this is—"

The voicemail message interrupted her. "If you have an emergency or if this is official police business, please call the Garden City Police Department at 911."

Really?? she thought again as she waited for the beep.

———

CHESNEY'S PHONE chirped to alert him to the voicemail. He hit the button and listened.

"*Ok, Mr. Call Me anytime. This is Laura Kate Starlington,*" her voice sassed just below sarcastic. "*Hey, I'm working tonight at Drunken Jack's and there's a really strange guy in here. I think he's using a stolen credit card.*"

He smiled to himself, a pretty clever fake setup to get to see him again.

"*I don't know if you can, like, run the name or whatever,*" she continued, "*but this guy doesn't look like a Victor Böhring to me.*"

Victor Böhring, Chesney thought, *why does that sound so familiar?*

"So, if you're ready to protect and serve or whatever, give me a call. Later."

He saved the message and put the phone back into his pocket. Before pulling out of the bank parking lot, he tapped the name into his laptop search. Google reported: About 24,500 results (0.31 seconds).

None of the results jogged anything in his memory. Dead end.

Guess I'll just have to go see what Mr. Böhring is up to at Drunken Jack's.

He picked up his radio. "Todd, I got a 10-21 on a 10-83 at Drunken Jack's. Gonna check it out."

His radio squelched. "Sounds hard, Dick! Slip on in there and see if you can get your hands on the situation."

He put his radio down without answering. *It never stops, does it? I'm working with juveniles.* As he drove toward the bar, he wondered if it was time for a career change.

————

LAURA KATE DROPPED her phone into her purse as the stranger yelled from across the bar. *"Wheya the fook ah them beeyahs?"*

"Coming right up," she yelled as she pulled her shirt tail out of her skirt and tied it up in a knot, exposing her midriff. *Okay, abs do your thing. Gotta keep 'em here long enough for the cavalry to ride in.*

15

Zig Zag

TROY CLINT BODEAN couldn't remember the last time he'd darkened the doors of Drunken Jack's Restaurant and Lounge. After a few months in Pawleys, the allure of the touristy places had worn off.

He stood in his bathroom studying his ruddy reflection. A rumpled white linen shirt (the one with no stains), his cleanest pair of Columbia brand khaki shorts and his LSU ball cap made up his best *going out* outfit. His reflection shrugged.

He didn't know if this was what people wore out, but it was the best he had. He scrubbed his hand through his more than stubbly chin and wondered if he should shave. He hadn't seen his face clean shaven in so long, he was afraid he wouldn't recognize what he saw ... so he left it.

He picked up a bottle of Old Spice cologne that sat on his bathroom counter. He couldn't remember the last time he'd used that either. A tiny splash of it behind his ears ... he guessed that was what he was supposed to do with it.

"Okay," he said and clapped his hands together. "Let's do this."

As he walked into the living room, he noticed the cowboy hat laying up-ended on the futon. He smiled to himself as he took off old faithful and put on the new straw beauty. It was the last time the Outback Tea Stained straw cowboy hat would ever leave his head.

He locked his door and carefully placed the key above the porch light behind a slightly loose board; thinking ahead to any guests he might have later tonight. He strolled across the road to the creek-side dock where he'd lost his fishing rod earlier to wait for his ride. Uber was a wonderful thing, and he figured he might not be in a condition to drive after a night of Drunken Jack's signature Margaritas.

The moon glistened off the gentle current and the breeze was soft and warm. He eased down into the hammock and was almost sound asleep when the *beep beep* of his chariot-for-hire broke the calm. A long black Lincoln Town Car sat in front of his modest cabana. *Whoa*, he thought, *seems a bit fancy for Pawleys.* The car's windows were too dark to penetrate, but the windshield did have the familiar Uber logo and looked pretty legit.

Suddenly, the driver's door opened and a black man dressed in a black suit wearing a black driver's hat and black leather gloves jumped out and hurried to the back to open the door for Troy.

"Good even', Mista Troy," said a familiar voice from behind a gleaming white smile.

Recognition dawned. "Willie?"

"Yessa," said the one-eyed ice cream truck driver as he tipped his cap to his passenger.

"You drive for Uber? How is that even possible for someone with only one ey—" He stopped short, realizing Willie was glaring at him (out of one eye, obviously).

He ignored the remark about his eye and ushered Troy into the back of the Town Car. "Only fo' coupla days now. Ma' otha car's in da shop." The man's eye squinted angrily and looked off in the distance. "But da man ain't gon' keep me down, no sir."

He closed the door and Troy watched as he

limped around the car and slid inside. Willie
punched a few buttons on his phone and turned
around to speak to Troy.

"You inna hurry, Mista Troy? Gotta stop or two ta
make if ya don' mind. Don't worry, I won't start da
trip til we get goin' yo way."

Troy shrugged his shoulders. "Works for me."

"Grand, Mista Troy, grand," he said, beaming,
"Got a few bottled wata's in da cooler if ya get
thirsty."

"Much obliged." Troy opened the top of the
small Yeti cooler and grinned. "Can I have one of
these Orange Crème Push-Ups?"

"Why, a' course, Mista Troy," Willie tipped his
cap at him in the rear-view mirror and they headed
back for the causeway. Troy took in the beautiful
car's appointed leather, and the expensive cooler
filled with Evian and ice cream.

As he pushed up his popsicle, he asked, "So,
Willie, what gives? How's an ice cream man afford all
of this?"

The old, one-eyed ice cream man winked at him
—which was an odd sight for a one-eyed man. "I got
dem trucks in every neighborhood and beach town
from here to da Keys. Ice cream bidness is good."

"I can see that," Troy said, finished his push-pop,

and carefully placed the sticky wrapper in a small trash can between the seats. He washed it down with a cool bottle of Evian and after a second, finished that off too. *Stay hydrated*, he thought.

"Got one on da way up from Islamorada that'll put me back in da ice cream bidness by tomorrah," Willie said and winked at him.

"Gotcha," Troy said, tossing the empty bottle into the trash.

No more than a mile later, they pulled into the Pawleys Pier Village—the only condos on the island. *Odd*, Troy thought to himself as One-Eyed Willie punched in the code to the security gate, but he had no idea just how odd it was about to get.

———

FORTY-FIVE MINUTES LATER, a loud bang startled Troy. He rubbed his eyes and looked at the clock on the dashboard. The luxurious Lincoln Town Car was still idling, but there was no sign of his driver. Troy stretched and peered out the windshield toward the courtyard between the buildings. It was dark, but he thought he could make out someone running away from the pool. Probably some kids swimming after hours. Suddenly, another bang shattered the silence.

It clearly wasn't a gunshot; it was more like a trash can lid being slammed shut. Troy clicked the button on his door and the window slid down. Murmurs floated to his ears across the darkness.

"Git mah jeans, git the chair and git back in here!" he heard a woman's voice call into the dark. "That gall-dang guard's comin' back."

Troy shook his head and laughed. Pawleys Pier Village sometimes attracted the rougher, more touristy crowd from up and around Myrtle Beach.

Another voice entered the fray. "Drop the butcher's knife and put your hands up!"

It was an old man, but not Willie.

"You girls are out here runnin' around like a couple of crazy people givin' everyone the heebie-jeebies!"

Troy could stand no more; he had to see what this was all about. He gently opened the car door and hunched his way through the walkway to the courtyard. When he got to the corner, he peered around the edge.

About ten feet apart from each other stood the hundred-year-old man (presumably the security guard) and a naked blonde girl holding a butcher knife and a pile of clothes in front of her bare body. On top of all that ... she looked vaguely familiar. He'd seen her before, but couldn't place where.

"Don't git no closer, old man!" she said and pointed the knife at him menacingly. "I knows what yer after! Ain't nobody gits to see this without payin'."

Troy almost laughed when the man shrugged his shoulders.

"You girls are trespassing and I just need you to leave."

Another voice called out from the balcony right up behind Troy. He hit the deck as she called out, "We ain't causin' no trouble old man. That gate was open and she's jus' gittin' a bath!"

"Lady, you can't be bathing in our swimming pool. Now, look, you just get your things and go and I won't call the cops."

Ignoring him, the naked girl called up to her friend on the balcony. "Daisy Mae, how'n the hell'd you git up 'ar?"

"I climbed the gutter, dumbass."

"Oh, well, git on down. I found you some clothes hangin' out by the pool."

Troy couldn't see it, but apparently the young lady on the balcony was climbing down again.

"Be careful, Daisy Mae. Don't hurt 'at baby, now."

Baby? What the hell? Troy could see that the security guard was obviously concerned about the woman scaling the gutter.

"I got dis, Ellie Mae," called the voice, grunting with effort, "I ain't gon' hurt little T.C."

T.C.? That's weird, Troy thought, *that's what dad used to call me.* When she finally thudded to the ground, Troy could see she was also naked and dripping wet and more than eight months pregnant!

"Now, listen you two," the security guard said, his hands up in front of him. They were shaking wildly with fear—or maybe a palsy of some sort.

"Just leave that," —he pointed to the knife— "in there, —he motioned to a trash can nearby— "and get your dirty jalopy and trailer out of here."

The first girl (Ellie Mae?) started handing clothes to the pregnant girl (Daisy Mae?).

"Let's blow 'is joint," Ellie Mae said as she tossed the knife into the trash can. "We got what we need."

"If you call 'em cops, old man," Daisy Mae spat at the security guard, "we gon' come back'n gut ya."

"Whatever," he said, still holding his hands out in front of him. "Just go."

The two girls, who had to be twins, started toward the walkway that Troy was laying down next to. He froze, hoping the darkness would hide him.

Suddenly, One-Eyed Willie came down a set of nearby stairs singing, Zip-a-dee-doo-da ...

Every head turned. Willie froze.

"What de hell ... " he mouthed into the night.

The oldest security guard in the world turned toward Willie. "Who in the hell is this now, your pimp?"

Ellie Mae's face twisted in rage. "We ain't no ho's, ya old bastert!"

Daisy Mae agreed whole-heartedly. "Yeah, stupid. There ain't no sex in the champagne room!"

"Just cuz we strip don't mean we do nothin' else!"

"Yeah, loser," Daisy Mae laughed as she sang out, "if ya ain't got no twenty, you ain't gettin' any!"

Troy froze. *Oh, shit*, he thought, *it's Cinnamon and Starr from the Peppermint Hippo back in Vegas*! He never knew their real names, but it was definitely them. Starr (or Daisy Mae) was always trying to get with Troy after getting all coked up on stage, claimed she wanted to have his babies.

"What in God's name are they doing here?" he mumbled to himself.

There was a moment of silence as everyone suddenly realized no one was moving to leave.

"Okay, well, it's been real nice meetin' y'all, but I

got ta go," Willie suddenly said and started walking away from the group.

The cacophony rose again with all the parties yelling at each other, no one seeming ready to give in.

Troy took this as his cue and jumped up as quietly as he could and ran back to the car.

He ducked into the back of the Lincoln, but he could still see the chaos erupting in between the buildings of the Pawleys Pier Village. A set of naked, blonde twins (one of whom was busting out pregnant), Methuselah the security guard, and a black, one-eyed ice cream truck/Uber driver all scrambled in different directions. Troy could almost hear the theme song from The Benny Hill show playing, or maybe it was the Keystone Cops song— either way, it was hilarious.

As Willie jumped into the car, he jerked it into reverse and said, "We getting' outta dis crazy place!" He slung the long black car out of the parking spot so fast that Troy slid across the slick leather back seat and went tumbling to the floorboard. His cowboy hat flew off and he reached down to get it.

"Hold on, Troy," Willie said, hitting the gas.

Troy pulled himself up, holding tight to the head rest. "Geezus, Willie, you're gonna kill us!"

When they rounded the turn toward the exit gate, a crappy old Camaro towing a junked-out trailer rounded the turn across from them. As they barreled toward each other, Willie slammed on his brakes and skidded sideways, throwing Troy up against the window nearest the Camaro. The rusty former muscle car turned hard away from them, leaving the two cars side by side mere inches away from each other.

Troy shook his head and looked over to the passengers of the car. Cinnamon and Starr, both still buck naked, were looking straight at him.

In slow motion, Troy could see the recognition dawn on their twin faces. Their teeth clenched and anger filled their eyes in unison.

"Willie," he yelled, "go NOW!"

"You got it, boss!"

As they squealed away from the ex-strippers, Daisy Mae and Ellie Mae Gallup were flashing four matching middle fingers his direction and screaming. Luckily, he couldn't make out what they were yelling about.

As they raced away from the condos, Willie took something from his pocket and slipped it into the dash—Zig Zag rolling papers and a small bag of what looked like Oregano.

"Really, Willie?"

"Mista Troy," he said and smiled his beaming white smile, "it's fo my glaucoma."

From behind them, Troy heard the loud bang again, which he thought might be the Camaro backfiring as it tried to catch up.

"Just get me over to Drunken Jack's."

"I jus' started da meter."

16

Buckets Of Spew

KARAH CAMPOBELLO CHECKED her makeup in the visor mirror of her silver Land Rover (affectionately named Luna after her first dog) and applied even more bubble-gum flavored lip-gloss. All was good. She tucked her wallet up under the driver's seat—because no one breaking into a car would ever check there—and headed up the stairs to Drunken Jack's.

The tinny tunes of some old salty singer doing his best Gordon Lightfoot rendition drifted out of the door and the early evening drone of patrons getting in the mood buzzed a little lower than the crescendo they would reach by midnight.

Karah looked down at her Omega De Ville Prestige Watch, a present from her last boyfriend—

he was a nice guy, studying political science, but just a little too straight laced for Karah—and saw that it was 11:47pm. The dinner crowd was rolling out and the late-night crowd was starting to roll in. The party was just about to kick off.

————

DARREN "THE BODY" McGlashen was looking a little green around the gills. Man'ti realized that all they had eaten all day was the junk food he'd taken from the CVS. Ten shots of whiskey and tequila later, Darren was starting to slur and drool, and standing up was not an option.

On top of that, the skinny man was starting to stink. His nose had the crusty remnants of blood clinging to it from Man'ti's crushing punch, and his foot—that was wrapped in a sock that was purpled with blood and bound with duct tape—smelled like a bag of rotten almonds soaked in ammonia.

And on top of all that, there were two young frat guys in the early stages of a bar fight at the other end of the room. They were puffing up and bumping each other around. *Stupid fooks*, Man'ti thought to himself. And that's when the beer bottle flew out of one of the punk's hands and bounced off Darren's left eye. It immediately swelled, and blood pooled into the white sclera, making him look like some kind of black-eyed demon.

"Shit," Man'ti muttered, watching Darren growl and push up from his bar stool.

The sweet blonde bartender that Man'ti had been softening up saw this begin to escalate and tried in vain to calm things down. "Boys, boys, nothin' a free shot of Jäger won't fix!"

She wagged the dark green bottle at them, but no one was paying any attention.

"Which onya stoopid fooks let goa thet bottle?" Darren moved toward them.

Man'ti grabbed the bottle of Jäger out of Georgiana's hands and took a long swig.

"Hey!" she protested, "you can't do—"

Man'ti slammed the bottle on the bar. "Jus' put it on me tab."

One of the frat guys had claimed the throw and was sizing Darren up. "Don't know what yer worried about, dude. It didn't hurt yer looks any, ya creepy fu—"

Darren interrupted him with a swinging roundhouse punch to the side of his head. All the energy he had left exploded the young man's eardrum, and he screamed.

"Shit." Man'ti cracked his knuckles.

The frat guy was in shock at the blood trickling down the side of his face and his eyes locked with Darren's, who was now exactly one second from passing out.

"I'm gonna kill you, dude!"

He pulled his leg back and in the slow motion that happens in some movie fights, Man'ti saw that the young man was wearing a soccer jersey. He let out a snort. *This ain't gonna end well*, he thought. Darren was lifted about a foot and a half off the ground when the soccer playing frat guy's kick rocketed into his groin. As he crashed back down to the ground, agony spreading across his bloody eyes, he began gurgling loudly.

Man'ti moved to keep him from falling back, and put his hands up under Darren's arms. In the process, he dropped his cell phone; it hit hard and shattered into a million pieces. His beaten colleague gagged hard again.

"Oh, fook no." Man'ti shoved him toward the grinning frat guy.

And that's when Darren threw up. Buckets of spew splashed across the frat guy's face and shirt and even more soaked him down to his shoes. The horror—a horror that can only come from being barfed on in public after suffering an exploded ear drum in a bar fight with a creepy homeless looking dude—splashed across the kid's face like ... well, like vomit.

"Are you FREAKIN' kidding me?!?" he screamed.

Darren sagged to the floor, sliding around in the contents of his own stomach. Man'ti threw a quick rabbit punch at the kid's face, and he slumped down unconscious.

Bouncers from the front door suddenly reached toward hidden earpieces and turned toward the melee.

"Time to go," Man'ti said to the semi-conscious Darren.

He wondered if he should just leave him. But doing that would probably lead the cops back to him. Darren groaned as Man'ti heaved him up onto his shoulder. The blonde bartender was staring wide-eyed at him and holding her phone up to her ear.

"Gimme 'at cell, ya bitch," the giant man said and grabbed it out of her hand.

He looked down at the screen. She had called 9-1-1. *Shit*, he thought.

"9-1-1, what's your emergency," the speaker squelched.

Man'ti clicked it off. "Back door?"

"You can't leave! The cops are coming to—"

He shoved her back against the wall behind the bar, dislodging a bottle of triple sec. It crashed to the floor and the smell of orange floated up around them.

"Back fookin' door, or I break ya face like thet bottle."

Georgiana squeaked, tears forming in her eyes. He almost felt sorry he'd gotten so rough with her, but she *had* called the police. She pointed to a door behind the bar.

"Sayonara, sweet tits."

17

The Hat

KARAH CAMPOBELLO—DRESSED in her multi-colored skirt of purple, yellow and pink that blended into a print of leopard and flowers at the bottom with jewels on the top that sparkled like a rainbow—was about to take the first step up into Drunken Jack's when the giant man flew past her from around the back of the bar. He bumped her shoulder hard, tumbling her back off the step and almost sending her sprawling to the ground.

"HEY, watch it buste—" She suddenly stopped when the huge tattooed man turned back to glare at her. He was carrying another man on his shoulder who looked like he might be dead. *Did he kill somebody? Is he going to kill me?* She felt herself involuntarily crab walk backward away from him and fear made her whimper out loud.

A bouncer from the top of the stairs slammed the front door open and yelled. "Dude, get your ass back here!"

The big man turned and ran into the parking lot. The bouncer bounded down the stairs and knelt down to Karah.

"Are you okay, miss? Did he hurt you?"

"I'm fine, I'm fine." Karah took a deep breath. The bouncer, whom she had met before, recognized her and helped her stand up. "Thanks, Eric."

He nodded and looked back into the parking lot. A bronze van with white pin striping and a painted sunset on the back was squealing out of the lot.

Karah dusted off her elbows and checked the backside of her incredible dress to make sure no damage was done. When she was sure of that, she composed herself and walked into Drunken Jack's. The music was cranking up again and the Pseudo-Jimmy Buffet singer was droning on about being sorry for the interruption while tuning his guitar. The bar side of the restaurant was in complete disarray.

Like the parted waters of the Jordan River, the ends of the bar were populated with people rubbernecking like there had been some sort of car wreck. The center of the bar looked exactly like that's what had happened. Laura Kate Starlington was pushing a moldy mop through a mess of stinky vomit and glass and maybe even a little blood.

Karah caught her eye and mouthed, *OMG, what happened*??

Laura rolled her eyes and nodded to an empty spot at the far end of the room.

Karah mouthed, *Margarita*?

Laura nodded again.

Side-stepping through the crowd, Karah made her way to the empty table.

"If we couldn't laugh, we'd all go insane," the singer crooned as she sat down and the crowd clapped half-heartedly.

A few minutes later, Laura slid two-mile-high Margaritas onto the table and slumped down in the chair across from Karah. Her usually blonde, vivacious, and beautiful cousin was looking particularly hollow-eyed, harrowed and disheveled.

"You would NOT believe what kind of day I've had," said Laura, and took a long gulp from the tequila-laden beverage that conspicuously didn't have a salt ring or an umbrella in it.

"Tell me." Karah reached across the table and

took Laura's hand.

Her cousin's shoulders slumped and heavy tears began to form in her eyes. "Daddy's gone."

Over the next thirty minutes, she told the story of Rick Hairre's untimely demise. Though Rick wasn't a blood uncle to Karah, she was still shocked and saddened to hear he was tortured and murdered.

"Sweetie," Karah said as she wiped a tear from her face, "you need to go home."

"Can't." Laura sniffed and rubbed her red-ringed eyes. "Can't afford to."

"Have you called his family?"

"Oh shit," she said, suddenly realizing she hadn't told anyone about it. "I guess I should call the Starlingtons, not that they give a rat's ass. I don't know if there's anyone else to tell." She reached down into her apron pocket, then said under her breath, "Dammit."

"What?" Karah asked.

"My phone got stolen by some giant tattooed asshat who was in here throwing punches at college guys."

Karah slid her phone across the table. "I think that asshat ran over me in coming in."

Laura's expression looked surprised.

"It's okay," Karah said and waved her hand, "Eric came to my rescue."

Laura clicked open the phone. "He likes you, ya know."

"Uh huh." Karah's eyes twinkled. "But I've got a bigger fish on the hook than him." Karah reached over and clicked the Instagram icon, opening the app. She slid over to the photograph of Troy she'd taken shortly after he'd been attacked by the Jon boat. *Hmm, 147 likes. Nice*, she thought.

"I know, I know." Laura pointed at her screen name under the picture. "I saw it *and* the other fourteen pics of him you sent me. Cute."

"You have no idea." Karah pulled out a tube of shimmering lip gloss. "He'll probably be here any minute."

"Really?" Laura raised an eyebrow and clicked out of Instagram.

The phone's background was a picture of Troy that had been taken the day after the fishing incident. He hadn't known she was taking his picture from the porch of his own beach house.

He was standing out on the beach wearing a straw cowboy hat and khaki shorts. Karah's cousin shook her head and grinned.

"It's the hat, isn't it?" Laura asked.

"Definitely the hat."

Something tickled the back of Laura's mind. Something about the hat. It was one of those things that you searched your mind for, but couldn't come up with it ... the name of a movie or a song. Eventually, you just searched the internet and everyone would say, *ohhhh, yeahhhhh*, that's what it was. She didn't think about it long. It would come to her.

———

THE DARKNESS slowly receded from Darren's beat up brain. He tumbled around unrestrained in the back of the bronze van as his *partner*, Man'ti, slammed on the gas. The sound of gravel pelting against the underside of the van told him they were off-road, or at least on an unpaved road.

He could feel the infection burning again in his foot and leg. When he put pressure on the disgusting makeshift bandages, a rotten smell oozed out and fire shot up his ankle. He pulled himself up and peered out the front windshield of the van. Darkness was all he could see.

"Where the fook are ye takin' us, mate?" he asked to his hulking New Zealander driver.

"We gotta disappeyah fer a bit." Man'ti looked back over his shoulder.

Darren could taste the foul, stale vomit crusted in and around his mouth. "Stop at the next petrol station. Ah need a drink."

"We ain't stoppin'."

This bloke's forgot who's in charge here, Darren thought as he climbed into the passenger's seat.

"Now, listen, ya freak of nature." Darren pulled a small pistol from his belt and pointed it at Man'ti. "Ya moyt be big, but me gun's bigga. Ah need a drink and a hospital."

It was a tiny pistol, maybe a .22 caliber that looked to maybe be a woman's purse gun. Man'ti did not appear to be impressed. In fact, Darren watched in disbelief as he slowly smiled, then grinned, and then began to laugh.

With impossible speed, Man'ti grabbed the back of Darren's head and slammed it forward into the dashboard. Darren felt a crack somewhere under his left eye in the split second before the airbag deployed, throwing him backward into the seat and pinning his hand with the gun against his face. Either the van's ABS or Man'ti, he didn't know which, slammed on the brakes, bringing the van to a squealing halt.

Without thinking, he emptied the revolver and fire burned his cheek. The barrel had become red hot and was melting his face, but he didn't care as long as Man'ti was full of bullet holes. The sound of glass shattering out of the driver's door was pleasing to hear, and he waited to hear the big man screaming. That sound never came.

The airbag began to deflate, releasing Darren only to see an extremely mad Man'ti staring at him. There were no bullet holes in the man.

Darren lifted the revolver and grinned. "Say g'night ya bahstad!"

He clicked the gun ten times before he realized it wasn't firing. Tears began to form in his eyes as he remembered he'd just emptied the gun a few seconds ago. *Shit*, he thought..

Man'ti grabbed the tiny gun and jerked it out of Darren's hand. It was so small that the gun's trigger guard was tight on his forefinger and in one quick motion, the giant Kiwi had not only ripped the gun out of Darren's grip, but had also removed his forefinger and the top half of his thumb. He hadn't thought he could feel much more pain, but suddenly he did.

"Ah, fer shit's sake!" Darren grasped his hand. "Not me hand."

Suddenly, Man'ti's hand was around his throat and Darren "The Body" McGlashen began to think his time on earth was done. But amazingly, he didn't die.

"Mate," Man'ti said through gritted teeth, "you and me's through. Ah'm callin' the boss, see what bridge he wants me to bury ya unda."

Darren could feel the whimpers coming out of his mouth. "Jus' leave me, mate. Out by the road ... anywhere ... I probly won't make it anyway."

"Shut yer fookin' trap," said Man'ti as he pulled a cellphone from his pocket.

The big man stepped out of the van and walked around to the front, cellphone up to his ear. Darren watched as he spoke, trying to read his lips, and thus, his fate. Man'ti looked back toward him and nodded in apparent response to whoever was on the phone.

Darren groaned and whimpered and shook uncontrollably ... until he noticed the keys were still in the van's ignition. Man'ti did not appear to be in a hurry to get off the phone, and a plan began to percolate into Darren's hazy mind. He waited for Man'ti to rotate and face away from the van, and as quietly as he could, he inched over into the driver's seat.

With his intact left hand, he quietly locked the door. With his torn up right hand, he gingerly reached for the key. In an instant, Man'ti whirled around.

"Don't even ... " he started to yell as Darren fired up the van.

Darren laughed maniacally as he gunned the van and put it in drive. Pain shot into his ruined right foot as he slammed the accelerator to the floor.

Man'ti had run around to the driver's side where the window had been shot out and was reaching for Darren, but he was too slow. The bronze van was powerful, if nothing else, and before Darren could hear the rest of the New Zealander's yell, he had left him in the dust.

Darren wasn't sure if he was still laughing or crying when he looked up into the rear-view mirror and caught sight of his face. His left eye was still blood red from the beer bottle at Drunken Jack's, his left eye socket looked like someone had thrown a baseball at him and left a crater in his skull ... but his right eye was still okay. His right cheek had the perfect red, blistered outline of a pistol melted into it.

Darren grabbed the rear-view mirror with his now three fingered right hand and jerked it straight up so he couldn't see himself in it. *Hospital*, he thought, *thas what ah need.*

"Then ahm gonna find 'at fooka and murder his tattooed ass," he said to no one.

As he drove, he could see a hazy light growing in the distance ... hopefully a city ... a city with a nice hospital. Civilization began to appear and his hopes were answered by the first gas station attendant who would speak to him. The St. Francis Hospital in Litchfield wasn't far away, and they had a pretty nice emergency room according to the attendant. The drive would give Darren a chance to regroup and get ahold of his boss ... and plan the demise of his former colleague, Man'ti.

He grinned and clicked on the radio. He couldn't help but laugh at the Judas Priest song that blared into the night.

"Yeah, mate! You got anotha thing comin'!" Darren screamed the rock anthem out the busted window into the cool rushing air.

———

MAN'TI WATCHED in disbelief as the airbrushed sunset scene on the back of the bronze van got smaller and smaller. A ping from the cellphone in his hand brought him out of his shock. He held it up. Text notification from *Cute Cop*:

-*On way.*

Man'ti shrugged his shoulders, and hit the back button, more out of curiosity than anything else. The last text was from someone called *Sexi Cuz*.

That's more like it, he thought. He scrolled back through the past few messages. A couple of the messages were photos, so of course, he opened them.

"Ah, shit's sake," he muttered out loud as he scrolled through the pictures. "*Cuz* is a fookin' dude."

As he thumbed further backwards in the photos, he realized *Sexi Cuz* was not the dude, but a girl sending pictures of a dude. He found one that made him stop short. It was a picture of a man standing knee deep in the surf at a very familiar piece of beach in front of a very familiar beach house on Pawleys Island. The man was dark haired, tan, looked to be about forty, and he was wearing a cowboy hat with sungla— The hat.

Man'ti scratched his chin, which was beginning to stubble over from the lack of a shower and shave. The hat was an incredibly distinctive straw cowboy hat with a peacock feather stuck on the back. Not exactly the kind of hat you see every day ... but he couldn't place where he'd seen it before and why it made him so curious. He scrolled back to another closer picture of the man wearing the hat, and it hit him.

"Thet hat belongs to fookin' Rick Hairre!" He pointed at the screen. "How the fook did 'is fooker get it on 'is head?"

He started walking a little faster down the street, not exactly sure where he was headed, but very sure where he needed to go. As he pinched, out enlarging the photo to study the hat more closely, a thought crossed his mind about the recently departed Mr. Hairre and the Outback Tea Stained Cowboy Hat.

"Ah shit. Ya gotta be fookin' kiddin' me." He clicked out of the text message and quickly dialed the number he'd just called ten minutes earlier.

The voice on the other end of the line said, "Vell, iz it done?"

"Nah exactly." Man'ti gritted his teeth. "Darren took off with me van."

"Then vie are ve speaking?"

"Ah need t'come visit. Ah think ah found it."

"By all means," the voice said. "Find your friend, Darren, bring him here. Und den ve vill discuss zee otha matter."

"Right."

Part II

Check Please

"I don't want to smoke cigars or go to stag parties, wear jockey shorts or pick up the check."
-Shelley Winters

18

Hard Labor

DAISY MAE GALLUP had one hand on the slippery, cracked dashboard of the 1977 bumblebee yellow-on-black-on-rust Chevy Camaro and one hand on the bottom of her burgeoning, pregnant belly. Ellie Mae Gallup was driving and had the car and trailer rocking violently with each turn.

"I'm gon' git that sumbitch, Sis," she yelled over the loudly protesting engine. "Jus' you hang on now, ya hear?"

Daisy Mae Gallup did not answer for fear of vomit spewing up and out of her mouth. She was afraid to tell Ellie Mae that her stomach, or at least something deep inside her stomach, was aching somethin' fierce.

Chasing the Lincoln Towncar containing Troy

(Daisy Mae's alleged *baby-daddy*) off of Pawley's Island was an oddly slow high-speed chase. The listed speed limit of 25mph was rigorously enforced and the last thing Daisy Mae wanted was to get pulled over when she was so close to nabbing Troy and making him accept responsibility for his unborn child.

"Not so fast, Ellie Mae!" she kept yelling, but her sister wasn't having any of that.

"I ain't slowin' 'is thang down 'til he's in here with you!" she yelled back.

The Camaro and trailer hit a bump hard after crossing the Pawleys north causeway bridge and something kicked hard inside Daisy Mae's belly.

"Hey, stop 'at little T.C." She looked down and tapped her own stomach.

Ellie Mae grinned over at her. "He's a-kickin' hard now that he knows his daddy's nearby."

Up ahead, the black car with Troy inside picked up speed as they left the island. Ellie Mae punched her foot on the accelerator until it hit the floor. The Camaro picked up speed incredibly slowly and the Lincoln they were chasing began to get farther and farther away.

"Go, ya Gall-Dang Chevy!" Ellie Mae beat her fist on the steering wheel. The horn honked loudly twice and then wouldn't stop. It just blared on without remorse.

The kicking feeling in her stomach started again and Daisy Mae began to realize it wasn't a kick at all.

"Ellie Mae!" she shouted over the horn.

"Don't bother me now," she yelled as they turned hard right onto Ocean Drive. "Once I git on the straightaway, I think I kin catch 'em!"

Daisy Mae began the breathing exercises she had seen in the YouTube video about going into labor. She didn't tell Ellie Mae that she was having contractions. But for now, they were pretty far apart and not very regular. *Jus' hang in there, little T.C.,* she thought to herself. As she looked up from her belly, she could see the black Lincoln Towncar getting smaller and smaller as it raced away from them.

"Where'n the hell are they goin' so dang fast?" Ellie Mae shouted over the horn.

————

TROY LOOKED BACK through the rear window of One-Eyed Willie's Lincoln Towncar. "They're not moving very fast, so can we lose them?"

"Mista Troy," the old man said, chuckling, "I

been practicin' the art of losin' little chirren in my ice cream truck fo years 'n years."

Good point, Troy thought.

"And if'n this car cain't outrun dat heap 'o junk, imma sell it tommorrah."

Another good point. Troy took out his cellphone and clicked open the message to Karah.

-*"Hey, you still at Jack's?"*

-*"Yeah, where are you? It's been like 45 mins!"*

-*"Sorry, crazy story. Uber took a side trip. I'll fill you in when I get there."*

-*"Don't rush, talking to my cuz. She's had a rough day."*

-*"Ok, be there soon."*

Rough day? Troy thought, *seems like they're going around.*

"Hey, Willie," he said and leaned forward and tapped his driver on the shoulder, "there's an extra twenty spot in it if you can get me there in a hurry."

One-Eyed Willie winked at him—which Troy thought was unsettling at best—and said, "Mista Troy, for a twenty, I git you there in ten!"

With that, Willie punched the accelerator and threw Troy back against his cushy leather seat. He grabbed the two ends of the seatbelt he hadn't been wearing and buckled them together quickly.

"I know a real good shote-cut," Willie said, veering onto the Business 17 exit, "we be there in two shakes of a lamb's tail."

———————

DEPUTY CHESNEY R. Biggins turned his cruiser down Wachesaw Road after a quick stop at the Kangaroo Market on the corner to grab a coffee. It was looking like a long night, and he wanted to be alert.

His mind kept going back to his notes and Rick Hairre's file he'd picked up from Tammy-Anne Tidmore at the GKCU. There had to be a clue to the councilman's murder in all his notes, but it all just seemed like ordinary life information.

He'd always thought he'd be good at CSI type work, but this was proving to be harder than he thought. First thing to do was get the password to the zip drive. He looked over at the yellow pad notes:

1. Georgetown Kraft Credit Union
   Debit Card
2. BankAmericard Rewards Visa – Expired
3. Driver's License – Issued to one Rickard

Bertram Hairre. *Rickard? Must be a family name.*

4. Hair Club of Georgetown membership card, ID #4747
5. Humana Medical Insurance Card issued by city council of Murrell's Inlet.
6. Five city council business cards
7. Post-It Note with address: 700 S. Kawasaki – googled for SC, no match. Closest match JFK Auto in NC.
8. Receipt from Lee's Inlet Kitchen

Something dawned on him as he read through the list. The zip drive hadn't asked for a password. He tossed the yellow pad into the passenger's seat and pulled his laptop open. He clicked the zip drive icon – F: and the box popped up asking him to login. It read: Username:_____ PIN:_____

"That's it!" he exclaimed, reaching for the credit union customer file.

As he did, he accidentally pulled the steering wheel and veered the cruiser into the oncoming traffic lane. But Wachesaw Road is a side street and has zero traffic late at night, so no one was coming. His coffee sloshed over the edge of the cup and burned his hand, startling him as he pulled back into his lane. He mopped at a few stray drops on the passenger's seat.

Ouch, Chesney thought as he put the laptop down and wiped the coffee from his hand. *That was a close one; it could've poured into my lap ... CRAP!*

While distracted with the coffee cup, Chesney had missed the stop sign and pulled straight out onto Business 17 and rammed t-bone style into the side of a black Lincoln Towncar.

In the driver's side window of the car, Chesney could see a very pissed off black man wearing a black suit and tie ... with a black patch over one eye.

"Willie?"

He couldn't hear the extremely animated ice cream truck driver, but he could clearly see him mouth the words, *You Sumbitch!*

———

ELLIE MAE GALLUP kicked the gravel parking lot with her beat up cowboy boot and banged her fist on the hood of the Camaro. Smoke billowed out from the edges and from the front grill.

"I cain't believe 'is P.O.S. decides ta give up right when we got 'im!"

She turned to peer down Ocean Drive, but there

was no sign of the Black Lincoln Towncar they had been chasing.

"Gall dangit!" she spat and kicked the driver's side tire, accidentally shearing the top off of the dry-rotted air nozzle. Air hissed out and the tire flattened in seconds.

"Are you freakin' kiddin' me?!" She kicked the tire again. "Piece 'a junk."

From inside the car she heard a low moaning. Daisy Mae Gallup was sitting in the passenger's side seat holding onto her stomach.

"What's takin' so long?" she yelled out her own window, "he's gettin' away!"

"I kin see 'at, Daisy Mae." Ellie Mae looked around the parking lot of Frank's. It served a clientele that had pricier vehicles, which were naturally harder to hotwire, but right next door, oddly, sat a Dollar General. The cars parked there looked much easier to—

"Miss?"

Her thought was interrupted by someone tapping her on the shoulder.

She whirled around. "What inna hell do you wa—"

She stopped mid-sentence. He was a cute young man, maybe twenty-five, lots of blonde hair and fairly muscled. He was wearing a Pawleys Island tank top and had sunglasses propped up on his head, even though it was nearly dark. Obviously a tourist. He'd apparently just stepped down out of a brand new, fire engine red, jacked up, decked out Jeep Wrangler Unlimited ... and it was still running.

"Are you having some trouble with your car?

Ellie Mae had a sudden flash of brilliance. "Oh, yes, thank you so much! This dang tire jus' blew up on me!"

The young man knelt down to inspect it and Ellie Mae gestured wildly over his back to Daisy Mae to get out of the car. She pointed to the Jeep and mouthed, *get in.*

The man looked up at her holding a broken air nozzle in his hand. "Here's your problem. You got a spare?"

"Oh my," Ellie Mae said and leaned over, exposing her cleavage—familiar territory to a former stripper—and said, "I do, but shore 'nuff, I cain't change no spare."

"Ma'am, I'd be happy to change it for you," he said, moving back to the trunk.

In a few minutes, he was hard at work on changing out the flattened tire for the spare. So hard, in fact, that he never noticed Ellie Mae climbing into the driver's seat of his Jeep.

He did notice when the Jeep suddenly gunned and kicked up gravel as it screeched out of Frank's parking lot.

Ellie Mae thought she could hear the man yelling as they turned onto Ocean Drive.

"Poor fella," Daisy Mae groaned.

Ellie Mae looked over at her sister. She was sweating bullets and breathing hard in a regular, pulsing rhythm. She had one hand on the door handle and one on her belly.

"Daisy Mae?" She brushed her sister's hair out of her face. "How you feelin'?"

"Ah think ah'm havin' a baby."

————

TROY WAS THROWN into the passenger's side door of One-Eyed Willie's Black Lincoln Towncar, but not hard enough to injure him. However, it *was* hard enough to throw him from the car.

He had seen the other car coming and knew there would be a crash, but didn't have time to warn Willie. He jumped sideways a split second before the collision and as he slammed into the passenger's side door, it popped open, spilling him gently onto the pavement. It then rocked back and forth a few times, essentially dropping Troy off on the ground unharmed.

He could hear Willie had gotten out of the car and was yelling at the other driver.

"Ya got ta be kiddin' me!" he heard the old man exclaim. "Two times in da same week?? And by da same dang po-leese car?"

Police car? He hadn't noticed it was a police car as it barreled toward them. Glancing back down Business 17 the way they had come, he didn't see any sign of the Gallup sisters on the road. He wondered if they'd given up the chase. Then he remembered why Willie had stopped at the condos in the first place ... probably enough weed to get them both arrested. He mentally apologized to the ice cream man/Uber driver, and crawled as quietly as he could to the side of the road. Ducking behind a scraggly bush on the corner, he peeked back at the scene of the accident.

Willie was gesturing wildly at the damage to his Black Lincoln Towncar and the cop was having no luck getting a word in edgewise. Neither man was paying attention to the passenger. Troy quickly sprinted away. He wasn't far from Drunken Jack's and figured he could make it pretty quickly on foot. He glanced at his cellphone. No messages. 1:47am.

Dammit. He quickly tapped out a text to Karah.

-*"You still there?"*

No response. He quickened his pace to a slow trot in the direction of DJ's and tapped out a second message.

-*"I'm almost there. More craziness. Tell you all about it when I get there."*

Then he added,

-*"Sorry, I'll make it up to you."*

He shoved his phone into his pocket and started jogging. *So much for a few casual beers and a quiet night.*

———

DAISY MAE GALLUP was breathing hard in between what Ellie Mae was now certain were contractions. Although they hadn't quite reached the magical 5-1-1 rhythm yet—five minutes apart, one minute long for one hour—Ellie Mae thought this baby was coming sooner rather than later. But they still had time to catch that rat, Troy, and get him to the hospital with them.

"Ah don't think I'm gon' make it, Ellie Mae,"

Daisy Mae wheezed between her Lamaze breathing. "We gotta git to the hospital now!"

In between her breaths of *hee hee hee* and *hoo hoo hoo*, she grabbed the wheel of the Jeep and jerked. Ellie Mae jerked it back, but not before they had swerved off Ocean Drive and onto the alternate road, Business 17.

"What in tarnation are you tryin' ta do, Daisy Mae?" she yelled as she steadied the racing Jeep into the proper lane. "Now ya done got us lost!"

Daisy Mae couldn't answer, she just grunted a long, slow, *pushing* grunt. Ellie Mae finally registered what was happening ... this baby was coming now. She put her hand on her sister's stomach, and said, "Okay sis, ta haile with that creep. Let's get you and Troy junior to the hospital."

Daisy Mae grunted again and nodded.

Ellie Mae slammed the Jeep's accelerator to the floor.

"Shit, hold on," she said and put both hands on the steering wheel. "There's a dang cop up ahead."

"Don't stop, sis-uhgghhh," Daisy Mae groaned out the last.

"I ain't plannin' ta."

———

CHESNEY WAS HAVING no luck getting through to One-Eyed Willie. The department's insurance would naturally pay for all the damages, but Willie was in a tirade ... and rightfully so. Just a day ago, Chesney had slammed into the rear end of his beautiful ice cream truck and here he sat with the hood of his cruiser buried into the side of Willie's Towncar. Luckily it had been just behind the driver's side door, so no bodily harm had come to the old man.

"Willie," Chesney said and held up both hands as he backed slowly toward his cruiser, "let me radio the station and get you a tow. They'll get you a rental in the meantime."

"A rental?!" Willie yelled. "Ah, don't need no rental. I jus' need cops ta stop crashin' inta mah vee-hicles."

Chesney ducked into his car and radioed Todd. "This is Chesney. I need a tow truck out on Business 17, a block south of Drunken Jack's."

Thankfully, Todd didn't retort with any middle school humor. Maybe he was finally getting bored with it.

"Willie, the tow should be here any minute," Chesney called out his window as he started to pull away from the Towncar.

One-Eyed Willie just threw his hands up, and

said, "Well, don't dat jus' beat all? I gotta sit 'n wait ona tow truck and you git ta ride off in da sunset? Sheeii—"

His expletive was cut off by the sudden screeching of tires as a brand new, fire engine red, jacked up, decked out Jeep Wrangler Unlimited swerved around the right side of Willie's Black Lincoln Towncar. The driver of the Jeep must not have realized the passenger's side door was still open from the wreck. The Jeep slammed into it, shearing it away from the car, and sent it flying down the road bouncing and spraying sparks as it tumbled.

Chesney had hunched down instinctively from the sound of the impact. He rose to see Willie hunched over with his hands on the side of his head ... thankfully unhurt.

"Ya got ta be effin' kiddin' me ... " was all Chesney could hear him say as he turned on his lights and took off after the Jeep.

"Todd, I got a lifted red Jeep Wrangler running high speed down on 17. In pursuit, may need backup."

"10-4 Officer Dick Biggins, we got your rear," came the radio squelched reply with a smattering of snickers in the background.

"Dammit, Todd," he yelled into the receiver, "this

is serious. Get your shit together and stop with the wisecracks."

"Settle down, Ches, jeez! Nothing ever happens around here. Just trying to stay awake."

"Well, give it a rest and send me some backup."

"10-4."

The more things change ... Chesney clicked the receiver down and focused on catching the Jeep. His cruiser groaned with the effort ... it had taken too many beatings to give much chase. He stomped the accelerator to the ground and hoped for the best.

———

DAISY MAE GALLUP was now having regular contractions and was pushing involuntarily.

Ellie Mae found herself breathing along with her, when suddenly Daisy Mae screamed. Ellie Mae looked in the rear-view mirror, and saw no sign of the cop car that had been following them since they took the open door off the black car sitting in the middle of the road.

"Oh, mah Gawd! I think he's comin' now! Pull over, PULL OVER!"

Ellie Mae jerked the Jeep into the next parking lot and skidded to a stop. Gravel was still flying as she jumped out of the Jeep and ran around to the other side.

"It's gon' be alright, Daisy Mae," she said, opening the passenger door and taking her sister's hand. "Let's git you inside and call a doctor. They gon' have ta come ta us tonight."

As Daisy Mae gingerly dropped down from the Jeep she looked up at the building situated at the rear of the gravel lot. "Drunken Jack's? Why'd you stop here?"

"It ain't like ya give me much choice!" Ellie Mae helped her sister walk toward the building. "Hell, it's good as any. I'm shore they gotta pho—"

Suddenly, through a blinding red haze forming in her eyes, she saw him standing at the top of the stairs leading into Drunken Jack's.

"TROYYYYYY!!!!!"

———

SOMEONE behind him screamed his name. It was a guttural scream, like a gladiator calling him out to die. Troy turned around to face his opponent. Cinnamon and Starr—or rather, Daisy Mae and Ellie Mae Gallup—were lurching across the parking lot toward him. Daisy Mae was leaning on Ellie Mae and breathing hard. She had one hand on her belly and looked like she might pop her baby out at any moment.

As they got closer, Ellie Mae pointed a finger at him. "You did 'is ta mah sister. Ya don' got her pregnant and runned off."

"What?" was all Troy could muster.

"Ain't a man's job to take care o' 'is family? Ta support his little 'uns?"

"Wait ... what?" Troy raised his hands.

"Donchu act like you don't know this here baby is yours," Ellie Mae said, and pointed to Daisy Mae's belly. "She don' told me he was yers!"

A light began to flicker on in Troy's mind. *Oh, sweet Jesus*, he thought, *they're crazier than I remember. They're trying to say Daisy Mae's baby is mine.*

"Now, Ellie Mae, hold on just a second," he said in low, gentle tones. "Don't you realize I haven't worked at the Hippo in over ten years?"

"We know 'at, stupid!" Ellie Mae shook her finger at Troy. "She's talkin' bout that night you spent back in Vegas fer yer brother's bachelor party! He's yers alright!"

Troy's mind raced ... *what the hell were they talking about*? He hadn't spoken to his brother, Ryan, since he left Afghanistan ... his brother, who had been discharged (reason unknown) had returned stateside and gone completely off the grid.

"Ellie Mae, my brother and I haven't spoken since before I worked at the Hippo. Hell, I haven't seen him since I was shipped off to Afghanistan."

Confusion spread across the girl's face. He could see her certainty falter.

"I'm not sure who you think, um … did this to your sister," he said, pointing to Daisy Mae, "but it couldn't have been me."

She thought for a second, then an evil smile spread on her face. "Oh yeah? Then explain 'is pitcher!"

She reached into her bra and brought out a faded but clearly recent Polaroid photograph of Daisy Mae looking slim and not pregnant. In one hand she held a cigarette, while her other arm was draped around a man holding a bottle of champagne. The man had longer, curly black hair, a short stubble beard, a decent tan and dark eyes … much like Troy.

She flipped it over and pointed to a date printed on the back. "See 'at? And you ev'n signed it!"

She handed the photo to Troy and smiled the smile of a victorious lawyer giving a perfect closing argument to seal the fate of the defendant.

Troy took a close look at the photo. It was clearly not him, though the man did bear a striking resemblance to him. He flipped it over to check out his *signature* on the back. The date did correspond to the impending baby ... just about eight and a half months ago. He could barely make out the scrawling text, but it became immediately clear what their mistake had been.

He handed the photo back to Ellie Mae, and said, "You've got the wrong man. Read it again."

Ellie Mae snatched it out of his hand suspiciously, and turned it over.

THANKS for one hell of a bachelor party! My brother and I will never forget it!

With love from Troy.

AND A LITTLE FARTHER DOWN, in almost illegible script, the signature:

Eric Bana

. . .

WHEN HE SAW the look of understanding slowly creep over her face, he said, "Hey, it's not all that bad. Apparently, you spent the night with Eric Bana. You know, from the movie, *Troy*?"

"Ho-lee-she-it," Ellie Mae said slowly.

"Yeah," said Troy, letting the silence hang for just a few seconds, "and I guess maybe also having his love child?"

"Hey, you two," Daisy Mae suddenly said out of nowhere, "can we 'scuss this later? My water jus' broke."

19

Hospitable Hospital

DARREN "THE BODY" McGlashen was teetering on the edge of unconsciousness when he pulled into the emergency room valet area at the St. Francis Hospital in Litchfield. His list of injuries was growing more severe by the minute and all of them threatened to render him unconscious ... but he couldn't afford to waste time with passing out, there was too much to do.

Unbelievably, there was a pay phone in the lobby of the emergency room, and though Darren had no change to his name he felt sure the boss would accept his collect call.

"Sir?" Someone tapped him on the shoulder. "We need you to fill out these forms."

An emergency room nurse with almost black

curly hair stood behind him holding out a bright pink clipboard and pen. He turned around so quickly that it must've startled her. She stepped back and shoved the clipboard at him as if she didn't want to catch whatever pestilence he hosted. Darren almost laughed at her.

"Look, um ... " —he tapped her nametag with the bloody nub of his right forefinger— "Rachel, is it? Ah ain't got no insurance. Ah ain't from 'is godforsaken country and from da way ah feel, ahm bettin' I got infections all ova me body. So, why don't we dispense wif dees forms and get me a docta, eh?"

The nurse seemed to find some courage. "If you want to be treated here, you're going to have to fill out at least your name, sir."

Darren snatched the clipboard out of her hand and she squeaked and ran back behind the reception desk. She picked up a phone and dialed quickly while staring at him out of the corner of her eye.

"Dammit," Darren muttered, scrawling his name out on the top of the forms the best he could with his missing digits. "Shouldna done that probly."

He reached up to push the zero on the payphone and quickly realized he didn't have a forefinger to push it with. He thumbed the zero, sending a jolt of pain lancing into his hand. With all his other pain, he'd forgotten he'd lost a little chunk of his thumb as well.

The operator picked up and he gave the boss's number for a collect call. When the beep sounded, he said, "McGlashen." After a few seconds, he heard the other end pick up and the operator ask if they would accept a collect call from the St. Francis Hospital from McGlashen.

"I vill accept da charges."

The call was connected and Darren began to run down the events of the past few days, the boss listening quietly with no comment. A nurse hurried past and he grabbed the clipboard and shoved it into her hands. She took it to the admitting desk, holding it as if it were a piece of rotten banana peel.

"And Man'ti's gone rogue," Darren growled at the end, "he friggin' tried ta kill me!"

Silence greeted him when he finished. Darren swallowed and waited.

"Und you haf not found eet?" the boss said finally.

"Well, um ... not yet."

"Dis story dat you haf told me ... is not exactly how Man'ti described eet ven he called a few minutes ago."

Ah, crikey, Darren thought, *the bloke musta called in first*.

"Ah dunno what 'e mighta said, but ... "

"Silence!"

"Sorry, boss," Darren croaked.

"I do not care vat is going on betveen da two ov you. Vat I do care about is de retrieval of my money."

"Yeah, um, we been all ova town and um ... can't seem ta locate it."

"Man'ti said he may know vere to find eet ... somzing about a hat?"

Darren's mind raced ... *hat*? *What fookin' hat*? He had no idea what Man'ti was talking about, but thought it best to fake it.

"Aw yeahhhh," he said, making it sound like he'd clued in on the detail, "the hat!"

"Yes, zee hat. You are at St. Francis, no?"

"Yeah, boss. Waitin' ta get treated."

"Man'ti vill be on zee way. Verk out your differences und get me my money."

"Done."

The line disconnected and Darren slumped down into the nearest waiting room plastic chair. His head was swimming and he had absolutely no idea what Man'ti was talking about with some hat. Maybe the big man was lying about it to put the boss off for a bit. But that's all fine; he was on his way here now. He'd find out what Man'ti was talking about and then murder that fooker.

"McGlashen?" His voice was called over the speaker. "Please report to the reception desk for admittance."

"Thank the good." He lurched up to the front desk, and said, "at's me, McGlashen."

Before the nurse could check him in, the front doors of the Emergency Room admittance area slid open and an alarm went off. Two blonde women dressed in clothes that didn't quite fit were rushing in through the doors. One woman was sitting in a wheelchair, sweating heavily and very pregnant. Running in just behind them was a man wearing a white shirt, khaki shorts, and a straw cowboy hat.

"Hey y'all, we needa doctor," shouted the woman who was pushing the wheelchair. "Mah sister's 'bout to ave a baby!"

The two women were obviously twins, blonde and maybe pretty at one time. Nurses rushed to their side and began helping the pregnant woman onto a gurney.

Ah shoulda said ah was havin' a baby, thought Darren, *woulda got in fasta.*

The women and nurses disappeared in a

whirlwind through swinging doors back into the bowels of the hospital.

The man who had come in with them (probably the baby daddy) was left standing in a daze. He looked at Darren and shrugged as he walked up to the admittance desk. Darren turned to the reception nurse to ask when he'd be able to go back.

"Howdy, friend," the man in the cowboy hat said and slapped him on the back, "you look like you could use a doctor."

"Well, that's why ahm fookin' heyah, mate ... " Darren looked up at the man and froze. He couldn't help but grin as he remembered the details from his *interrogation* of Rick Hairre.

"Ah like ya hat, mate," he said, cocking his head to one side. "Where'd ya get it?"

20

PINs And Needles

CHESNEY BIGGINS EASED his battered police cruiser into the parking lot of the now winding down Drunken Jack's. His chase of the Jeep Wrangler had ended with his car whining in protest and threatening to overheat. Smoke wafted up from the cracks in the front bumper and around the edges of the hood. He had Todd send Litchfield PD the plate number, but they were covered up ... unlikely the vehicle would ever surface again.

He looked at his watch: 2:30am. There were a few straggling patrons stumbling out to their cars, seeing a police car in the parking lot, then stumbling back into the bar ... presumably calling that cab they needed. Chesney wasn't here for that, but it was a good side effect of his presence. He shut the car off and walked into the bar.

The overhead lights were on, the last few hangers-on were paying their tabs, and the salty musician was wrapping mic cords around his arm and making eyes at a couple of saltier groupies. The air had a tang of smoke and vomit that was unmistakable in any bar at closing time. Above the quiet din of the restaurant, Chesney could hear a radio droning country music from the kitchen where the hired help dishwashers were clinking and clanking through the evening's dirty slop.

Laura Kate Starlington was running a rag over the bar top and dumping the bar rail mats out. Another college-age girl was sitting across from her on a barstool stirring a straw in a mostly full margarita. Laura smiled when she saw him, but it was a bit of a sarcastic smirk.

"Really?" she said, looking at her watch.

"You have no idea." Chesney raised his hands in a surrender gesture. "I've been all over town today, and to top it all off, I ran my car into an Uber driver on the way over here."

The other girl at the bar snapped her head around to look at him. "You were in an Uber crash? Where's the other driver? Is he okay?"

The girl stood up suddenly and clicked her phone on. Chesney had no idea why it would be of concern to her.

"Yeah, he's fine," he said, shaking his head, "except for the fact I've crashed into two of his cars this week."

She looked up from her phone. "Oh, poor Troy!"

"Troy?" Chesney asked. "Who the heck is Troy? I crashed into Willie."

"Who's Willie?" She looked confused.

"The one-eyed ice cream man who also, I guess, now drives ... or did drive ... for Uber."

If it was possible, she looked even more confused.

"Anyway, I didn't see any passengers in his car, so maybe your friend Troy took another car."

She didn't answer. She was busy clicking out a text message.

Chesney shrugged and turned to Laura. "Sorry, it's been a pretty strange night. What's been going on?"

Laura arched an eyebrow and put her hands on her hips.

"Well, pretty much a typical night at DJ's except for a couple of rough foreign guys bangin' up the frat boy tourists," she said, dropping her rag into the bar sink.

She fished around in her apron and pulled out a credit card. Chesney took it and looked at the name she'd told him earlier.

"Yeah, Victor Böhring," he said shaking his head. "It sounds so familiar, but I don't know. I googled him and came up with a few thousand results."

He placed the card into his shirt pocket. "Let me do some checking and I'll get back to you."

"So ... how are you?" he asked sheepishly. "I mean, with your dad and all that."

"I'm okay," she said, and smiled. "I haven't really had a chance to let it all sink in yet."

"Yeah."

An awkward silence settled in. Chesney realized that Laura's friend had been watching them talk.

"Sorry, and you are?" he said and stuck a hand out to her.

She shook it and chewed the end of her straw. "I'm Karah. And you are?"

"Uh hem!" Laura cleared her throat loudly. "This is Chesney. He's the cop working on my dad's case."

Karah winked at him. "Ohhhh, nice to meet you, Chesney."

She flashed a grin at Laura and then turned back toward him. "I've heard a lot about you."

Chesney could feel his cheeks redden slightly, and wished the bar lights had still been turned down so it wouldn't be so obvious.

"Well, um ... "

His radio crackled into the awkward conversation and for once Chesney was relieved to hear Todd's voice.

"Ches, we got a disturbance at St. Francis. Litchfield PD is covered up, can you get there?"

He clicked his shoulder mic. "On my way."

"Sorry girls." He nodded to Karah and then to Laura. "I'll um ... I'll check on this and then I'll call you later. You know, with whatever I can find out."

Laura tore a piece of receipt paper from the cash register and scribbled something on it. "Call me on Karah's cell. The asshat who was in here bashing things up earlier stole mine."

She smiled and arched an eyebrow at him as she handed him the number. "Or you can just stop by and see us later. We'll be enjoying the beach."

He was glad he had his back turned as his own grin was hard to conceal. Over his shoulder he heard Karah say to Laura under her breath, "Cute!"

. . .

CHESNEY SLID into his patrol car on a slightly sticky seat. He remembered the overturned coffee he'd purchased and decided that he'd get a new one for the drive to Litchfield. Still feeling the glow of seeing Laura, he decided he'd splurge this time and get Starbucks. He clicked open their mobile app on his phone and began typing in his password to see if he still had any credit. *Buck forty-two. Hardly enough to buy anyt ...* His thoughts trailed off as he suddenly remembered his train of thought on Rick Hairre's zip drive and the PIN.

He opened his laptop (also a little sticky from spilled coffee residue) and clicked the F: symbol indicating the plugged-in zip drive. Again, he was prompted:

USERNAME:
    PIN:

HE OPENED the manila folder Tammy Anne Tidmore had secreted to him at the Georgetown Kraft Credit Union. Among other penciled information, the outside read: Rick Hairre, Account #04132016.

He leafed through the papers until he found what he was looking for: a single sheet reading Debit Card Personal Identification Number.

In the middle of the sheet in what must have been Rick's handwriting was scrawled the four-digit PIN: *4747*. He looked back at his yellow pad and noted that his ID card for the Hair Club had also been 4747. The number must've had some significance for Rick.

Chesney proudly started to type in the PIN on the zip drive prompt, but his elation was quickly doused. *What the heck is his username?*

He tried several combinations of Rick Hairre, R. Hairre, Rick H. and R.H., but none unlocked the drive. He flipped back to his yellow pad.

Number 3 read: Driver's License – Issued to one Rickard Bertram Hairre.

He clicked Username and typed Rickard Hairre and then the PIN: 4747.

His laptop made a whirring sound and the login box was replaced by a spinning circle indicating it was working. The contents of the drive popped up in a file manager window.

Four files were displayed:

GKCU_Deposit_Slip_LKS.jpg

IMG_4833.jpg

TCWEdPro.pdf

VNHSBC002-08171971-47.pdf

He double clicked the first file and the image popped up on his screen: a deposit slip for $500,000. Chesney whistled through his teeth. *Where'd you get all that money, Rick?*

He scanned the deposit slip, noting that the account number didn't match the account number on Rick's file from the credit union. *And where did you deposit it? Looks like I may have some more detective work for Tammy Anne.*

His radio crackled and jolted his attention from his screen. "Hey, um, Ches? I hate to be a *dick*, but ... " There were not-so-restrained snickers after the pause. "I know you've had a *hard* night but, um, are you at the hospital yet? They called back and said there was no sign of you."

Chesney didn't answer. He put his cruiser into drive, hoping the engine would hold together long enough for him to get to Starbucks. *Screw 'em, they can wait*, he thought, *I'm gettin' a coffee.*

21

Deal or No Deal?

TROY WATCHED AS THE HUGE, muscled security guard (whose nametag designated him as an orderly) wheeled the odd little man back through the stainless double doors into the emergency room proper. He'd gotten worked into a frenzy yelling something at Troy about stealing his hat and that he'd have his guts for garters before he'd let him walk out of the hospital with it.

Orderly Eric had slammed a needle into the man's backside and Troy watched his eyes roll back into his head. He slumped down into a wheelchair that had been slid behind him, and off he went.

He looked like a wreck and Troy thought he must've been on drugs or something. *Probably gang violence*, he thought, *too much of that goes on around here.*

"So, how are Daisy Mae and Ellie Mae coming along?" he asked the reception nurse.

"She's pushin'," the nurse said without looking up from her computer, "probably gonna have a baby soon."

"No way! Really?" Troy smiled through his sarcasm.

The nurse shrugged her shoulders and eyeballed Troy above her tiny reading glasses. "When the baby is born, if the mother says you're allowed, you can go in. Not before."

"Okay, okay ... " Troy tapped his fingers on the counter, "I'll be over here ... just waitin'."

"Fine."

Troy sidled back over to the emergency room waiting area and slid down onto the vinyl couch. It felt a little sticky and he wondered what fluids might have caused that ... he stood up.

He put his hands in his pocket and suddenly remembered his cell phone.

"Ah, crap," he said, clicking into his missed text messages.

There were fifteen new messages from Karah.

.   .   .

- *"ARE YOU OK?"*

    -*"Cop said there was an Uber crash."*

    -*"Did your Uber crash?"*

    -*"Where are you?"*

    -*"Troy??"*

    -*"We're leaving DJ's. Call me."*

    -*"Ok, I'm starting to worry now."*

    -*"If you didn't want to come, you could've just said so."*

    -*"Sorry about that last text. Just let me know you're ok."*

They went on like that, but he didn't finish reading them. He tapped out a quick text back.

- *"I'M FINE. Sorry. Yes, Uber crashed, but I'm fine."*

    -"WTH. Why didn't you text me?"

    -*"Sorry, you have no idea what I've been through tonight."*

    -"Well, that makes two of us."

    -*"I'm really sorry, Karah. Where are you now?"*

    -"Back at my place. Laura is with me. You should come over."

    -*"On my way."*

    -"For real this time?"

-*"Yes, for real. I'm taking a cab."*

-"Good."

TROY WALKED BACK UP to the reception nurse. Before he could speak, she removed her glasses, held up her hand in the universal *stop* signal, and said, "No, you can not go back there yet."

Troy smiled his biggest smile. "Well, that's good, cause all I was gonna ask for was a cab to go home."

She rolled her eyes and handed him a business card for Creekside Cab Company.

"Thank ya, darlin'."

She didn't answer and went back to clicking away on her computer keyboard.

Troy walked outside and dialed the cab company. His ride (a bright orange Crown Vic with a surfer dude painted on the hood) pulled up to the ER doors within fifteen minutes. The morning light was beginning to paint a new sunrise over the trees and Troy wondered what craziness today would bring. He'd come to South Carolina for peace and quiet ... to get away from all the madness in his past. And now he was caught up in all this new crap ...

"Where ya headed, my friend?"

"Pawleys. The Turtle Nest house, you know it?"

"Ya mon, get ya dere real quick."

"No, no, just take your time."

"Whatever your pleasure, mon."

Troy settled back into the cab's back seat. Within minutes, he was asleep.

———

DARREN WOKE to feel throbbing pains in his right eye, his right cheek, his right hand, his nose, and his right foot. His vision was blurry and he had drool crusted on his chin. His various injuries had pristine new bandages, but the one on his foot was starting to bloom new dark circles where his toes had been.

He felt groggy and bleary-eyed and wondered how many painkilling drugs they had pumped into him. He actually felt pretty good ... all things considered. He looked to his left and saw a pretty blonde girl sleeping in the next bed. In what looked like a fried chicken warming tray, there was a tiny little baby sleeping as well. In a chair, next to the tray, was an exact replica of the girl sleeping in the bed. They were beautiful.

"Gr'dayee," he mumbled through his drug-induced haze. It came out sounding like he had a mouth full of marbles. He swallowed and tried again. "Howrdyyy, bonny girrllss."

He didn't know what he was saying, but it woke the girl in the chair.

"You ain't Troy," she said suspiciously. "Whar the hell is Troy?"

Darren could only shrug his shoulders. "Got no idea what thet eez."

"Well, then who the Sam hell are you?"

With extreme effort, Darren sat up in his bed. Pain lanced through his various injuries and sent him into a groggy flop back down onto his back.

The girl jumped up out of her chair and ran to her sister's side. She grabbed the nurse call remote and clicked the button several times. The nurse's voice came over the intercom, sounding very much like she'd been enjoying a coffee or a smoke and was being interrupted.

"What is it now?" the nurse asked.

"Thar's a strange man in my sister's room."

Darren took offense to that. "Ahm not thet strange!"

"The hospital is over full tonight, ma'am," the nurse said, sounding as if she had explained this a thousand times before, "and that man has significant injuries. Your room was the only room with a bed left."

"But he's lookin' at me all funny like."

Darren sat up again and looked over at her. "Huh?"

"Thar, see?" she said, pointing at him. "He done it agin."

"Ma'am, if there's no emergency attention needed, I have work to do. The doctor will be doing rounds soon for your sister's baby and you'll probably be moved to a regular room by yourselves soon."

"Better sooner 'n later," she harrumphed.

The nurse had disconnected the intercom when the baby squawked. Darren watched as the girl raced over to the chicken warming tray and lifted the baby up to cradle it.

"Thar, thar little one," she cooed at the baby, "mama's getting' some shut eye. Aunt Ellie Mae is here."

Something in Darren softened. He never had a mama—or an aunt for that matter—pay him any attention. Psychologists in the pen tried to tell him that was why he was a criminal ... something about neglect and all that.

"Thet's a beautiful baby," he said, adjusting his

bed with the electric remote so that he could see them better.

The woman, Aunt Ellie Mae, glared at him, but then she softened a bit too.

"I know he is." She traced her hand over the top of the baby's head. "Cuz his mama's beautiful too."

Darren felt tears begin to well in his eyes. "Thet she is."

"Who are you?"

He thought Ellie Mae seemed to be asking less out of suspicion and more out of curiosity.

"Name's Darren," he said, nodding.

"You in a car wreck or sumthin'?"

Darren opened his mouth to say no, that he'd had his toes torn off by a rogue recliner, his eyeball and socket crushed by a beer bottle and a fist, his other eye slammed into the dashboard of a van, his cheek burned by the barrel of a gun he'd been shooting at his criminal partner, and his fingers ripped off by that partner grabbing the gun out of his hand, but then he thought better of it.

"Yeah, that's it," he said and smiled, sending a sharp pain into his cheek, "car wreck. Damn drunk driver."

"I'm so sorry," she said, "I hope they ketch the bastard!"

"Ah, don't ya worry, lass." Darren pictured Man'ti in his mind. "Ahm gonna get 'im good."

Ellie Mae shrugged. Beside them, the other girl in the bed yawned and opened her eyes.

"C'mere little T.C." She stretched out her hands and Ellie Mae handed her the baby. "Yer mama's here. You hungry, little one?"

She promptly pulled out her boob and shoved the baby on it. Little T.C. began to nurse.

"Daisy Mae," —Ellie Mae pointed a finger— "This here's Darren, right?"

He nodded.

"He was in an awful car wreck."

"I can see 'at. Ya look like shit," Daisy Mae said matter-of-factly.

Darren flushed. "Ah don't normally look like 'is! Ahm pretty good lookin' actually."

Daisy Mae shrugged and turned to her sister. "Whar's Troy?"

"He done run off."

"What? Why?"

"Guess he figured since little T.C. ain't his, he's off scott free."

"Well, shee-it." Daisy Mae switched the baby to her other boob. "Who's gone take care of us and little T.C."

Darren watched this exchange with growing interest and an idea bloomed behind his broken eye socket.

"Ah ken take care of all three of ya," he said, surprising himself.

She turned toward him, looking at him as if they thought his meds had made him crazy.

"Ah got so much money comin' in that it'll set us all fa life," he said defensively, "but we might have ta move to Mexico ... or Australia."

His clouded mind was still working on the small detail that Troy had disappeared, but he'd figure that out later.

"I ain't never been to Mex-eee-co," Daisy said to her sister.

"And we can all get married," he started, "or at least two of us ken get married. The other could be a live-in or something."

He could see that the sisters were clearly warming up to the idea.

"You'll hev all tha money ya eva need," he said, trying to clinch it. "Ah got seven million comin'."

Ellie Mae whistled through her teeth. "Seven million?"

Daisy Mae looked down at her baby. "At's enough to make 'lil T.C. very happy!"

"Um, yeah." Darren crinkled his eyebrows. "About thet. Any way you'd consider changin' 'is name to little Darren?"

"Darren Gallup," Daisy Mae said, testing out the name. "It does have a nice ring to it. What you think, Ellie Mae?"

"I think it sounds like a million bucks!"

"Seven million," Darren corrected her. "Is thet a deal, ladies?"

Ellie Mae looked at Daisy Mae. They nodded at each other.

"Yup, it's a deal," Daisy Mae said, smiling. "Little T.C.—er, ah mean little Darren—is gonna be so happy!"

"The deal is," a deep voice said from the door to the hospital room, "ya comin' wit me."

The girls jumped at the sound of a new voice and gaped at the figure in the doorway. A giant man with close-cut black hair and black tattoos scrawled all over his muscled arms stood silhouetted in the opening. He had on a black t-shirt and black jeans that strained against his NFL sized shoulders and legs. His skin was dark olive and slick. His eyes were hidden in the shadows.

"Ah, shit," Darren whimpered.

"Get ya shit and let's get outta heyah," the giant said and turned to walk out.

Darren eased out of the bed and said to the wide-eyed girls, "Take good care 'o little Darren. Ah'll be beck."

22

A Böhring Family Vacation

VICTOR BÖHRING CONSIDERED himself a man of impeccable taste. His hands caressed the dark wood inlays on the steering wheel of his brand-new Mercedes Benz AMG G65 SUV. It was the only vehicle he'd found that matched his considerably high standards.

He eased the accelerator toward the floorboard and the 621-horsepower engine pushed him backward into the black handcrafted Napa leather diamond stitch patterned driver's seat. He lovingly traced the gleaming chrome Mercedes logo on the horn, and allowed himself a small tight-lipped smile. He loved this car.

His newly constructed beach home on Pawleys Island had been built with the same attention to detail. By the island's standards, the house was palatial. Eight bedrooms and six bathrooms, each with its own particular theme, made the house into a veritable beach mansion. Lazy palm leaf ceiling fans kept the air breezing comfortably over the terrazzo marble floor. A modern palette of creamy whites with splashes of bright colors in the furnishings. Custom artwork on every wall represented the theme of each room.

The master suite was an exact duplicate of the honeymoon suite at the private island estate in Jamaica that had served as the Böhring's marital holiday destination. A massive four-poster mahogany bed with draped sheets, deep chocolate furnishings with only the smallest antique brass knobs, hinges and pulls, and original Angela Moulton paintings of local birds and landscapes, made this room anything but shabby island chic. It was more like a European interpretation of shabby island chic, which suited Victor just fine. It was in this bedroom that Mrs. Böhring slept, awaiting her husband in a mid-morning, mimosa-fueled daze.

Victor had been feeling particularly generous, so he called ahead to have the maid warn his wife he was coming. She usually required half an hour or so to compose herself. Her melancholy moods were becoming tiresome. He would do something about this soon.

As he turned onto Myrtle Avenue, the main drag on Pawleys Island, he slowed to the required twenty-five miles per hour. Normally, it didn't bother him to cruise at the island speed limit, but today he was in a bit of a rush. Tourists on rusty rental bicycles, runners carrying bottled waters and iPods, and the occasional high strung toddler mom pushing a stroller, crowded the street. This time of year, it made the two-lane road a veritable obstacle course to navigate.

He tapped his horn twice to gently nudge a double-wide stroller over just a little and gave the obligatory sorry-about-that wave as he passed. "Go home, Yankee," he whispered under his breath, and smiled a broad, gleaming white smile.

The crunch of gravel was satisfying under the wheels of his new Mercedes as he pulled into his new beach home. The outside of the house was broad and covered four side-by-side parking spaces beneath. The green metal roof covered two stories of window after window winged by green storm shutters, all of which overlooked creek-side and beachside wraparound porches. Stately square columns held charcoal grey railings and offered foot rests to at least twenty white rocking chairs. Victor was looking forward to resting his travel-aching body in one of those chairs while sipping on a beautiful Pinot Noir he'd brought for just that purpose.

Again, feeling generous, he shut off the car and tapped the horn twice and waited. Everyone deserved at least a little warning. He pulled the driver's side sun visor down and adjusted the mirror so he could see himself. He had the smooth tan that came from perfectly even man-made tanning lotions and clear, crystal blue eyes. The lines around his eyes had deepened in the past few years, more from stress than laughter, but he'd had a few Botox treatments to slow that down. He ran his tongue over the new perfectly white caps on his front teeth; coffee, wine and cigars had yellowed his own until he'd decided to get them fixed. Finger combing his hair straight back revealed a hairline that had also been surgically augmented, but only a very close inspection would reveal that to any observer. He'd kept it salt and pepper though; it looked distinguished and age-appropriate, even if his smooth skin did not.

He glanced down at his Junghans Meister Handaufzug watch, a timepiece that equaled the

Mercedes in craftsmanship and elegance, and decided that he'd given them enough time. He wondered if the children would come up from the beach to meet him. Often when they did, he felt very much like Captain Georg von Trapp from the sound of music, interviewing his offspring about their recent behavior and escapades. He didn't have the whistle to blow to send them scampering to and fro, but he thought he might acquire one soon.

As he closed the door of his SUV, a stray beach ball floated in and bounced off the hood. He grabbed it quickly before it could bounce again and squeezed it until it popped. Pushing the button to call the elevator to the ground floor, he idly threw the busted ball into a nearby trash container. *I vill devinitely be getting a vhistle*, he thought to himself.

———

LAURA STARLINGTON YAWNED as she clicked through the first few pages of a new book on her Kindle, trying desperately to become attached to the new characters, but it just wasn't happening. The first book in the series had been amazing, but this one just hadn't caught any steam yet. She had gotten up and dragged her chair down to the beach to watch the sunrise. It was a good one this morning; Pawleys never disappointed in the sunrise department.

Her toes were digging in the crunchy bits of shell that had washed up with the tide as her right hand traced the condensation on her mimosa. Her cousin, Karah Campobello, was still in the bed after their crazy late night at Drunken Jack's.

Frat boy bar fights and weird foreign dudes barfing all over and creepy, psycho wrestler looking guys using stolen credit cards; it had been a circus. In fact, thinking back about the night, she realized all those characters were more interesting than the ones in her new paperback. If this book didn't get any better, Laura thought she'd run to Starbuck's for a couple of coffees to help pep things up around her Pawleys Island cabana.

A couple of houses to the North, four cute little kids were digging in the sand, throwing a beach ball around and splashing in the gentle surf. They looked to range from about five-years-old all the way up to ten. They all had shockingly blonde hair, and matching teal swimsuits with matching teal beach towels. She thought if she ever had kids, she wanted them to look like these kids. They looked like kids from a Parenting magazine ad. A horn honked twice and the kids froze, all of them looking up like a group of meerkats scanning the beach for a predator. Nobody moved.

Suddenly, running down from the house was an older boy. He ran like he was trying to warn the others of a boulder chasing him out of a cave like Indiana Jones. He stumbled and fell to his hands and knees in a splash of sand.

"D.A.D.!!! Repeat, we've got a DAD alert!!" he yelled. "Did you hear me? D.A.D.!!"

The kids playing in the sand scrambled to pick up belongings; towels, beach balls, sand castle building tools, paddle balls and paddles, bocce balls and Frisbees. They looked like the victims of Pompeii, furiously—but futilely—trying to escape some impending doom.

The older boy looked almost in tears as he cried. "Hurry guys! He's coming!"

In a whirlwind of dropping toys, picking up towels, running, falling and stumbling, the children made their way up the beach collecting their fallen comrades along the run like the soldiers storming Normandy on D-Day. And suddenly it was quiet again.

Laura tipped her hat back on her head and looked at her watch: 6:48am. *Mmmm, Starbucks will be open by the time I get there!* She dragged her chair up toward the dune, and plopped it down on the deck, not bothering to spray it off (they'd be back out on the beach in a little while anyway).

She dipped her feet into a tub of cool water to wash the sand from between her toes and slipped her flip flops on. Entering the house always felt like stepping into a refrigerator, and she wrapped the towel around her shivering body. She listened for Karah and heard her soft snoring coming from the upstairs bedroom. *Lazy thing won't be up for at least another hour, plenty of time to grab a couple of lattes.*

She jotted out a quick note and grabbed Karah's keys, since her cousin's Land Rover was parked behind her Jetta. No need to get dressed; she'd be hitting the drive-through anyway. She clicked the door shut and padded down to the car.

Karah's cell phone was lying in the console compartment between the driver's seat and the passenger's seat. Idly, Laura picked it up and clicked it on. One missed message from Troy early this morning:

-*"In cab, on way."*

Laura clicked out a reply:

-"Hey it's Laura, Karah still sleeping. Heading to

Starbucks, you'll probably beat me back. You want something?"

-"*Yeah, get me that white chocolate thingy they have.*"

Laura couldn't help but smile—that had to be Karah's doing.

-"You got it. See you in a bit."

She dropped the phone into the passenger's seat and headed north to the causeway.

————

VICTOR BÖHRING PACED BACK and forth as his children dripped on the marble floor. They were shivering in the air conditioning, all in various states of dampness and sandiness from the beach. The maid stood at the end of the line, lips pursed and looking as if she were guilty of the children's current disheveled state. Victor preferred everything to be in very precise, neat order, including his offspring.

The shock on their faces resembled those of an audience watching Harry Houdini perform an incredible escape, when he said, "one hour. Zat eez your beach time today."

The youngest girl, Eliza, said, "Yayyy, thank you, Daddy!!"

"Shhhhh!" the others scolded her.

"You are velcome," he said and ruffled her nearly white hair. "Off vit you. Enjoy your day."

The children jumped for joy and laughed hysterically as if Christmas had come in the summer. Within seconds, they were back on the beach and the maid was standing alone, dumbstruck by the generosity of her employer.

"Meester Böhring," she started to say, "thees ees wonderf—"

He held up a hand to stop her. "I did not tell you to speak." He motioned to the sandy, wet aftermath of the children. "Clean it up, now."

She bowed and meekly replied. "Yes, Meester Böhring."

"Where is Mrs. Böhring?" he asked derisively, knowing the likely answer.

"She ees in da bed, Meester Böhring."

"Wake her ven you hev zis cleaned up." He waved a hand. "I need her out ov here as vell."

"Yes, Meester Böhring."

Victor checked his watch. Man'ti and Darren would be here soon and he needed time alone with them to discuss their next move. They had proved to be bungling idiots, and he felt like they needed a little more motivation. He sat down heavily into the plush leather recliner facing the ocean-side windows. As he watched the kids playing in the sand, he opened the cigar humidor sitting on the coffee table and took out a pristine, unsmoked Montecristo #2 cigar. From his pocket, he produced the razor-sharp cigar cutters engraved with the initials VB, and snipped the ends of the cigar. He prided himself on keeping his cutters so sharp that he barely felt the resistance as he squeezed them through his cigars.

He put the popular Cuban smoke in his mouth and rolled it around on his tongue to moisten the end. He quickly clicked the cutters open and shut to remove any debris from them, and grinned around his teeth. *Motivation comes in all different shapes and sizes,* he thought, picturing the damage his snippers could do to a finger. He didn't light the cigar, he just sucked the end ... waiting.

23

Bad Timing

KARAH CAMPOBELLO ROLLED out of bed with a pounding headache. *One too many margaritas*, she thought.

"Hey, I'm just gonna take a quick shower," she called down the stairs, "and then we can hit the beach, k?"

She waited for the response from her cousin. None came.

"Laura?"

Strange ... maybe she went down to the beach already. Karah walked down the stairs calling out again. She found a note on the kitchen counter:

Gone to the bucks, brb. Taking your car.

She rummaged around in the junk drawer of the

kitchen and finally found an old, out-of-date packet containing two ibuprofen capsules and swallowed them whole, downing an entire glass of water in the process. *Hydrate, gotta hydrate and rally*, she thought. *Troy will be here soon and I can't be all hungover.*

She filled her glass again and headed back upstairs to get going on the shower and beach prep. "I hope Laura's gettin' me a double shot of espresso and something,'" she muttered .

Her shower steamed up the mirror in the bathroom and she almost fell asleep under the hot stream of water. After a few minutes, she began to feel human again. Rummaging through her bag, she found a new bikini she'd bought from Venus along with her new dress that Troy had only seen in a pic. It was a little racier than the one he'd seen her in before. She grinned at the thought of seeing his reaction to her tan lines that were exposed, because this suit was much smaller than her other bikini. She felt a thrill at the thought and was excited to see him.

Wonder where he is anyway ... he should be here by now.

She ran downstairs to check her phone and realized Laura had it with her. *Crap.* She caught a glimpse of herself in a mirror hanging in the living room. *Dayummm, girl,* she said and winked at her own reflection, *he doesn't stand a chance when he gets here.* She filled a tumbler with a little leftover sangria and ice, grabbed a towel, her book, a straw hat (that she idly thought matched Troy's cowboy hat) and her sunglasses, and headed down to the beach.

It was still quiet, except for those weird kids next door; they were all running around splashing in the surf, kicking a soccer ball and building sand castles. Laura must've been out earlier, as there was a chair sitting down on the dune by the bottom of the steps. She grabbed it and dragged it to a spot at the edge of the surf.

After a few pages in her book and a few sips of Sangria, she nodded off into a warm nap.

———

DARREN DROPPED himself down into a recliner after Man'ti had helped him up the stairs into the Böhring's beach house. He froze when Victor inhaled heavily.

"Not zee recliner," he said, and flicked his eyes to a small couch across from the chair.

"Right." Darren pushed himself up, groaning

with the effort, and limped over to the couch to sit beside Man'ti.

For a long moment, Victor did not speak. The only sound was the clink of ice cubes in his scotch. Darren couldn't help but lick his lips at seeing the drink, but Victor didn't offer him or Man'ti any.

"You," he finally said, placing his drink down on a small cocktail napkin on the side table next to what looked like a cigar box, "look like shit."

"Boss, ah know that," Darren began, "but ah—"

"Shut up."

"Right."

Darren massaged his leg, the fire burning down into his foot and his head hurt like hell. He wondered if they'd done enough for him at the hospital. He felt better than he had, but had a long way to go to reach one hundred percent.

"Tell me vat you hev discovered," Victor said, turning to Man'ti.

The giant man held out a cell phone to Victor. He put a pair of reading glasses on, then took it and swiped a few times.

"Vat am I looking at?"

"Thet man theya," —Man'ti pointed to a picture — "is out in front of ya neighbor's house."

Victor looked up over his glasses at Darren.

Darren nodded, having absolutely no idea where this was going, but decided it was in his best interest to play along.

"Und, I give a shit about dis because?"

"Thet girl he's with must be stayin' next door."

Victor placed the phone down on the coffee table and slid it back toward Man'ti.

"Und you think she has my check?"

"Not exactly." Man'ti picked up the phone and scrolled until he found another picture.

Darren could see it was a picture of the man he'd met in the hospital ... the man wearing the cowboy hat. He watched Man'ti pinch out on the photograph, enlarging the hat and turning the phone back toward Victor.

"Thet theya," —he pointed toward the back of the phone— "is Rick Hairre's hat."

Darren's brain finally broke through the haze he'd been in and he remembered the epiphany he'd had seeing Troy at the hospital.

"Thet fooka put the check in 'is hat!" he exclaimed.

Man'ti looked over at Darren with what might've been suspicion and repeated what he'd said. "Thet fooka put the check in 'is hat—"

"You know we nevah found it on Rick, but we nevah thought ta check 'is hat," Man'ti added.

Victor rolled a wet cigar around in his mouth. "Und zees man has zee hat now?"

"Right," Man'ti said and nodded.

"Und, vere is zees man now?"

Darren touched the right side of his head gingerly. "He was at the hospital ... but then he left."

Victor turned toward Darren and glared. Darren looked at Man'ti, seeking a little help with the rest of the story. Man'ti said nothing. *Prick.*

"I'm vaiting."

Man'ti finally said, "Like ah said, thet man theya, wearin' Rick Hairre's hat, is the boyfriend of the girl in the otha picture outside thet house ova theya."

Man'ti motioned toward the house next door through a beach side window.

Victor took a long look at the house. "Zat house belongs to Rick Hairre."

Darren did a double take. "Well, then, the girl must be his daughta."

"No," —Victor swiped a couple of times on the phone, looking at the girl in the phone's plethora of selfies— "zees girl eez not his daughter. I hev seen his daughter many times. I do not recognize zees girl."

"Then who the fook is she?" Darren grabbed the phone out of Victor's hand and suddenly regretted it.

"I do not know," Victor said and pulled his cigar cutters from out of his pocket and tossed them to Man'ti, "but she eez valking down to zee beach as we speak."

"Crikey!" Darren jumped up and regretted that too as a shot of fiery pain seared up his ruined leg. "He might be in thet house right now!"

"Vie don't zee two of you check zee house," Victor said, then nodded to the razor-sharp cigar cutter in Man'ti's hand. "If he eez there, bring me zee hat. If he eez not, ask her vere he eez. Cut off one of her fingers every time she refuses."

Darren shuddered at the thought of fingers being cut off. He was a few digits short on his right foot and hand himself.

"Und ven she tells you," —Victor paused and struck a match to light the end of his cigar, sucking in the flame and rolling it between his fingers— "make her disappear. Und do it better zan you did vit Mr. Hairre."

Victor opened a drawer in the table next to his chair. With a white handkerchief, he picked up a small .38 caliber pistol and handed it to Man'ti. He reached back into the drawer and pulled out an exact match. He paused a minute before handing it to Darren. Darren snatched the gun and spun the chamber around checking for bullets. He noticed that the serial number was filed off, clean and ready for business.

He grinned. "Got it, boss."

24

Where The Hell Is Troy?

KARAH CAMPOBELLO WAS AWAKENED by the sound of a whistle or something shrilling in the air. It was apparently coming from next door. Whatever it was, the kids all scrambled frantically to scoop up their beach toys and towels and ran toward the house. She yawned and stretched. *Wonder how long I was asleep?* she pondered. The tide hadn't moved too much and she assumed it had been less than an hour.

Where the hell is Laura? And where the hell is Troy? She glanced back up at her cousin's beach house. No sign of anyone there. She stretched again and stood up. She didn't bother to fold the chair up or bring her book with her as she trudged through the sand, but she did carry her tumbler. A little more sangria, and she'd thought she'd be ready to rock. Tromping up the stairs to knock the sand off her feet, she glanced over at the next-door neighbor's house. It was gorgeous. Surrounded on all sides by a screened in porch, a massive sunning deck on the flat roof extending toward the ocean, and at least twenty rocking chairs sprawled all around. A strange looking old man smoking a cigar was rocking back and forth in one of the chairs. *Oops.* She jerked her glance away as she noticed he was looking in her direction. *Creepy*, she thought and wished she'd brought her cover-up.

She walked up the stairs, careful not to look back in his direction, and pulled open the heavy sliding glass door. The rush of cold air hit her and the suddenness of going from bright sun to dim interior light had her fumbling for a few seconds before she could see clearly.

When her eyes adjusted, panic set in. She instantly recognized the massive tattooed dude that had bowled her over outside of Drunken Jack's sitting on the couch.

"G'day," he said, "wheyah's ya boyfriend?"

Karah whirled around and grabbed the handle of the sliding door. A bandaged hand thumped on the glass next to her, holding the door shut. She'd been so shocked at seeing the first guy, she hadn't noticed the second. He was bandaged all over and seeping through in several places. His eye was blood red and swollen and filled with goop. He was missing a couple of teeth on that same side and his right foot was completely covered in bandages oozing a dark purple fluid. Without thinking, she slammed her heel down on his foot and punched him hard in the eye.

The man howled in pain and let go of the door, reaching first at his foot and then his eye. She grabbed the door handle and yanked hard to open it.

"Not so fast," she heard the bigger man say close by her ear.

She felt his fist grabbing a handful of her hair. He shoved her hard at the door and slammed her head into the glass. Her last thought before she passed out was that she was going to have a black eye when Troy got here ... and she was really pissed about that.

———

SHE WOKE with a throbbing pain around her eye. She could feel it wasn't too bad—just a little swelling —but it seemed her forehead had taken the brunt of the bash. The room was dark, no windows and only one door. Furnishings were sparse. By the door was a small wooden chair next to a small wooden table with a single bulb lamp without its shade. In the chair was the man she'd recognized from the parking lot at Drunken Jack's—the huge, wrestler type dude with all the tribal tattoos.

She tried to sit up, but had trouble, suddenly realizing her hands were tied behind her back. They must've been bound with some kind of zip-tie as they were raw where the sharp edges of the binding cut into her wrists. Her captor noticed she was struggling and propped her up to sit with her back against the wall. He'd been surprisingly gentle, though quite firm. She wondered if he'd stay that way.

"Right," he said, sliding his chair around backward to face her and laying his arms across the top of the chair. "Sorry 'bout the bump ... couldn't have ya screamin' 'cross the beach."

Karah said nothing. Fear was starting to seep into her mind as she contemplated the situation; locked in what might be a basement room, no windows, hand-cuffed, wearing a tiny string bikini and an imposing kidnapper staring at her. Tears began to pool in her eyes.

"Don't worry yaself." The man must've seen her distress. "Tell me what ah wanna know and we'll all be outta heyah in no time."

Karah shook her head. "I have no idea what you're talking about."

"Ya boyfriend," he said, "where is he?"

Karah was confused. *What in God's name did this man want with Corey?* She hadn't dated him in over a year.

"What do you want with him?" she asked the man.

Before she could react, the man's hand flashed up and smacked the side of her head. She tumbled over and pain shot up her cheek and into her ear. She cried out.

"Ah'm askin' the questions, skank," he said and made no move to help her up.

So much for gentle yet firm. Karah's face was pressed into the cold cement floor and the coolness helped the pain a little. She tasted a trickle of blood on her tongue. As the throbbing slowly subsided, she turned her head to face him.

"I have no idea where he is ... that's the truth."

"I don't believe you."

"It's true; we haven't seen each other for over a

year. I mean, if I had to guess, I'd say he's at home in Alabama."

"Alabama?" the man asked, "What tha fook are you talkin' about?"

"I haven't seen him since last May." She spit the pooling blood from her mouth.

The man seemed genuinely confused. He pulled a cell phone out of his pocket. Karah instantly recognized Laura's phone. The case was a custom printed shell with a picture of Laura's dog, Tyson, on it.

"Where did you get that?"

He raised his hand, preparing to swing again, and she cringed backward into the wall. The blow didn't come.

"Ah said, I'm askin' tha questions."

He clicked and swiped through the phone. Turning the screen to face her, he asked, "Looks ta me like ya saw him yesterday."

Karah would've laughed if she wasn't lying in a growing puddle of blood from her mouth with her hands zip-tied behind her back in a dark cellar-like room with a massive captor beating her up.

"That's not Corey, that's Troy." She immediately regretted saying it.

"Troy?" the man asked. "Alright then, where tha hell is Troy?"

———

TROY CLINT BODEAN was a simple man. He liked to get plenty of sleep, which he'd gotten very little of last night. Back in Afghanistan, there were days on end with no sleep. Then in Vegas, he was up at all hours workin' the D.J. booth at the Pink Hippo strip club, and fishing boats in Louisiana hadn't offered much time for rest either. Since he'd come to Pawleys, he'd gotten into a comfortable routine of hittin' the hammock early and rising whenever he chose. He usually rose just after dawn, but only after a full night of shut-eye, otherwise, he might sleep in until noon.

He felt his ride—the bright orange Creekside Cab—pull onto the causeway and ease down to a slow crawl. Traffic on Myrtle Avenue was light at this hour; most of the runners, walkers and bikers had already had their turn and were probably out on the beach by now.

"Hey buddy," he said and tapped the cabbie on the shoulder, "you can drop me here."

A little walk to the house would be good to get his muscles working again.

"Whateva yo pleasure, mon." The cabbie shrugged and pulled over in one of the gravel driveways.

Troy paid the man and tipped his hat to him. "Gracias, amigo."

"Ya, mon," the driver said and backed out and pulled away.

Troy rubbed his eyes and stretched. He took the straw hat from his head and ran his fingers backward through his black hair. He felt old today. He pulled his phone from his pocket and checked his messages—nothing new since Laura had asked him about a coffee. He thought maybe a shower would do him good, wake him up, shake the cobwebs out of his head and give him a chance to change clothes. He clicked out a new text.

-*"Gonna hit my place for a few. Grab a shower and some trunks. See you girls shortly."*

-"K. Got coffee, almost back. See you there."

-*"RT."*

Troy settled the cowboy hat back on his head, slipped his Costas on, and started walking. He had no reason to pay any mind to the silver Land Rover that passed him going a good clip over the posted twenty-five miles per hour speed limit, even if the radio was blaring some kind of eighties pop boy band.

———

LAURA KATE STARLINGTON was feeling good. She had the windows of her cousin's car rolled down and the sunroof open. The crooning of an old group she'd loved screaming for in high school was blasting on the high-end stereo. She took a slow slurp from her chai tea and belted out a few more lines of the song. As the final chorus was fading out, she was pulling into the driveway behind her own car.

She carefully picked up the drink carrier with the three coffees, tucked the pastry she'd chosen for herself into her mouth, and grabbed the phone and keys in her other hand. She clopped up the wooden steps thinking she'd have to kick on the door to get Karah to open it rather than put anything down. But as she reached the top of the stairs, she noticed the door was slightly ajar.

That's weird, she thought, *Karah must've seen me coming and opened the door for me.* She bumped the door open with her elbow and walked in.

"Honey, I'm home," she called around the pastry in her mouth.

Nothing. *Dang, is she still asleep?*

"Karah, come on down. I got you Starbucks!" she yelled up at the ceiling.

She craned her ear up toward the second floor listening for movement. Still nothing.

"Karah?" she called again while walking toward the small table in the kitchen.

"Ya waistin' ya time, sweet tits," said a weasely voice from the other side of the room.

A man who might've been trying to impersonate a zombie was leaning against the bar that led into the kitchen. He smelled like a zombie too, but after the initial shock, Laura wasn't very afraid of the man. He looked like he might fall over at any second. He was bleeding from more than one location, including his eye.

"Number one, who the hell are you?" she demanded, dropping the pastry. "Number two, what the hell are you doing in my house?"

The man grinned, exposing a few gaps in his mouth where teeth had once been. He lurched toward her and she took a step back.

He feigned sadness. "Ah, now c'mon sweetness. You don't recognize me?"

Her mind flashed back to the night before at Drunken Jack's. It was the vomit dude who'd gotten into the brawl with the frat guys. What the hell was he doing here? His pretended frown disappeared, replaced with a maniacal, Cheshire-cat-like smile. He lunged at her again, this time getting even closer to swiping his oozing hand across her shirt.

She clicked the phone open. "Stop right there! I'm calling the police."

"Yeah, that ain't happnin', chicky."

With impossible quickness, the man lunged at Laura and knocked the phone out of her hand before she could hit send. It clattered across the floor and through the open door to the stairs, and Laura heard it thunking down out of reach. She turned to run, but he grabbed her shirt. It tore a little, but didn't rip through. He had her. He was reaching behind his waist and she saw the glint of metal flash from the barrel of a pistol.

She threw an elbow behind her high and felt it connect with his face. She heard a disgusting crunch and felt like she was hitting the open half of an orange. His grip loosened and he howled.

"Thet's mah good eye, ya fookin' bitch!"

Laura didn't look to see, and instead just jumped for the open door. She bounded through and reached for the knob just as the man was recovering and giving chase. She jerked the door closed as hard as she could and just before it slammed shut, the man reached his hand through. But it was too late, as Laura had pulled with all her might and she saw blood spurt out of the man's fingers as the door banged hard on them. The top of what might've been his middle finger snapped completely off and skittered past her. *Ugh, gross*, she thought. He yelped like a wild dog from behind the door.

"Shit!! Not mah good hand!"

Laura was already bounding down the stairs, taking them two at a time pausing only for a second at the bottom of the stairs to retrieve the cell phone that had jumped away from her in the scuffle. She hopped into Karah's Land Rover and suddenly realized she had no keys. She must've dropped them back in the house. She heard the man beating on the door and screaming even louder. She jumped out of the car and sprinted out into the street kicking up gravel with every step. She ran straight into the arms of another man who was obviously the weasel guy's accomplice. Without thinking, she pulled back a tightly grasped fist to punch the man.

"WHOA there little darlin'!"

Laura gasped out her breath and let her fist drop.

She was looking at the bluest lensed Costa
sunglasses wrapped around the bearded face of a
ruddy-skinned man. On top of his head was a straw
cowboy hat with a peacock feather stuck in it.

"Troy?!"

"That's right, and you are?"

She didn't answer; she just grabbed his hand and
jerked him away from her house down the street.

"I'm Laura. Listen, someone's got Karah," she
said, panting and running as hard as she could.
"Kidnappers or something."

"What the hell?" Troy was doing his best to keep
up, but his legs ached a little from the long ride and
the walk.

"There's a man in there," Laura said, jerking her
head back toward her house. "A drunk from DJ's last
night. I think he's got Karah."

"A drunk? In Rick's house?"

"How do you know my father?"

"Your father?"

"Well, my stepfather."

"Doesn't everybody know him?"

That was true. Laura looked back, but saw no
sign of the creepy man who'd been in her house.
When they reached the driveway of the next house,
she jerked him toward the car park underneath. A

small Chevy S10 pickup truck sat lonely in one of the parking spots. She wondered if anyone was home.

"We can probably break in here and lay low," she said and pulled Troy up the stairs to the door.

"No need to break in," he said.

"What? Why?"

He held up his hand, dangling a key chain with two keys and a rabbit's foot on it. "Cause, I got a key."

25

Follow The Money

CHESNEY BIGGINS BLEW on his overfull coffee and slurped a whipped cream sip into his mouth, slightly burning the tip of his tongue. *Dammit, that'll hurt for a week.* He took another sip, careful to blow on it a little more before drinking it.

Todd had radioed him off of the St. Francis hospital run; apparently all the trouble makers had gone. So, there was nothing to do now but chill on the side of the highway and wait for the next call.

He parked his cruiser under a clump of Palmetto trees and slid his coffee into the cup holder, careful not to spill any.

He opened his laptop and a screen popped up showing a deposit slip. Remembering where he was, he pulled out his yellow pad and scribbled some new notes as he examined the files on the zip drive.

Check out deposit slip at GKCU.

He closed the .jpg of the slip and clicked on the file labeled TCWEdPro.pdf. A two-thousand four-hundred and twelve page document opened. At the top in bold letters were the words:

Tourism Conservation and Wetland Education Project

Chesney had remembered hearing something about that, but he had no idea what it was all about. Under the title in smaller text:

Author: Marianne Deckerton

Co-Author: Rick Hairre

Interesting, he thought as he scrolled down through the document. Wetlands, blah blah blah, richest biodiversity, blah blah blah, sustainable development, blah blah blah ... it went on and on with every environmental buzzword Chesney had ever heard packed into a completely unreadable paper.

He scrolled faster, not even reading the words and hoping something would stand out. Just as he was about to close the document, feeling there was nothing to be learned there, he saw a table of financials. It looked to be what the authors considered a reasonable estimate of what the requested grant should be for this project.

There were seven major headings and about a bazillion smaller headings under those. The larger headings were things like: *building environmental awareness, providing direct financial incentives for environmental protection*, and *minimization of tourism's environmental impact*.

Each line had a number attached to it. Chesney gathered that this was the proposed amount they were requesting for that portion of the project. The bottom line was $7,000,000. Chesney whistled through his teeth. *Seems like a lot of dough to protect the wetlands for tourists.* He wondered why the government wasn't footing the bill, but then of course, the environment wasn't on the top of anyone's political list right at the moment. He clicked through the last few pages of the .pdf and finally got to the clincher. The last page was literally stamped DENIED in huge red letters and several signatures from different offices in Washington gave their name to the denial.

Chesney picked up his coffee and leaned back. *What the heck does all this have to do with anything?*

He wondered if there was anything significant enough in the project to warrant a murder. *Doesn't seem likely.* Government grants were boring business and were denied all the time. No one would be murdered for such things. And in the grand scheme of the trillion dollar deficits, seven million dollars seemed like small change.

Chesney clicked the file closed and sighed. "No help there."

He clicked the next file - IMG_4833.jpg. Chesney blinked in surprise, as it was a picture of Laura. But it wasn't a personal snapshot that someone would take of their step-daughter; it looked like a surveillance photograph. She was clearly unaware the picture was being taken. Chesney recognized the photograph's surroundings as the outside of Lee's Inlet Kitchen—where Laura worked during the day.

"What the hell is going on here?" Chesney muttered and took another sip of coffee.

We've got a deposit of half a million going to a random account, a denied grant for some kind of ecological tourism project, and a picture of Laura. It felt like a puzzle with pieces that didn't look the same or fit together. Chesney was baffled.

He opened the last file - VNHSBC002-08171971-47.pdf, and warning bells began to go off in his head. It was a .pdf of a cashier's check. As he looked at it, he still didn't know how all the pieces fit together, but he knew something sinister was going on.

Oddly, the cashier's check did not have a payee listed, that blank was ... well ... blank. The guarantor of the check was CPM via The Traditional Department of The Interior of South Carolina. And the coup-de-grace ... it was made out for you guessed it: Seven. Million. Dollars. Chesney sat his coffee down and looked out the windshield of his cruiser.

"What the hell ... " He tapped his finger on the side of the laptop.

A thought snapped into his head and he looked back at the list of files. Deposit slip for half a mil, but no deposit slip for the seven million. He looked at the date ... *shit, one week before Rick was found.* Something that sounded like a bad episode from one of those cop shows began to form in Chesney's mind.

We got a councilman denied for an eco-tourism whatever grant, an un-deposited cashier's check for the exact amount of the grant from some bureaucratic foundation, a half a million deposited somewhere ... and a picture of the dead guy's step daughter.

He scratched his chin. "Where the hell's that check?" he finally said out loud.

Another thought struck him and he opened a

browser. He tapped out The Traditional Department of The Interior of South Carolina and a few thousand hits came up that had nothing to do with the actual company. Wikipedia had an interesting line buried among some official sounding jargon: The Traditional Department of The Interior of South Carolina is associated with being a front for money laundering.

Wait ... what?

He searched for *CPM* ... 177,000,000 entries. *Dammit*. He added *South Carolina*. 461,000 results. Better. He tacked on *environment* and in quotes *"The Traditional Department of The Interior of South Carolina."* 9,975 hits and there it was at the top: *CPM —Consolidated Paper Mill.*

"What are you up to, CPM?" he muttered as he clicked the link.

A very bland page with a bunch of jargon that described the goings on at the paper mill in stale outdated language popped up. He clicked around and almost left the page before a thought hit him. He hovered over the "About Us" tab and a dropdown appeared: Mission Statement/Company History/Board of Directors.

He clicked Board of Directors and gasped. There at the top was a picture of a man with close-cropped white hair, a goatee that was peppered with grey, and small, circular glasses propped low on his nose. Underneath the photograph was the caption: Victor Böhring – CEO and Owner.

"Oh. My. God." Chesney opened a window and searched Victor Böhring, Pawleys Island. A property deed popped up from fifteen years ago with an address to a beach house on Pawleys. He dropped the laptop and slammed his cruiser into gear. His tires scattered gravel as he squealed onto the road.

The goon Laura had served at Drunken Jack's had been carrying this man's credit card ... maybe it wasn't stolen. Maybe this guy was a hired thug. This was getting deep—deeper than his pay grade.

He picked up his personal cell and clicked through the contacts. He found John Dodd Welford and pushed *call*.

After exactly two rings, a vague voicemail answered, as any secure line phone call would. Chesney left a quick message. "John, it's me, Ches. Call me back as soon as you get this. I think I'm on to something big here in Pawleys ... maybe a homicide. Something above local jurisdiction. I need a fed's eyes on this. Check out Victor Böhring and give me a call."

He hung up the phone and accelerated. He

couldn't be sure, but he thought Laura was in danger. He opened her contact screen and clicked *call* again. Chesney cursed as he remembered her phone was stolen. Of course, it went straight to voicemail.

"Shit," he said, turned on his lights, and sped up.

26

Don't Eat No Yellow Snow

DAISY MAE GALLUP held little baby Troy, er ... little baby Darren ... in her arms. He was nursing and alert. He had a messy shock of almost black hair on top of his head and his eyes were dark too.

"Dangit if he don't look like Troy," she said, stroking the top of his head.

"I know it," Ellie Mae said from the chair beside the bed, "I cain't believe he ain't."

"That's alright though," —Daisy Mae switched the baby to her other breast— "his new daddy, Darren, is gon' take care of us better'n that loser anyhow."

"You betchur ass he is!"

"When they gonna let us outta here?" Daisy Mae

jerked her thumb toward the call button. "This here baby needs ta see his daddy."

"Jus' cool yer jets, sis," Ellie Mae said, and held up her hands palms facing her sister. "They gotta make sure little baby Darren is truckin' along jus' fine and dandy afor they let us outta here."

"It's a dang prison!" Daisy Mae groaned.

The baby turned his head away from the breast and nuzzled into her arms to take a nap.

"It ain't that bad, Daisy." Ellie Mae rolled her eyes. "If everythin' looks okay, they'll probly let us go tomorrow mornin'."

"Tomorrow mornin'?"

"Yup, that's what they said."

"I cain't spend another night in here drinkin' that apple juice crap they keep bringin' me!" Daisy Mae slapped a small paper cup off the lunch tray sitting next to her.

"Oh, come on now," Ellie Mae said and reached down to retrieve the cup, "it ain't that bad."

"I need a Pepsi."

"What?"

"Go down to the cafeteria and get me a Pepsi." Daisy Mae pointed at her forehead. "I got a ragin' headache and a Pepsi's all that's good for it."

"I don't think yer 'posed ta have any caffeine,"

Ellie Mae said and picked up the nurse call button and started to push it. "I'll find out for ya."

"If you push 'at button, I'm gone come up outta this bed and clobber you."

Ellie Mae dropped the button and snorted. "You couldn't stand up, let alone catch me right now. Whatchu gone do?"

Daisy Mae pouted her lips out. "Come on, sis. Just a little Pepsi. Just a little one and I won't even drink it all. I'll share it with you."

Ellie Mae arched her eyebrow in obvious suspicion.

"Swear it!" Daisy Mae drew a cross over her heart with her finger. "Hope ta die. And make it a Diet Pepsi if ya want!"

Ellie Mae snorted again. "I ain't drinkin' no Diet Pepsi. If we's sharin' it's gonna be full test."

"If you insist," Daisy Mae said.

Ellie Mae shook her head, slung her purse over her shoulder, and walked out the door. Her sister hadn't been gone for more than a minute when the nurse came in.

"Ok, ma'am," she said and reached for the baby, "we need to take this little guy over to the nursery for his tests."

Daisy Mae jerked him closer to her body. "Oh no yer not!"

The nurse blinked in surprise. "But, Miss, they all have to get their shots and tests done."

"Oh, hell no." She pointed a finger at the nurse. "I know how this works. I give you my baby, you take 'im away, and then he's gone, kidnapped."

The nurse cocked her head. "Ma'am, I assure you that won't happen. He has a tag on his wrist that matches yours. No one can leave this hospital with your baby without a matching bracelet. That only happens in the movies."

"Sure, it does!" Daisy Mae was starting to get hysterical. "But why do you think they made them movies in the first place? Cause it happened to someone, that's why."

The nurse was baffled. "But ... ma'am, if you want to take your baby home, we have to do his tests."

"You can take yer tests and shove 'em up yer—"

"Hey now," came Ellie Mae's voice at the door, "What's this all about?"

"This lady is stealin' mah baby!"

The nurse held her hands up. "I most certainly am not! I was trying to take the baby to the doctor to have his tests—"

"She probly ain't even a nurse!" Daisy Mae pointed an accusatory finger at her.

Ellie Mae walked into the room and sat two large drinks in Styrofoam cups on the bedside table.

"You might be right." Ellie Mae narrowed her eyes. "Why dontchu jus' get on up outta here, nurse whatever yer name is."

Then she turned to Ellie Mae. "I seen 'is in a movie once. They take yer baby and sell 'im on the black market fer kidney's and such."

Daisy Mae nodded fiercely. "Yup!"

The nurse put her hands on her hips and sighed loudly. "Well, I never," she said, exasperated.

"And you ain't never gonna." Ellie Mae raised a fist and shook it at the nurse. "Now git!"

The nurse turned and scurried into the hall. They could hear her voice echoing down the corridor, calling for security.

"Sounds like maybe we best git little Darren outta here," Ellie Mae said and nodded to her sister.

"I think yer right," Daisy Mae agreed, handing the baby to her sister. "Lemme git his things."

With that she waddled out of the bed, unplugged herself from various IV's and machines, and started rifling through the cabinets. She dragged diapers and wipes and lotions and towels off the shelves and into a bag that said, *St. Francis Hospital of Litchfield* on the side.

When it was fully stuffed, Daisy Mae set the bag down by the door and peered out into the hall. It was quiet for now, a lone wheelchair resting empty a few doors down, but the security team would be coming any second now.

"I need some clothes," she said, pointing to the open backside of the hospital gown. "Cain't git far with my butt hangin' out!"

"Here, put these on," said Ellie Mae, and handed her a pair of sweatpants that said *Pawleys Island* down the side.

Daisy Mae pulled the sweatpants up over the gown and cinched the extra-large waistband until it was snug on her newly shrunken belly.

"Imma git that wheelchair and git you and baby Darren outta here." Ellie Mae crept into the hallway and slunk down to the chair.

A few seconds later she rolled it into the room. Daisy Mae slumped down into it with the baby swaddled snugly in her arms. Ellie Mae slung the overstuffed bag of baby products over one of the handles and grabbed the two large drinks.

Without much fanfare, they marched down the hall, showing matching bracelets to the front desk.

Through the nursery window they could see the nurse who had been trying to kidnap the baby earlier. Her face lit up with alarm and she gestured wildly toward the trio, saying something to the doctor who was holding up a baby by its legs.

"It shows show that you're supposed to be here until tomorrow," the nurse at the desk said and frowned at her computer screen.

"Yeah, well, the doc said little baby Darren here is advanced and can graduate early." Daisy Mae smiled her best honor roll mother smile.

Of course, she was faking it; she had no idea what that kind of smile looked like.

"Well, I'll have to check it ... " the nurse was saying while tapping on her keyboard.

"Here, gimme that!" Ellie Mae grabbed the scanner from the desk and shone the laser on her sister's and the baby's bracelets.

The door buzzed and they shoved their way through.

They slid sideways out into the hall and hurried down to the valet stand. Ellie Mae proudly produced a ticket and within minutes the just-out-of-high-school part-time-looking valet retrieved their brand new, fire engine red, jacked up, decked out Jeep Wrangler Unlimited and handed them the keys.

Daisy Mae climbed up into the passenger's seat and carefully strapped herself in, snugging the baby in behind the shoulder strap.

"Nice ride," said the valet, his hand out and obviously expecting a tip.

"Bet yer ass it is," Ellie Mae said and looked down and smacked his hand. "Don't eat no yellow snow!"

They both cackled hysterically as the Jeep roared to life. Just as they pulled away, a security team bumbled their way out the door. They were out and gone in a matter of minutes.

Ellie Mae watched them get smaller and smaller in the rearview mirror as Daisy Mae shot a bird at them out the window.

"Where to, sis?" Ellie Mae asked.

"I got Darren's phone number right here." Daisy Mae was unfolding a small piece of paper. "Let's see where he's at."

27

Can You Hear Me Now?

TROY CLINT BODEAN pulled his straw cowboy hat off his head and flung it on the kitchen counter. He filled two glasses with water from the refrigerator door.

Laura Kate Starlington was pacing back and forth in the living room on the verge of hysteria. She was running her hands through her hair, brushing it back from her face.

"They've got her. They've got Karah." She was starting to cry. "There's a crazy dude in my house and Karah is gone. We've got to call the police. I've got to find Chesney's number. This is crazy. What the hell ... "

"Now, just slow down, little lady," he said and handed Laura a glass, "and tell me what's goin' on."

"I'm not thirsty, Troy! There's a strange man in my house and someone's kidnapped Karah!"

She smacked his hand, sending the glass crashing to the floor and slinging water all over him. "Shit, I'm sorry."

She rushed over to the broken pieces and crouched down. She was gingerly stacking the glass in her hand when she broke down and started sobbing.

"Here," —Troy sat the remaining glass of water down and eased his hand under her arm helping her up— "let's get that later."

He helped her to the futon and sat her down. She shuddered with each breath, gasping as she cried. "I don't understand," she sniffled. "Why? Why Karah?"

Troy shook his head. "I don't know. She's a pretty girl. I guess this kind of thing happens to pretty girls."

He looked through a window that faced Laura's place. "let's get that dude out of your house first."

Jumping up the stairs three at a time, he called down to her. "Be right back."

He slid apart the doors to his bedroom closet and pulled the string to turn on the naked light bulb. Standing on his tiptoes, he reached up on the top shelf, fingers scraping the edge of an old Sperry Docksiders box. Finding solid purchase on the top of the box, he pulled it off the shelf and down into his hands. He blew a slight coating of dust off the box and placed it on the end of his bed. He took a deep breath and opened the box.

Inside it, wrapped in an old desert issue tan t-shirt, was a Beretta M9. *Been a long time*, he thought, staring at the nearly new looking handgun.

Troy picked it up out of the box, checked the safety, and ejected the magazine ... two rounds. *That should do it.* He slid the nearly empty mag back home. He checked the safety again, pulled his shirttail up, and slid the gun into his waistband. He closed the box and put it back up on the closet shelf.

He padded back downstairs to find Laura on the phone. She was less animated and was nodding her head.

"Okay. Yes. I don't know. I guess he's still in there. Okay. No, I didn't see her in there. No, no screaming ... nothing like that."

He couldn't hear the other caller, but assumed she must be talking to the police. She saw him come into the room and walked toward him, still talking into the phone.

"Okay, I'm just next door. Yes, I'm with Karah's

boyfriend, Troy. Okay, hang on." Laura took the phone away from her ear and hit the mute button. "He wants to talk to you."

"Cop?"

Laura nodded.

Troy took the phone. "Y'ello?"

Nothing.

He shrugged at Laura. "Nobody there."

She took the phone, unmuted it, and handed it back to him.

Troy tried again. "Yello? Can you hear me now?"

On the other end of the phone, a man with a calm voice, said, "Yes, hello Troy?"

"Yup, this is Troy."

"Okay, good," the man said. "This is Officer Chesney Biggins of the Pawleys Island police department. I'm a ... good ... um, friend ... of Laura's."

"Pleasure, Officer Biggins."

"Call me Ches," he said. "Listen, from what I can gather, Karah has been kidnapped?"

Troy looked over at Laura and turned away from her. He lowered his voice.

"I reckon that is the situation," he drawled, "and apparently there's a dude still in the house."

He peeked over his shoulder at Laura and lowered his voice.

"Maybe waitin' on Laura to kidnap her too."

"That very well could be the case," the officer said matter-of-factly. "I'm on my way. You and Laura need to sit tight. Do not approach the man. Do not go into her house. In fact, if you have a vehicle, you may want to consider leaving the island for a while."

Troy pulled a key ring from his shorts pocket; it held the key to his beach house and a key to his pickup truck.

"Yeah, um ... about that," —he shoved the keys back into his pocket— "I've been meanin' ta get that battery looked at."

"No worries," the man on the phone said, "just stay in the house. Lock the doors. No one gets in. I'll be there ASAP."

"Thank you, officer."

"Call me Ches."

"Gotcha." Troy held up a thumbs up sign to Laura. "Thanks, Ches." He ended the call and handed it back to Laura. "Pretty nice guy," he said.

"Yeah."

"He said for us to just park our be-hinds here and wait it out."

"But what if Karah is still in there?" Laura motioned toward the house. "We have to at least find that out."

"I thought you said she wasn't in there."

"Well, I didn't see her ... or hear her for that matter. But she could've been tied up, or gagged. Shit, I left her in there with that man."

She started crying again. "Troy, you have to go over there and see if she's there."

Troy sucked his teeth and absent-mindedly brushed his hand up the back of his shirt, checking to see if the M9 was still there. He took a deep breath and went into the kitchen. In one long gulp, he swallowed the glass of water he'd left sitting there. He picked up his cowboy hat, ran his fingers through his hair, pulling it back. He sat the cowboy hat on top of his head.

"Here's the deal," he said, and turned to Laura, pointing to the sliding glass door facing the beach. "When I go out that door, lock it and bar it behind me. Go upstairs and don't come out until Officer Ches gets here. You get me?"

Laura nodded. "Be careful, Troy."

"Always am, little darlin.'"

He took a quick peek through the window and, satisfied that no one was looking, he hurried out the door. He heard it slide closed behind him and then the click of the lock.

He jumped down the deck stairs that led under

his house and shuffled through the dune that connected to Laura's place. When he crawled over the railing under the house, he stopped and listened.

Nothing. Quiet. He eased himself up the stairs to the deck at the back of the house. When he reached the top, he stopped and listened again. The only sound was the rush of waves crashing on the beach ... good cover for his approach, but also good cover for the man who might still be inside the house.

As he army-crawled across the deck, his right knee throbbed and he had a mild flashback to Afghanistan. He could still hear Harry Nedman screaming, legs torn off from an I.E.D. The explosion had shot a piece of shrapnel into Troy's knee, completely severing his ACL. Under heavy machine gun fire, he'd rolled Harry up onto his back and crawled through the sand back toward the chopper, praying to God that there wouldn't be another bomb in the sand. Harry didn't make it back to base and Troy never went back into combat. Here he was, light years away from the desert, on a beach house deck, and crawling again.

He carefully opened the screen door on the porch. It squealed mildly, but probably not loud enough to hear inside. From here, Troy could see that a curtain had been pulled almost shut across the sliding door. There did appear to be a four-inch opening between the jamb and the drape where he could see in ... if he could just look without attracting any attention from the dude inside ...

He crawled past two brightly painted rocking chairs, one with a Longboard beer design and another with a Harpoon IPA picture. The wind kicked up and the chairs started rocking back and forth. He froze. He heard a thumping sound from inside and ... was someone moaning? When the sounds quieted, he inched closer to the opening in the drapes. He was just about to peek around the edge when a huge engine growled from in front of the house on the road. He heard a throaty rumble and then the sound of voices shouting.

"DARREN!" a loud female voice called. "Where you at?"

Then the horn started honking. It blared over and over again in between the shouts.

"HEY!" the woman yelled again. "Come out, come out, wherever you are!"

Troy stopped crawling. *Do I know that voice?*

The honking sounded closer. It sounded like maybe they were pulling into the carport under Laura's house. *Gall-dangit*, thought Troy. He jumped up and ran, slamming the screen door back and leaping down the stairs toward the beach. No sneaking down under the house and scooting across the dunes now. He hit the sand and didn't look back. Someone was definitely here. He waddled through the loose sand, knee screaming in pain. He grabbed the handrail of his own steps and took them two at a time, hopping as fast as he could.

At the top of the deck, he grabbed the door and yanked. Locked. *Dangit*. He'd forgotten that he told Laura to lock it. He ran back toward the side of the house away from Laura's to where the kidnapper and the car had been, and took the stairs down under his house. His old Chevy pickup was there and he hauled himself up (on his good knee) and threw himself down into the bed. He was pretty sure they couldn't see him from next door. Sliding the cowboy hat off his head, he peeked up over the bedrail of the truck. A huge red Jeep was in the carport under Laura's house, probably the kidnapper's backup or maybe the kidnapper himself coming back for Laura. He subconsciously tapped the gun in the back of his waistband to make sure it was still there. Then he remembered his cell phone. He tapped out a message to Karah's cell (Laura had it upstairs with her).

-*"Laura, it's Troy. Open door downstairs."*

-"How do I know it's really you?"

-*"Just ask Ches."*

-"K, be right down."

Troy peeked over the truck bedrail again and listened intently. He could hear muffled voices, but nothing he could make out over the sound of the ocean. His knee pounded and he thought about Harry Nedman losing his legs to that dang I.E.D. back in Afghanistan. He wondered if it was time to move on again. Pawleys Island hadn't proved itself to be very quiet and he needed some quiet to drown out those flashbacks from the war. He'd been one of the lucky ones ...

"Troy," Laura hissed from the door, "come on!"

He rolled himself out of the truck and limped up the stairs. When he reached the top, Laura was frantically waving him in.

"Did you see anything? Is she still over there? What's going on?"

"I never saw inside." Troy pointed his thumb toward her house. "Somebody just drove up in a big red Jeep. You know anyone with a car like that?"

Laura shook her head.

"Then it's likely that the kidnappers are still in your house."

"And Karah?"

"I couldn't hear any screamin' or anything," he said and walked into his living room, closing the door behind him, "so they probably took her away somewhere and they're waitin' on you to come back."

Laura slumped down on the futon and started crying again. "Oh my God. First dad and now Karah. Why is this happening to me?"

Troy took his hat off and rested a hand on her shoulder. "I don't know, little darlin', but we're gonna get her back and figure all this out."

He limped into the kitchen, dug out a Ziploc bag, and began to fill it with ice.

"Where's Ches at?" he asked over his shoulder.

"Almost here."

"Good." Troy sat down at the kitchen table, propped his leg up and put the ice pack on his knee. "Let's sit tight and wait for the cavalry."

Laura nodded. "You think she's okay, Troy?"

"I do, little darlin'," he said, hoping he sounded convincing but not at all convinced himself, "I do."

28

Sayonara, Jackass

DARREN REGAINED consciousness to the sound of a horn blaring somewhere outside the house. His head was pounding and his entire body ached. Feverous shakes racked his bones and his vision was cloudy.

He propped himself up on his knees to assess his current situation. He'd come to this cursed house to grab the blonde bitch but she'd elbowed him in his good eye and now both were swollen and oozing pus. And to add insult to injury, she'd slammed the door on his left hand ... his good hand. He'd already lost a few digits from the right and he was sure he'd felt his middle finger come off his left when the door closed on it.

But that wasn't the worst of the situation. His left

hand had been positioned at the exact height of the handle when she'd slammed the door. Somehow, the bones of one of his fingers had gotten jammed into the bolt hole and the door was stuck shut. He'd tried to open it, but couldn't grasp the knob well enough with his blood slicked, finger-lacking right hand. The more he tried to turn it, the more slippery it became.

"Mutha fookin' bitch," he growled, and slumped back down.

Before he'd passed out, he'd reached into his pocket for his cell. It was a burner phone Victor had handed them to use for communication during the search for Troy and the hat. With his right-hand situation—missing digits, wrapped in a blood-soaked gauze, and sore as hell—he'd squeezed the phone a little too tight and it had jumped out of his hand. It bounced twice and landed about five feet away. His left foot could barely graze it, but that was all.

He laughed and thought absently that it was a maniacal sound. He knew he was on the edge ... who wouldn't be with all that happened to him. He wondered if he was going to die here ... oozing out blood from almost everywhere.

"Ain't this jus' grand?" He slumped further down.

The good news was that his left hand (the one stuck in the door) was elevated so the flow of blood had basically stopped. The bad news was that it was starting to go numb and he was cramping badly in his shoulder. He decided that eventually he was going to have to just bite the bullet and rip his hand free from the door ... but not yet. He would rest a few minutes, gather what little resolve and strength he could, and then—

His thoughts were interrupted by the squeaking of the screen door on the back porch. The drapes were pulled so that only a slit of light showed through the sliding glass door that led out to the beach. He could hear the gentle thump of someone walking, or maybe crawling, out on the deck. He blinked away the sweat beginning to drizzle into his eyes and squinted hard into the light. And then, there it was ... the hat ... the God forsaken straw cowboy hat. It was low to the ground and looked as if someone was about to peek into the house. Must be Troy.

He drew in a breath, about to scream at Troy, when the sudden clomp of heavy footsteps sounded on the steps leading up to the door he was stuck in.

"DARREN!" a loud female voice called, "where you at?"

Then the horn started honking again. It blared over and over again in between the shouts. Darren jerked his head back toward the sliding door. Troy was gone ... his money was gone. If the stupid cowboy had any sense in him, he'd be on the first flight out of South Carolina. *Shit.*

"HEY!" the woman yelled again, "come out, come out, wherever you are!"

Darren heard whoever had been on his back porch jump up and run. He never saw his face, but he knew it had to have been Troy.

"You're a dead man," he growled toward the sliding door.

Then a loud pounding knock sounded on his door.

"Hey, Darren," Ellie Mae's voice called from the other side, "you in thar?"

"Yeah," he croaked through a dry, cracked throat. He swallowed and tried again. "Yeah, it's me. Look, I'm stuck in the door."

"Stuck in the what?"

"Me hand's stuck. It's wedged in the—"

He was cut off by the door slamming open and into his back. Pain shot into his left hand, but he was free. The blood rushed back into his arm and an arterial spray began shooting from the tips of his fingers.

"Fa fook sake!" he shouted, grabbing the end of his destroyed hand.

He was covered in blood and bandages, most dark brown and oozing. His mangled hands were wrapped tightly together and his eyes were both bruised and swollen. His right leg was wrapped in a flimsy gauze and was also moist from what looked like green and brown mud. In his lap, he cradled a small handgun, also covered in blood.

"Towel," he said and nodded toward the kitchen. "Get me a towel, wench!"

Ellie Mae looked down at him. He saw the sudden twitch in her hip and she threw it out to the side, slapping a defiant hand on it.

"Whatchu just call me? A wench?" She arched an eyebrow. "And now yer orderin' me around?" She shook her head. "Yeah, that ain't happnin'"

"Shit's sake, woman," —Darren started to prop himself up on his elbows— "I'm gonna bleed out here!"

Ellie Mae took in a deep breath. She inched around him and walked into the kitchen. Grabbing a white dish towel, she flung it at him.

He grabbed it and the blood spurted from his torn finger. The tip above the first knuckle was gone in a jagged tear. He groaned and wrapped the towel around it as best he could. With great effort, he lifted himself up and looked at Ellie Mae. Her eyebrow was still arched.

"What in God's name done happened to you?" she asked.

"Ah was attacked by an evil she-bitch!" Darren said, wobbling on his feet, "but she'll pay fa that. First, I'm gonna go slit her cousin's throat. Then, I'm gonna chase her down and rip her fookin' eyes out. Then, I'm gonna tear her fingers off, one by one. And then ... "

Ellie Mae's eyebrow slowly went down. He saw a new emotion flick across her face ... fear.

Good, he thought. *She needs to be afraid of me.*

"And then," he continued, "I'm gonna fookin' rip off Troy's goddamn head and take his fookin' hat. Take the fookin' check out of it and then burn that fookin' hat. Then, me and baby Darren are gonna cash that check and disappear on a beach somewheyah south of the border."

"What about us?" Ellie Mae's voice sounded different. "What about me and Daisy Mae? We're goin' too, ain't we?"

Darren blinked twice. "Ah, yeah ... that's what ah

meant. All four of us. Disappear. On a beach, or something like thet."

Now a new emotion started to drip into Ellie Mae's eyes. She crossed her arms.

"So, you mean to tell me you ain't got the money? But it's in Troy's hat?"

"Yes, woman," Darren snapped. "Haven't you been—"

He stopped suddenly. *That fookin' bitch*, he thought, *she's gonna steal my money.* His eyes closed to a slit ... even though they were mostly closed already from the beating they'd had in the last few days.

"Ah'll fookin' kill you!" he yelled, trying to point his pistol at her as he lunged toward her.

His slickened bandages slipped across the hardwood floor and she jumped back. He scrambled like a fish on a slip n' slide toward her, the gun clattering away from him. She turned and bolted out the door.

"Sayonara, jackass," she called behind her as she ran down the steps, "your ass is grass!"

He had no idea what the hell that meant, but it enraged him. He pounded his bloody fists on the floor until they started throbbing. Bandages were flying, syrup ribbons of blood slung in every direction. Rolling onto his back he let out a guttural scream. He had now officially lost everything. His money, his woman (women), his baby, his fingers, his toes, his clear eyesight ... all was slipping away. He thrashed like a wild animal for a few seconds until he panted, his lungs aching.

Can't get to them fookin' wenches, dunno where fookin' Troy has run to, damn blondie ran off, the two sluts with the baby are dust in the wind ... that left only one person to feel his wrath ... Karah.

He rolled over to rise up onto all fours, growling low and deep, like a wolf on the prowl. *Ah'm gonna slit that chick from ear ta ear*, his thoughts burning red in his mind, *and then I'm gonna shoot her.*

Part III

Check Out Time

"Yo, man, it's check out time. It's time to get out this mother."

-2Pac

29

Shocking Troy

TROY CLINT BODEAN paced back and forth on the screened in porch on the beach side of his rented beach cabana. His knee ached a little from all the running and crawling around spying on the house next door. He could hear the sounds of people yelling coming from inside the house, and prayed that Karah wasn't in there.

Laura's cop boyfriend was supposed to be on his way, but there wasn't any sign of him yet. The commotion next door grew ... God, it sounded like a bar brawl had broken out over there. He couldn't see anything happening, but he did hear a car door slam and then the screech of tires and the scattering of gravel as someone apparently drove away from the house in a hurry ... whoever was in the red Jeep, he guessed.

Dangit, he thought, *hope to hell they ain't takin' Karah somewhere and we missed 'em.*

He poked his head into his house through the sliding glass door. Laura Kate Starlington sat crying on the futon. She was staring at the cell phone in her lap. It was Karah's phone. She looked up at Troy.

"Should I call her folks?" she asked through streaming tears.

Troy took a deep breath. "Yeah, probably so."

"What do I say?" Laura asked, sniffing.

He had no idea. *Your daughter has been kidnapped, she might be right next door and we're just waitin' on the police while the kidnappers have their way with her.* Troy checked to see that his gun was still tucked in his waistband. The cold steel made him feel uneasy. He pulled a breath in across his teeth.

"It's quiet over there now," he said and nodded toward the next house, "so ah'm goin' ta get her."

"I'm going with you."

"Nope." He pointed at the front door. "You wait 'til Ches gets here and then you send him over. This ain't my first rodeo, so I'll be just fine."

"Bu—" Laura started to protest, but he interrupted her.

"No, now you sit tight," he said, "and call her folks. When the cavalry arrives, send 'em on over if I ain't made it back with Karah yet." He slid the door shut, then opened it again. "Lock this behind me."

Laura stood up, walked to the door and clicked the lock while staring through the glass at Troy. She mouthed the words, *be careful*.

He nodded and winked at her. He studied the house next door before leaving the safety of his own screened in porch. It was deathly quiet. Whatever had been going on over there was now done. They'd probably taken Karah away. *Dangit.*

He opened the screen door and casually took the stairs down to the beach, acting as if he was just out for a day on the sand. Glancing sideways at Laura's beach house next door, he didn't see any activity; no sign on anyone moving around in the house and no noise that he could make out over the crash of the waves. The big red Jeep that had been parked in the driveway was gone too. Likewise, the beach was almost completely empty as well ... except for one woman.

She was sitting in a teal blue beach chair wearing a teal blue one-piece bathing suit. Her towel was also teal blue ... it was the strangest thing ever, this monochromatic ensemble. Her hat was the only thing that didn't match. It was a large floppy hat, pink with a white bow around the brim. Her hair was pulled back into a single tight braid and was brown with an ashy look that might've been a color died over her natural grey.

She was flipping through the pages of a magazine and occasionally picked up a nearby tumbler and sipped at the straw. Troy was certain he'd never seen her in Pawleys before, but there was something oddly familiar about her. She suddenly dropped the magazine and stood looking out into the ocean. Stretching her arms high, she leaned her head back and inhaled the breeze. She flipped her head, looking north down the beach, and then turned to look south, directly at Troy.

He jerked his gaze away, realizing he was staring. She had large round sunglasses on, obscuring most of her face, but the sensation that he recognized her flooded into his mind. Maybe he'd run into her at the grocery store or the gas station or something. No, that didn't seem right. He thought she must be someone he knew ... like, really knew.

As he tried desperately to look nonchalant, peering sideways so as not to look directly at her, he noticed she was waving. He thought maybe she was also calling to him, but the sound of the ocean muffled her voice.

When he heard it more clearly, he turned to face her. She was walking toward him, her teeth showing brightly in a smile. She was still waving. And like a lightning bolt, it hit him.

"Holy dangit," he muttered to himself.

She was now just a few yards away and he could make out what she was saying.

"As I live and breathe," she said, still smiling, "if it isn't Troy Bodean."

Damn you, Debby, he thought as she walked up to him.

It was Debby "Gidget" Robinson, the friendly— yet married—stripper from The Peppermint Hippo. At the time, he'd thought she'd ruined his perfect little life spinning records for dancers at the strip club by making him believe she'd fallen for him, but a Mafioso husband and a couple of Italian goons later, he'd left Vegas. And that turned out to be the spark to get him off his ass and do something with his life. Whether or not he'd been successful was another story.

"Hello, Debby," he said and tipped his hat to her. "How's Teddy?"

Teddy was the husband that had caught Troy in

the buff, wrapped only in a towel in an expensive condo at the MGM with Debby. He saw a fleeting look of sadness cross her face.

"He's dead."

"Oh, dang." Troy suddenly felt guilty. "Sorry, I didn't—"

"Don't be," she interrupted. "He was gunned down by some other *family* years ago."

Troy knew what she meant by family. It was likely a hit had been put out on Teddy by a rival Mafia group that felt he was impinging on their territory. She took her sunglasses off and put her hand over her eyes to shade them from the sun.

"You look good, Troy." She smiled again.

"Thanks."

She looked good too ... but she looked older. Lines around her face showed more age than she had lived, evidence of a rougher life shown in the heavy darkness under her eyes. And the deep brown of her eyes was faded and ... empty. She looked like, well ... a Stepford Wife.

He glanced down at her hand and saw the huge diamond wedding ring. She must've noticed his look and subconsciously wrung her hands together.

"Yeah," she said through her teeth, "I remarried a few years after Teddy."

"That's good," Troy said, seeing her less than jubilant response, "I guess?"

She put her sunglasses on ... *another subconscious move to hide her true feelings,* he thought. She nodded.

"Mmhmm," she hummed, "it's been good. How about you?"

That was an odd way to talk about someone you'd promised to spend the rest of your life with, but he shook it off. "Nah," he said, shrugging his shoulders, "never found the right girl."

She smiled, turning one corner of her mouth up slightly, but said nothing.

"And you guys are vacationing here?" he asked, nodding to the massive house.

"Oh, that?" She glanced up at the porch. "It's my husband, Victor's, house. I've never been here before."

Another really strange thing to say. Her husband's house? And she'd never been there? He waited, but she didn't add anything to the explanation and a long pause indicated that the conversation wasn't going anywhere.

"Okay, well, it's good to see you." Troy reached out a hand.

She took it. "It's great to see you too."

"Maybe we can catch up sometime over a—"

"Oh, I don't know about that," she interrupted him, "I think we're leaving this week and Victor ... "

She let it hang for a second.

"Well, ya know ... jealous husbands are my thing." She smiled in a not-too-pleasant way.

"Yeah," Troy said, completely baffled at this strange meeting, "I suppose so."

As they stood in awkward silence, Troy was happy a voice broke through the sound of the waves. A high-pitched call drifted down from the porch of the beach house. "Meesus Debbyyyy."

A short round woman in a light blue dress with a white apron was looking toward them. Troy thought it must be the housekeeper standing on the deck waving.

"I guess I should be going," Debby said and waved back at the maid.

"Okay, well ... " Troy was at a loss for words, "have a good life."

"Same to you, Troy."

He watched her take a few steps away, and said, "Debby, wait."

She turned around and looked back at him.

"Did you see anyone ... did you see a girl ... " He struggled with how to ask if she'd seen Karah. "Did you notice if anyone was home next door?"

She shook her head no and shrugged her shoulders. "New girlfriend?"

"Ha," he blurted with a short laugh, "No, um ... just checking on a friend. I'm a little worried about her. She's been gone too long."

"Haven't we all, Troy?" she said, smiling ruefully.

"Yeah, I suppose so." He scratched the back of his neck. "Okay, so if you ... well, if you need anything, I'm just right over there. The Turtle Nest House. He motioned down the beach toward his house. "Look it up, call me if you ... " he stopped unsure what to say.

"Sure thing," she said and turned away, still smiling.

And just like that, *Hurricane Debby* had blown her gale force winds into his life yet again.

Troy watched her walk up the beach toward her husband's house and caught sight of the police cruiser as it pulled into his driveway.

That would be Officer Chesney. He slogged through the loose sand back toward his house, his knee aching again. He decided that when this was all over, he was gonna get that battery fixed in his Chevy pickup and leave Pawleys Island in his rearview mirror.

An old Skynyrd song about the Breeze drifted into his mind.

30

Sharpie Scribbled Initials

THE SLIDING glass door on the back of his house screeched open. Laura was sitting on the futon and a police officer was standing across from her. He was pacing back and forth quickly. They both looked over at him when he walked in.

"So?" Laura jumped up. "Was she there? Is she okay? What's going on?"

Troy was still in a little shock at bumping into Debby and realized he'd never actually made it to Laura's house to see if Karah was there.

"Yeah, um, I never made it over there."

"What?!" Laura raised her hands, palms to the sky. "Where in the hell have you been if you weren't over there?"

"I was, well," he stammered, "I bumped into an old friend and—"

"Troy!" Laura shook her hands. "This is no time to reminisce with old pals! My cousin is in danger."

"Okay, you two," Chesney butted in, "let's just ramp it down a second. I have backup on the way."

Laura looked at him. "But she's in trouble!"

He held up his left hand and his right hand subconsciously drifted over to rest on his gun.

"I'm going over right now. Both of you need to stay here. Go nowhere else. The other officers will join you here."

"I'm going with you." Troy wondered if his knee could take another jog back to the house.

"Nope," Chesney said and motioned to Laura. "What I really need is for both of you to stay out of this now. And Troy, I need you to stay with her. I'll explain later, but it's likely that these people aren't after Karah. It's Laura they really want."

"Huh?" Troy tipped the cowboy hat back on his forehead.

"Wait ... what?" Laura chimed in.

Chesney walked toward the street-side door and opened it. Backing out and down, he pointed at the sliding door.

"Lock that," he said, "and lock this one behind

me. Sit tight. I'll check next door and find Karah. But you two are going to stay here."

He closed the door and Troy turned the bolt to lock it. He then crossed the floor to the sliding door and clicked the lock. He grabbed a stick that was propped up behind the drape by the door and slid it into the track of the sliding door. An ancient—if not tried and true—method for ensuring that the door could not be moved.

"Why would they be after me?" Laura was in a daze.

"Darlin', I got no clue," Troy said and pulled the drape closed over the sliding door, "but let's just wait on Ches. He'll get her back safe."

The phone in Laura's hand began tinkling a pop song. She looked down at it. "Shit." She pointed the screen toward Troy, who shrugged. "It's Karah's dad."

Troy nodded. "Answer it. Tell him what's going on. Tell him the cops are here and that we're going to have Karah back in a few minutes."

She answered it and stood. Troy pulled the drape back a crack and peered toward the house next door. He couldn't see anything. Laura was relaying the events of the past few hours, her tears forming again.

Her voice faded into the background as Troy began to go over all that had happened recently in his head. None of it made any sense. It was a bizarre puzzle with pieces that didn't seem to fit together. There was some crazy dude from the bar following the girls and maybe kidnapping Karah, but he may actually be after Laura, whose dad, Rick Hairre—a politician from up in Murrell's Inlet—was brutally murdered just a few days ago. And women from all over Troy's past were seemingly swarming into South Carolina; first Ellie Mae and Daisy Mae Gallup, and now Debby "Gidget" Robinson—or whatever her not-so-blissful married name was now —had come to the island with her husband, Victor. Troy shook his head. *What in the Sam Hill is goin' on around here?*

"Okay, Uncle Roger," Laura was saying into the phone, "I'll see you in a few hours." She clicked the phone closed and sighed. "They're on the way."

Troy nodded, his head swimming with all the wackiness of the past day. He tipped the straw cowboy hat back on his head. Laura was looking at him ... no, she was staring at him. Her mouth was hanging open slightly and she was blinking rapidly.

"Your hat," she mumbled, and raised a hand to point at it. "I just realized ... it's ... it's exactly like the one I bought for my dad when I was little. He wore it everywhere ... I can't believe I just noticed."

Troy felt a shiver run up his spine.

"Where did you get yours?" she asked.

"I ... um—" he started to answer, but thankfully was interrupted by the door opening.

Chesney walked in.

"There's no one over there." He held out his hands.

"Oh no," muttered Laura, and then sobbed.

"The door was wide open, but no one was inside. It appears there was some kind of struggle in the kitchen. There's some blood smeared on the floor and on the door to the carport."

"That's from the dude," Laura said and wiped tears from her eyes. "He looked like he was bleeding all over."

"You saw him?"

"Yes, when I got home, he was waiting for me." Laura recounted the events. "I never saw Karah though."

"He was probably there to get you, and Karah just happened to be in the way." Chesney chewed his lip.

Laura looked puzzled, and asked, "What does he want with me?"

"I'm not really clear on exactly what's happening yet, but I have some evidence that your stepfather may have been involved in some kind of corporate blackmail scheme."

"What? You mean Rick?"

Chesney nodded. "There was some sort of really big check issued to him ... by a paper mill. I don't know, maybe a payment to keep quiet about dumping around here, or something like that."

"I have no idea what you're talking about," Laura said, her head shaking.

"It seems that maybe they were paying your dad to keep things quiet about the pollution coming out of the mill. And maybe Rick had a change of heart and decided to blow the whistle on it, or something like it."

Troy raised his eyebrows. "And they'd kill a man over something like that?"

Chesney shrugged his shoulders. "Well, it could be millions of dollars in fines. Not to mention, millions more to retrofit the mill to eliminate the pollution."

"Dang," Troy said, and whistled. "But with Rick gone—sorry, Laura—what in the world would they want with her?"

"That's the part I can't really figure out," Chesney said, and rubbed the back of his neck. "They apparently issued a big payment to Rick—a seven-million-dollar payment—in the form of a cashier's check. Maybe that was the hush money."

Laura gasped and Troy raised his eyebrows.

"Yeah," Chesney agreed, "but, the thing is, it was never cashed. It never showed up in any account that I could find on Rick."

He turned to look at Laura. "Unless ... um ... "

Laura realized what he was asking, "Ha! Right! I just bounced a check two days ago. That's why I got that twenty-five-dollar tip from Rick at the diner, remember?"

"Yeah," Chesney said, "unless maybe it hadn't cleared the bank yet?"

Laura started to protest. "Well, I think I'd know if there was a seven million doll—" She froze. "Wait ... I just used my debit card at Starbucks earlier. It shouldn't have worked. I have literally zero dollars in the bank."

She pulled out Karah's cell and clicked a few buttons. Troy thought she must be pulling up her account online. After a few seconds, Laura's mouth gaped open.

"Oh ... Oh my God."

She handed the phone to Chesney. He took it and pursed his lips looking at the screen.

"It's ... I don't ... I mean ... " she stammered. "It's not seven million though."

"That's the other thing," Chesney said and handed the phone back to her. "I also have evidence of a half-a-million-dollar payment to another account that I couldn't identify—looks like it must've been yours—that actually did get deposited."

Tears again pooled in her eyes; "He must've deposited it before he died."

"Yes," Chesney said, and spoke carefully, "it looks like that's the case."

"So," Troy interjected, "they want Laura to give the half million back?"

Chesney shook his head. "Unfortunately, that damage is done. It's traceable and with the evidence I have, I could make the link."

"Oh," Troy said.

"The half million is a drop in the bucket," Chesney added. "The seven million, on the other hand ... they probably want that back ... wherever it is. It's a check that anyone, anywhere can walk into a bank and cash."

"But, I don't have that check," Laura protested.

"They don't know that," Chesney said, looking at her. "They probably think Rick gave it to you for safe-keeping."

Laura put her head in her hands and a gentle sob escaped her mouth.

"Given the state that your stepfather was in when I found him," Chesney added gently, "I'd say they were trying to get him to tell them where the check was ... and I'm guessing they never found it. That led them to you."

Troy exhaled through his teeth. "And I'm betting they think Laura knows all about the deal ... so they need her out of the way too."

"That's exactly what they want," Chesney said. "They need Laura to go away to tie up the loose ends."

"Dangit," Troy said, "that's a tight spot."

"All of this goes back to the paper mill, and I've got a call in to one of my buddies at the FBI." Chesney hiked his thumb in the direction of the next house. "He'll know what to do about Victor."

"Who's Victor?" Laura looked confused.

Troy was in shock. "Victor? As in, Debby's husband, Victor?"

"Who the hell is Debby?" Laura was even more baffled.

"Victor Böhring is the CEO of Consolidate Paper Mills," Chesney said.

"Debby must be married to Victor," Troy added.

"Why does that name sound so familiar?" Laura asked.

"The credit card," Chesney said, "from Drunken Jack's. Remember?"

"Oh, shit ... " she said, eyes opening wide, "the two dudes who had his card must've been the ones he sent after me."

"Sounds that way, yes." Chesney sighed and turned to Troy. "And you know his wife?"

"Ha, well, ya see," he sputtered, "that's a story from another lifetime of mine, but if it's the same Debby, yes, I do know her."

"How does she figure into all of this?" Laura asked.

"Not sure," Chesney said, shrugging. "She may not know anything about it."

"I got the distinct feeling that she and Victor aren't very lovey-dovey," Troy said. "I bumped into her on the beach and there didn't seem to be any excitement about being down here with her husband."

"So, Victor is here?" Chesney asked.

"I reckon he is," Troy said.

Chesney's cell phone buzzed. He answered it. "Okay, yup, got it." He clicked the phone shut and turned to Troy and Laura. "Cavalry's here. I've got two uniforms downstairs. They'll stay with you until we figure out what our next move is." He turned the screen toward them. "And I've got a missed call from John, my buddy at the FBI. Give me a few minutes to talk to him and then we'll figure out what to do."

A gentle, single knock came at the door and Chesney let the two police officers in. They had different uniforms on and appeared to be from the Litchfield P.D. Chesney exchanged a few words with them, and they nodded first toward Laura and then to Troy. They moved toward the front of the house and peered out the windows, apparently on watch.

"Back in five," Chesney said as he walked out the door and closed it behind him.

Troy slumped down on the couch beside Laura. He tipped his hat off and ran his fingers through his hair. The hat was upside down in his lap and the inside band was showing. In small, sharpie scribbled letters—that he had never noticed before—were the initials R.H.

"Dangit," he muttered.

31

A Really Böhring House

MAN'TI STOOD in the living room alone. He was studying the tasteful and obviously expensive oil painting of a white egret hanging over the tufted linen couch. From somewhere down the hallway, he heard something that sounded like a whip crack and then a scream. The mister must not be happy with the missus. He sniffed and cracked his neck with a small smile. *Bitch probly had it comin'.*

Hearing the clip-clop of shoes coming, he turned to see Victor Böhring enter the room. He had a handkerchief out and was wiping his hands. Man'ti thought he might've seen a little blood on the cloth.

Victor shrugged. "Vell?"

"She ain't talkin'," Man'ti said. "Ah dunno where this Troy is and I dunno if she's gonna tell me."

Victor walked to the kitchen, took a small glass tumbler from the cabinet, and filled it with water from the refrigerator. He took a sip and licked his lips.

"Are you telling me," he said flatly, "zat you are unable to make zees girl talk? Big man, wit zee tattoos, and a little girl is keeping secrets from you?"

Man'ti could feel the heat rising in his face. "You said not to kill—"

Victor slammed his hand down on the kitchen counter. "I know vat I said." He inhaled slowly, a frown growing on his mouth. "You do not ave to kill her to make her talk, no?"

Man'ti nodded. "Ah'm actually not sure she knows where he is."

"Make her tell you."

"Yes, sir."

"And eef she doesn't tell you, get rid of her." Victor took another sip of his water.

Man'ti turned to go. "Oh, and theyahs a few cops down the way. Seen 'em come in this morning."

Victor raised his eyebrows. He seemed to consider this for a long moment. Reaching into his pocket, he pulled his key ring out and tossed it to Man'ti. "Get her out of here," Victor said, and waved his hand away from them. "Take her to zee apartment. Make her talk or make her go avay."

"Yes, sir."

"And for God's sake," —Victor finished his water — "don't get any blood on my car."

"Ah'll use a tarp."

Victor stuck out his hand, palm up. "Vatever you need to do, do it."

Man'ti nodded and walked out.

He didn't want to kill the girl, but if she wouldn't tell him what he needed to know, he'd shoot her in the head. And no one would find this body like they had found Rick Hairre's. He clomped down the stairs to the storage room underneath the Böhring house.

———

KARAH CAMPOBELLO SHIVERED in the darkness. It had been hours since the huge man had left her here. She was cold, achy, hungry and scared. Her hands were still zip-tied behind her back and her wrists were swollen and bleeding from the restraint's bite. Duct tape was strapped over her mouth, but she had screamed until her throat was raw. It didn't seem loud enough for anyone to hear.

After several unsuccessful attempts to kick the

door down, she'd cried for most of what she guessed was the entire night. She was sure she was dead. She'd probably be raped and murdered and no one would ever know how or why. All because of Troy ... she had no idea why, but it seemed like the man holding her here wanted to get to him.

Without warning, the door screeched open and bright sunlight blazed into the room, blinding her momentarily. Silhouetted in the light was her captor.

She edged back into the corner of the room, her tears coming again. He moved into the room and came toward her. Without hesitation, he grabbed the edge of the tape on her mouth and ripped it off.

She yelped uncontrollably with the sudden pain.

"Please don't," Karah cried hoarsely. "I told you before, I don't know where Troy is."

"Lies," the brutish man said simply.

He touched her cheek and she shied away. She could see the wolfish glint in his eyes and terror flashed its way into her heart.

"No ... please ... " she whimpered.

"Ya got ten seconds, sweetheart," the man said, "ta tell me what I wanna know. Otherwise, we're going on a little trip and one of us ain't comin' back."

"I swear to you, I have no idea where Troy is," Karah said through fresh tears. "I was supposed to meet up with him yesterday, but he never showed up."

"Right," the muscled man said, smacking the duct tape back over her mouth, "guess that settles it."

He stood quickly and without so much as a grunt of effort, he picked her up and threw her over his shoulder. She kicked wildly, screaming against her restraints, but he ignored her. He carried her out the door and into a carport. A carport exactly like the ones under the houses on ... *Holy shit, we're still on Pawleys Island*, she thought.

She screamed against the tape again, but her voice was still raw from crying out last night. Suddenly, the big man slapped her ass ... and it wasn't in a good way. It felt like he'd cracked her tailbone. She cried out again and kicked as hard as she could. The man was impossibly strong. He clicked a set of car keys and a nearby Mercedes SUV beeped as it unlocked. He opened the back and threw her in. She watched as he walked around and got into the driver's seat. She kicked the door with all the effort she could muster, but with bare feet, she wasn't doing much damage. He started the car and pulled them out onto Myrtle Avenue.

Looking out the back window, she was shocked to see that they were literally right next door to her cousin's house. She sobbed as she watched it get smaller and smaller as they drove away.

When they reached the causeway, the man turned onto the bridge and sped up. Karah had given up on screaming and slumped down in the rear compartment of the expensive looking car. She realized she was sitting on a large green tarp and next to the tarp was a bag with a spool of rope. There were also four, forty-five pound weights, like the kind she remembered seeing in the gym at school. He was taking her to kill her and dump her body in the water somewhere.

Her mind raced. She needed to get out of here. With no obvious solution at hand, she decided to save her strength. If her feet ever hit the ground again, she was going to run as hard and fast as she could. This dude was big, and big dudes weren't usually very fast. She closed her eyes and tried to bring her heart rate down to calm herself.

———

DARREN WONDERED how much he looked like a zombie trudging down Myrtle Avenue. With the bandages on his head, hands, and legs all dirty with old dried blood, and his limp from his bad foot, he was sure he resembled the living dead. God knows he felt like the living dead. His hand throbbed and his leg was on fire. Though he'd been to the hospital and taken the antibiotics, he felt sure the infection was back and raging through his system.

His mind was bleary and ravaged by all the losses his body had been through. Fingers and toes were missing, both his eyes were severely damaged, and his nose was crushed almost flat. He grinned to himself. *But ah'm still kickin'!* He coughed out a laugh, but didn't even notice the blood that trickled down his chin.

He urged himself to keep walking, just a few more steps to Victor's house. He didn't plan on knocking, he'd just open the storage shed underneath the house and kill the girl. He decided he wasn't going to shoot her, he was just going to choke the ever-lovin' shit out of her until she died. And then he was gonna choke her some more ... and maybe after that he'd shoot her. Hell, he might even tear her fookin' head off. He laughed again until he sent himself into another coughing fit.

As he walked into the carport, he thought it odd that Victor's ostentatious Mercedes was gone. A late model gold Toyota Corolla was parked in the driveway—he had no idea whose car that was—but shielding his eyes and looking through the back-seat window revealed a bucket and cleaning supplies. Must be the maid's car. He walked under the house to the back of the carport where the storage shed was located. He stopped short. The door was open. *Shit*, he thought. Inside he heard a faint scraping sound. Somebody was in there. He grinned. Maybe the girl was in there, and she was still tied up and couldn't escape.

"Come out, come out, wherevah you are," he sing-songed as he entered the door.

A woman in a blue dress was pushing a mop, and she stopped suddenly upon hearing him come in.

"Oh, señor," she said, and raised her hand to her mouth as her eyes darted from one of Darren's blood-soaked bandages to another.

"Wheyah ... is ... that ... fookin' ... bitch?"

"I don' know what you are talking about, señor."

Darren raised the pistol and shot her in the head twice before she fell. The red burning sensation came back. He walked out of the shed and headed up the stairs into the Böhring's beach house.

Victor Böhring was sitting on the couch in a ridiculously tight bathing suit, flipping through what looked like a German newspaper. His bright orange swim trunks reminded Darren of the shorty-shorts that he'd seen the waitresses wearing at a nearby Hooters wing place. It had looked teasingly tantalizing on the girls, but not on the old man. Darren laughed out loud and realized it sounded a little crazy.

"Vat in zee hell happened to you?" Victor barely looked up from his newspaper.

"Wheyah's the fookin' girl?" Darren said in a low voice.

"Your friend, Man'ti, has taken her somewhere else."

"He ain't mah friend," Darren said and pointed his pistol at Victor, emphasizing his point.

"Zat may be zee case." Victor carefully folded the paper and laid it on the coffee table. "However, he is taking care of zis matter, since you could not."

"Thet asshat ain't gettin' none of mah money!"

Victor sniffed. "Your money?"

"Ah'm gonna kill thet fooka, and then I'm gonna kill thet fookin' girl." Darren's voice was louder now.

Victor arched an eyebrow. "And zen you will hev your money?"

"Thet seven million's been mine since the beginning. Ah've paid a heavy price for it." Darren held up his bandaged left hand and shook it.

Victor inhaled and picked up a cigar from the nearby side table. He stuck it in his mouth and rolled it around, making sucking sounds as he moistened the end.

"You had your chance, Darren." Victor took the cigar out of his mouth. "I gave you every opportunity to retrieve zee check. You failed."

Darren could feel tears welling up in his eyes. Everything was falling apart.

"Man'ti will find zees man, Troy, get me my check, and zen he will be taking care of zee girl." Victor stood. "And you vill get nothing, as you deserve."

The check ... Man'ti hadn't found the check yet. Meaning, it was still out there somewhere, likely with Troy. The girl was the key. She had to know where he was, and Darren would get it out of her.

"Wheyah did he take the girl?"

"Zat is no longer any concern of yours."

Darren raised the pistol and pointed it at Victor. "Ah, but see, thet's wheyah you're wrong."

Victor snarled. "Don't be stupid. Zat check was never yours, it was mine! Vat are you going to do? Shoot me? Vat vill zat accomplish? Imbecile!"

Darren aimed the pistol at Victor's tan belly hanging over the waistband of his tight orange bathing suit. He pulled the trigger. The bang was a quick, short pop and the bullet plunged into the man's stomach. Blood shot out of the hole.

"Jeezus Christ!" Victor yelled. "Vat zee hell are you doing?"

He jerked his hands down to cover the wound in his stomach. Darren pointed the gun at Victor's head.

"Let's try this again," he said calmly, "wheyah did Man'ti take the girl?"

"You are a dead man."

"Not yet," Darren said through a grin, and lowered the gun to Victor's neck.

He fired again, the bullet ripping through the soft flesh between the man's neck and shoulder. He gasped and clutched his throat. Darren began to see the man's bluster fall away. He was bleeding profusely from his stomach and his shoulder, fear starting to seep its way into the man's eyes.

"God's sake, man!" Victor held up a hand. "Okay, okay! Zee money is yours. Man'ti has zee girl. They've gone to zee apartment."

Darren lowered the gun. "See now, thet wasn't so hard, was it?"

"Shit!" Victor was breathing hard and blood was

pouring out of his wounds. "Call 9-1-1. I must have zee ambulance!"

Darren watched as Victor squirmed around on the couch. The beautiful linen upholstery was turning from white to red. He wondered if he had nicked an artery in Victor's neck, because blood flowed freely from the wound in his shoulder.

"Quickly, you idiot!" he screamed at Darren, waving a bloody hand toward the phone.

"Sorry, mate," said Darren "The Body" McGlashen, and raised the pistol and pointed it at Victor Böhring's head.

"Vat zee fu—"

Victor's cry was silenced by the third bullet from Darren's gun. The bullet crashed through the man's skull and his squirming stopped immediately as his head slammed back onto the couch. Blood and brain splattered all over the wall, and Darren couldn't help but grin.

He knew where the girl was, and as a bonus, she was with Man'ti. Two more people were going to die today. Now, he just needed a ride.

A thought came to him as he looked around the quiet beach house; the maid's Toyota. He shuffled around the living room until he found what must've been her purse—a cheap *Coach* knock-off. Digging around in it, he found the keys and her wallet, which he opened to find fifty bucks folded neatly in the back. Victor must've paid her today. He stuffed the money in his pocket and headed for the door.

As he opened it, he heard something. A sniff? A cry? He strained to listen ... nothing. Just his imagination. He painfully limped down the stairs to the carport and worked the key in the maid's car. It turned over on the first crank. *Nothin' like a Toyota*, he thought. He turned on the radio as he backed out of the drive. It was blaring some sort of Spanish-language music and he fumbled the dial until he found another station. The jangly chords of The House of the Rising Sun echoed out of the tinny speakers. He cranked it up, rolled the window down, and drove off Pawleys Island for the last time.

———

DEBBY STIFLED the cry that had almost escaped her mouth when the man had walked into the kitchen and scrounged around in the maid's purse. She'd been pouring a glass of orange juice when the shooting started and she'd fallen to the ground behind the counter and listened to the whole exchange. Thankfully, the children had all been sent down the beach.

She wasn't particularly sad about Victor being shot, she was just shocked and afraid. But she'd managed to stay quiet until the man had left. After waiting long enough to be sure he wasn't coming back, she picked herself up and ran to the phone. Dialing 9-1-1, she told the operator what had happened. *Yes, he'd been shot. Yes, he was definitely dead. Yes, I'll wait here.*

She hung up. *Troy. Gotta get to Troy.*

She looked out the back window to see the children playing on the beach. She ran down the steps to the sand and headed to the house next door where she'd seen Troy go ... interestingly, there were three cop cars out front. *Good*, she thought, *the cavalry is here.*

32

Welcome To The Brady Bunch

CHESNEY R. Biggins paced back and forth on the rear deck of Troy Bodean's beach house. He clicked his missed call log to re-dial his friend, John Dodd Welford with the FBI. As the phone rang, he glanced toward the home of Victor Böhring; nothing out of the ordinary, bunch of kids playing out on the beach ... alone ... no parents watching ...

He turned to look up at the house. The massive deck was empty, no one rocking, no one peeking out of the back windows to check on the children. He could see the carport area under the front of the house and thought it odd that there was a beat-up Toyota Corolla parked beneath. *Hadn't there been another vehicle there when I arrived?* He couldn't remember for sure, but he'd thought there was at least one other. Strange ... the Toyota didn't look like a car the Böhrings would drive.

The receiver picked up. "Well, isn't it a fine day in Georgia when your old buddy, Chesney Biggins, picks up the phone to call?" came John's voice over the phone. "How the hell are you, ol' pal?"

Chesney jerked the conversation back to the business at hand. "John, did you listen to my message?"

John must've sensed the concern in Chesney's voice because he snapped into his FBI analytical voice. "I did not. Didn't realize it was a business call. What's the situation?"

Chesney took a deep breath and recited the fact sheet he'd collected from the murder of—and possible conspiracy surrounding—Rick Hairre. He fed John the details of the current kidnapping situation and where they were with the possible connection of Victor Böhring, the Consolidated Paper Mill, the missing check, and so on.

John was quiet, but Chesney could hear the clicking of computer keys in the background.

"Chesney," John started, "there's a file here on Victor. We've been watching him and a company called ... The Traditional Department of The Interior of South Carolina ... " As John apparently read through the file, he mumbled, "money laundering, conspiracy, yada yada yada." He inhaled. "Ches, I don't see anything here about a check or a murder. This is new. There are agents nearby on his case. I'm going to send them ... "

A muffled bang rang out from next door. Chesney instinctively ducked his head. He dropped to one knee, scanning the house next door.

"Get 'em here, fast." Chesney clicked the phone and shoved it into his pocket.

He drew his pistol and shuffled across the deck to get a better look at the Böhring house. The kids were still playing. Being closer to the ocean, the waves had probably muffled the already quiet pop. They never heard it, but Chesney knew exactly what it was—a small caliber pistol. Someone was shooting in the Böhring's beach house.

The door of the Toyota Corolla suddenly slamming shut and the quick firing of the engine drew his attention. The car jerked out of the driveway, but it was too far away to see who was driving.

Chesney stuck his head inside the house and

said to the police officers, "Something is up at the Böhring house. Sit tight. Lock the door."

He ran out onto the deck, down the stairs to the sand, and started the best waddling run he could manage on the soft white sand. He had one hand on his pistol and kept his eyes glued to the back door of the Böhring house. The door suddenly flew open and he froze, crouching down and drawing his pistol.

A woman came running down the stairs of the house. She was wearing a teal blue one-piece bathing suit and a white cover up draped over her shoulders. In her hand, she held an empty glass. She was crying hysterically as she ran. Chesney quickly figured out that she didn't see him as her gaze was cast down toward the sand.

"Ma'am," he called, holding up his hand, "stop right there."

Mrs. Böhring? She was middle-aged, but very pretty. She had the look of someone who used to be trim and fit, but the toll of children and a life of luxury had left her worn out and a little soft.

She stuttered to a stop, surprised to see him, but then suddenly relaxed. "Oh, thank God, officer," she said and motioned to the house. "My husband's been shot!"

Chesney grabbed the radio mic strapped to his shoulder. "This is unit 47, I need a bus over at—"

She interrupted him. "No need for an ambulance. He's dead."

"Check that," he said into the mic, "and gimme a second to assess the situation." He clicked the mic back to his shoulder and holstered his gun. "You're sure he's dead?"

"Yes, very," she said and sniffed back tears. "Some crazy man that works for him came in and shot him."

"Crazy man that works for him?"

"Yes." She shook her head. "I don't know, Darrel or Darren, or something like that."

"Is he still in the house?"

"No, he's gone."

"You're sure?"

"Yes, he took the maid's keys and I guess her car." A questioning look flitted across her eyes. "The maid ... I have no idea where she is."

Chesney put his hand on her shoulder and pointed the other back at Troy's house. "Mrs. Böhring, listen to me. There are two uniformed police officers in that house right there. Get your children and go knock on the door. I will call them and tell them to let you in."

She nodded and started walking toward the group of children. They seemed not to have noticed that anything strange was going on, but when she spoke to them, they all dropped everything and ran toward her. She herded them together and they all jogged toward Troy's house.

"I'm going to check out your place," he called to her as they passed by. "I'll still need an ambulance out here for the ... "

He stopped short, realizing the kids could hear him.

"Let's go, kids," she said and grabbed the nearest two and shouldered them around toward Troy's place.

"Why are we leaving, Mommy?"

"What's the ambulance for?"

"Don't worry, honey," she reassured them, "everything's going to be just fine. Let's go."

Chesney watched them walk away and turned back toward the Böhring house.

The scene inside was gruesome. Victor was indeed dead, there was no doubt about that. He'd been shot three times, including a head shot that had splattered gore and blood all over the expensive, white linen couch. He radioed the two officers in

Troy's beach house and the station. *All hands on deck for the crime scene.*

While he waited for the backup to arrive, he ticked off each room of the house; empty, no sign of any further violence in any of the other rooms. Nobody home ... no sign of the maid. *That's odd*, he thought. Then he recalled the Toyota Corolla speeding away from the house. He decided to walk down the steps to the carport and check it out. There might be some dropped scrap of paper or cigarette butt or something like that to help him find the shooter.

As he reached for the knob leading to the stairs, he saw it turn, slowly and quietly. It squeaked, and whoever was turning it froze. After a second they resumed twisting the brushed chrome knob. Chesney backed away softly and edged himself behind a nearby chair. He drew his gun and pointed it at the door.

With a soft click, the door creaked open. Chesney watched as the barrel of a gun peeked through. Shit, did the killer come back? He crouched and prepared to fill the guy with as many holes as he could. With a sudden jerk, the door swung open. Chesney's finger tightened on the trigger and he suddenly gasped, dropping his weapon to his side.

"Officer present," he called to the two Litchfield policemen coming in the doorway. "All clear."

They stood from their own crouches and holstered their guns.

"The house is empty," —Chesney motioned toward the gore in the living room— "except for Victor. Backup?"

"On the island, be here in seconds," the first officer said, "and there's another body downstairs in a storage closet. An older woman, possibly Latino."

"The maid," Chesney said. "Did Mrs. Böhring and her children make it to the house safely?"

"They did," the second officer said, nodding from behind the first.

"Good." Chesney put his hands on his hips. "Okay, let's get this scene secured. Don't touch anything." He pointed to one of the officers. "Front door." Turning toward the second officer, he nodded toward the sliding glass door facing the beach. "Back door."

"Got it."

Chesney walked into the kitchen and found the refrigerator door open and a carton of orange juice sitting open on the counter, which explained the empty glass Mrs. Böhring was carrying. He didn't touch it, but he did look inside the fridge. It was an odd collection of children's food—American cheese, hot dogs, fruit juice pouches—and food from another completely different social station—caviar, escargot and ... well, he didn't recognize the other dish.

Welcome to the Brady Bunch, he thought.

33

Behind The Balls

TROY CLINT BODEAN sat on the futon in his rented beach house, The Turtle House, and studied the sharpie-scribbled initials inside his hat. Ownership of the hat being what it currently was, new information had come to light, making it look like it might not be *his* hat much longer, since the initials R. H. were scrawled inside. It looked like it might've been Rick Hairre's hat.

Just seconds ago, the cops had stormed out of the house without much explanation and leaving the two of them alone ... waiting ... for what, he didn't know. He traced the initials on the inner headband of the hat again and looked at Laura Kate Starlington.

She was wringing her hands and staring at her

phone. Obviously worried about Karah, she hadn't said much when they found out she was no longer in Laura's beach house.

"Laura," he started, "I think I've figured something out."

She looked up at him, clearly puzzled.

"A few hours ago, you asked me where I got my hat." He turned it right side up and sat it on the coffee table in front of her. "Do you remember asking me that?"

She shook her head.

"Well, as the case may be, I um ... " He stood up and started to pace, his fingers steepled together. "You see, dangit all ... I found this hat."

Confusion spread across her face again.

"See, I was fishin' out in the creek," —he motioned through the window to the winding water on that side — "tryin' to catch a big 'ole red drum. And, well, I did. It jerked my brand-new rod into the water, so I dove in after it, and that's when the jon boat hit me in the head."

"Troy," she said, squinting her eyes, "what in the hell are you talking about?"

"That's just it," he said and opened his hands, palms to the ceiling, "I found your dad's hat in the boat."

Her mouth opened a little.

"I don't have a clue how it got there," he said, and sat back down next to her and flipped the hat upside down, "but that's where it came to me." He pointed to the initials.

Tears formed in her eyes. She thought back to the first time she'd seen a picture of Troy on Karah's phone. Something about the hat had registered with her, but with so much on her mind, she hadn't figured it out. She remembered buying the hat for her stepdad for his birthday. She was only six, or maybe seven, at the time, but she'd loved the peacock plume and hoped he would too. She'd forgotten all about it, like you forget what color someone's eyes are or what kind of shoes they wear. It was too familiar. And now, here it was, sitting on the table in front of her, with her dad's writing, his last message to her in the faded initials. Her cheeks were wet as she picked up the hat and traced the letters, R.H.

As Troy watched her study the lasting reminder of her stepfather, he noticed the corner of a piece of paper showing inside the band. He pointed to it.

"What's this?" he asked.

Laura's nose crinkled. "I have no idea."

She pulled the folded note out of the hat, which she handed to Troy.

"Why don't you keep it?" she said. "It really looks good on you."

Troy nodded, his attention still on the paper she held in her hand. She noticed his gaze as he unfolded it.

Her mouth fell open. "Seven ... million ...," —she paused— "dollars ... "

"Uh huh," Troy said. "Ches was right. We had the check the whole time."

She threw the check down on the table like it had burned her hand. "Rick died for that. I don't want it anymore. Get rid of it. Burn it!"

"Now, hold on just a second, little lady." Troy picked up the check. "The cops are gonna need this as evidence. I can void it if you want, but we can't burn it."

"I don't care what you do with it," she nearly growled, "I want it out of my sight, now!"

"Okay, okay," he said and held up his left hand, "settle down, Laura." With his right hand, he tucked the check into his shirt pocket.

"We'll give it to Ches when he gets back," —Troy looked up at the sliding glass door— "which should be soon."

He was startled to see Debby Böhring standing at the door with a whole mess of children hanging on and around her. She raised her hand and knocked frantically on the glass.

Troy shoved the hat on his head and jumped up. He reached the door in two long strides.

Debby stuck her head in as if she was coming up for air. "The girl. I know where the girl is!"

"Huh?" Troy asked, as kids started to pour into his living room.

"The girl you're missing," She held her hands out, palms up. "I know where they've taken her!"

"Aw, dangit," he said, looking back at Laura. "I need a car."

Laura shook her head slowly and then snapped her eyes up to look at him. "Karah's Rover. The keys are probably at my place next door. I think I dropped them when I was running away from the crazy guy with all the bandages!"

Debby spoke up. "I think that's the guy who shot Victor. He was covered in blood-soaked bandages and smelled like shit. He called him Darren or Darrell or something like that."

"Yeah, yeah," Laura said, nodding vigorously, "that's the guy."

"Where did they take her?" Troy asked, putting both hands on Debby's shoulders.

She licked her lips. "Do you know where Balls is?"

"Beg pardon?"

"You know, Balls," —she held her hand up motioning vaguely north— "that cheesy beach t-shirt shop up the road."

"Oh yeah." Troy snapped his fingers. "The one with the two beach balls and the surfboard on the front in the shape of a—"

"Yes," she interrupted him, "that's the one. Victor owns a small self-storage building behind it. He calls it the apartments ... I have no idea why. That's where he said the girl was taken before he was shot."

"Got it," Troy said. He took a deep breath and exhaled as he stood. "Okay, you two sit tight." He held up a hand to stop Laura as her mouth flew open. "No, you can't go."

"But—"

"Not a chance, little darlin'." He shook his head as he moved to the door. "This is gonna get real dangerous and I don't want you in harm's way."

"But she's *my* cousin!"

"Yup, she is," he said and opened the door, "and

her parents are on their way. They're gonna need you here. And Debby and the kids need you here."

Laura slumped back down on the couch and crossed her arms.

"This here part of the story is mine," he said. "Your part is to wait on the cops and the feds to get here and tell 'em everything you know."

He waited for her to retort, but she didn't. She uncrossed her arms.

"Just be careful, Troy," she said through her tears, not knowing what else to say. "And bring my cousin back to me."

"That's the plan," Troy said.

"Hey." Laura must've thought of something suddenly. "Take her phone. That other dude has mine. He's probably got it turned off, but you never know."

He tipped the cowboy hat toward them and closed the door.

TROY JOGGED/LIMPED the short distance down Myrtle Avenue and headed into the carport where Karah's Land Rover sat behind a green Volkswagen Jetta. He'd been too preoccupied to notice his gun bounce out of the waistband of his shorts and fall to the soft, pea gravel of the driveway. After just a few seconds, he found the Rover keys lying on the stairs leading up under Laura's beach house. The SUV fired up in the smooth, powerful way that only a Land Rover can, and he urged it quickly out onto the road. Once he got off the island, he gunned the car, and it leaped forward hungrily. He didn't care much how fast he was going as all the cops in the area were probably at Victor's house right now. The wheels ate up Ocean Highway swiftly as he raced toward the Balls beach shop, a touristy dive selling t-shirts, magnets, conch shells and a whole raft of other crap. He barely noticed the ding trying to inform him that he was dangerously low on gas.

———

MAN'TI SUCKED a toothpick as he stared at the girl sitting in the broken recliner. A crusty pool of blood under the chair reminded him of how that dumb-arse Darren had cut off his damn toes in this storage unit. *Fookin' idiot*, he thought, grinning.

Her wrists and ankles were bound tightly with heavy, plastic zip-ties and her mouth was covered with a piece of duct tape that wrapped around her whole head. She was crying, and muffled sounds came through the tape as she tried to yell.

He was at a mild crossroads here. He wasn't really a rapist, but this girl was fine. She was only wearing a tiny little bikini and looked to be college aged. Her body was the body of a girl who hadn't been through any shit yet to screw it up. Not like the girls he'd been with before. The only girls who'd pay him any mind were the kind that worked for twenty-five or fifty bucks an hour.

The way she looked at him turned him on. It was fear, or more accurately, terror. She knew he was going to kill her, but right now, she might be realizing that he was going to play with her before he did it.

He stood up and walked toward her. She flinched back and he was more turned on than ever. He grinned. Grabbing the back of her hair to keep her head still, he jerked the duct tape off her face.

She screamed, and he slapped her hard on the cheek.

Her scream turned into gasps of pain. "Don't kill me," she cried, "please, God, don't kill me."

Man'ti licked his lips. "If ya can't find me this Troy fella, I got no use fa ya." He laughed and tugged on his belt. "Actually, I do have one use ah'm gonna try out real soon."

Her eyes went wide as she realized what he meant. She scooted back into the chair as much as she could, shrinking away from him. "No, no, no ... " she whimpered.

He unbuttoned his pants and slid the zipper down.

Karah started screaming again.

"Shit," he muttered. He leaned down beside the recliner and picked up the duct tape. He stretched off a piece and stuck it over her mouth. "Shut the fook up," he barked and smacked her hard again on the same cheek.

She whimpered, but she stopped screaming. He went back to undoing his pants and slid them down around his ankles. As his pants hit the ground, a cell phone popped out of the back pocket.

The girl's eyes went even wider. She struggled and tried to speak from behind the tape. Her head bobbed quickly in the direction of the phone.

"What?" Man'ti picked it up. "This? Yeah, it's ya cousin's, so fookin' what?"

She tried desperately to say something again. Man'ti peeled the tape off her mouth.

"Call Laura!" Karah yelled, "she's got my phone and I'm sure she's with Troy!"

Man'ti considered this for a second. The girl had a point. If he could get to Troy, he could blackmail him with the girl. He'd have the check before nightfall. He turned the phone on and waited for it to boot up. "What's her number?"

"She's in the contacts under SexiCuz2."

Man'ti slapped the tape back over her mouth. He clicked the number and waited for the dial tone. It rang twice and someone picked up.

"Yeah?" the voice said on the other end.

It wasn't a girl's voice. It was a man. Could it be? "Troy?" Man'ti asked.

"Speakin'."

34

Break A Leg

THE METAL ROOM they were in suddenly became a cacophony of banging and clanging. Karah jumped uncontrollably and the huge man who'd been hovering over her about to rape her was startled too. The cell phone he'd been holding to his ear popped out of his hand like a bar of wet soap and crashed to the ground. The decorative case with the picture of Laura's dog, Tyson, cracked on the corner and the phone's screen shattered and went dark.

The banging started again, more insistently.

"Come out, come out, wherevah ya are," a voice yelled from behind the steel, roll-up style garage door.

"Shit," the big man said, and reached down to try and pull his pants up.

Karah started screaming, but the duct tape muffled most of the sound. She had no idea who was at the door, but he couldn't be as bad as this dude. She would realize only later how wrong she had been about that.

Suddenly, the door flew up and painfully bright sunlight flooded into the storage compartment. Karah squinted her eyes to see, but the figure in the doorway was just a silhouette.

"Bluddy fookin' hell," spat her massive captor, "what the fook are you doin' 'ere?"

The man standing in the doorway walked ... or actually ... he limped into the room. He was wrapped in bandages and his face was swollen and pulpy. Blood oozed from several different places and he smelled like vinegar ... and almonds.

Her first thought was that she'd been held captive long enough for the zombie outbreak to happen. Her second was that she was no longer the center of attention. She looked around the room for something to help her escape, the first order of business being to cut the zip-ties on her wrists and ankles.

Nothing. There was absolutely nothing in this room except for the two men, the recliner, the broken cell phone and her. She looked down at the phone and wondered if she could slide it closer to her with her foot. The two men were still yelling at each other, so she slowly stretched out her legs. Her big toe touched the phone and she almost gasped with relief. She was able to drag it inch by inch closer to the recliner. She had no idea how she'd be able to use it, but at least she was doing something and not sitting around waiting to be raped and killed. As the phone edged closer to the recliner, she dragged one last time and something sharp bit into her heel. She couldn't help but yelp in pain. Luckily, the duct tape muffled the sound so much, the two men never heard her.

A trickle of blood dripped down onto her foot and she saw what had happened. The recliner's leg was missing its rubber edge protector and the metal was exposed. It looked like a knife edge sticking out from under the chair. An idea jumped into her head. She carefully swung her legs so the sharp edge was between them. She lowered them until the zip-tie was touching the metal. She gently moved her legs up and down. After just a few scrapes, a notch began to form in the plastic binding. She looked back up at the two men as she worked.

The zombie guy had a gun pointed at the big guy,

and he spoke in crazy, slurred speech. The big guy had his hands up, but he didn't look scared.

"Who's got the fookin' uppa hand na'ow, mate?" the little guy cackled.

"Ya ain't got one full hand between the two of 'em, ya shit."

"Yeah, keep talkin'," the little guy said, "caught ya with ya fookin' pants down."

"Ah'm gonna fookin' murder ya if ya don't put that silly little pop-gun down, Darren."

Darren laughed a low, rasping laugh. He wobbled a little and inhaled to steady himself.

"Pop-gun or nah," he said, and lowered it to point at the bigger man's crotch, "it'll blow a hole right through ya wanka, Man'ti."

Darren and Man'ti, Karah thought, the two guys who'd been running out of Drunken Jack's the other night. The same two guys who'd been harassing Laura on that night. She had no idea why they wanted Troy, but she knew it was something worth killing her over. She worked her legs a little faster. These two weirdoes weren't paying attention to her at all. She glanced down at the zip-tie around her ankles. It was a third of the way cut. She was beginning to sweat and it was making it hard to keep the plastic up against the sharp edge. Several times it slipped off and jabbed her in the heel. Her foot was starting to slick with blood, but she didn't stop.

"Keep ya fookin' hands up," the guy called Darren growled at the other man.

He'd been trying to get his hands down to pull his pants up, but Darren wasn't having any of that.

"It's time we settled this once and fa all," Darren said, pulling the hammer back on his gun, "so say ya prayers, ya tattooed ass."

The big guy, Man'ti, lunged at Darren, but his pants were still around his ankles so he fell forward to his knees. He ended up eye-level with Darren's feet. He reached out and grabbed Darren's right leg with both hands. The disgustingly brown and gooey bandages on the man's leg squished like there wasn't a leg inside. Darren howled in pain and slammed the butt of his pistol down hard on Man'ti's head, but the big guy held on tight.

Man'ti's grip tightened more, and with a grunt, he jerked his hands downward like a chef breaking spaghetti to fit better in a boiling pot. Falling to the ground, Darren screamed again and shot Man'ti straight in the mouth. The back of the man's neck exploded in a bloody mess, but he didn't seem to want to die. The shot pinged against the back of the room and whizzed back at Darren ... a ricochet. He heard a bang and sizzle behind him, as the bullet found a new target out the door of the storage unit.

Man'ti was in full panic now, his eyes bulging out of his head. He released Darren's ruined right leg and clutched his throat. Ragged breaths wheezed in and out of him. He worked his mouth like he wanted to say something, but all that came out was the sound of a broken kazoo.

"Look what ya did to mah fookin' leg!!" Darren shouted in a rage, with spittle flying from his lips.

His right foot dangled at an awkward angle. It looked like a hanging sock with a potato in it.

Karah gagged at the sight of all the gore as suddenly the plastic zip-tie broke, freeing her legs. She shot up out of the recliner, but slipped on the puddle of her own blood beneath her feet, and she fell down, right next to Darren.

He grabbed her hair in a fist. "You ain't goin' nowhere, sweet tits."

Man'ti lurched up onto his knees, but he was still grasping at his neck and trying to fix the damage done to his head. Blood streamed down all around his shoulders.

Without a word, Darren raised the pistol. He put a bullet right in between Man'ti's eyes. The back of his head exploded out and he slumped forward.

Darren spit on the bloody mess of the hulking man. "Fook you!"

He pulled Karah's head up and tapped her forehead with the gun. "Gimme a sec ta catch mah breath. You're gonna tell me wheyah Troy is, or you're next."

35

Trade Route

THAT WAS ODD. The guy on the other end of the phone just hung up after he had said, "Speakin'."

Had to have been the guy who'd kidnapped Karah. Troy swung the Rover into the parking lot of the Balls beach store. The car sputtered and died just as he pulled in ... out of gas. *Dangit*, he thought, *no turnin' back now*.

He coasted in next to a brand new, fire engine red, jacked up, decked out Jeep Wrangler Unlimited idling in the lot. The back windows were so dark that he never noticed the girl sitting in the back seat nursing the baby. As he got out of the Land Rover, he reached behind his back under his shirt to discover that his gun was gone. *Dangit. Heading into enemy territory ... unarmed. Not good.*

Remembering his time in Afghanistan, patrolling sketchy neighborhoods, came in handy sometimes. Just like back on the dusty roads of Kabul, he eased around the side of the building until he could see the storage units. Clear. Most of the units were closed and quiet. As he walked back along the rows of rooms, he would peek around the edge, crouching down to lower his profile. Row after row, there was nothing. Clear. Finally, on the last row, he edged around the corner to see a gold Toyota spewing steam from under its hood. It was parked facing a unit with its door rolled up. Listening closely, Troy could hear the faint sound of a male voice coming from inside. He put his back against the row of doors and inched his way toward the open unit.

As he got closer, he crouched again. That's when he finally heard the girl's voice.

"I promise, mister," she said, "I don't know where he is and I don't know anything about a check or whatever."

Karah. Had to be her. Troy heard the sound of a smack and then a squeal from Karah. He flinched, wanting to run in to help, but he knew the guy was probably armed and extremely dangerous. Had to play this right. He took the Outback Tea Stained straw cowboy hat off his head and started to pull the check out. Gone. He was momentarily in shock, but then remembered he'd stuck it in his shirt pocket. He replaced his hat and pulled the check out. Unfolding it, he edged around the corner. He raised his hands high, holding the check in his left hand.

The scene was shocking. There was a dude lying on the ground with most of his head blown off, and a giant, dark, gelatinous puddle of blood oozing outward in the center of the room. A man was kneeling in the blood with a handful of Karah's hair held tight in his fist. She was covered in blood and Troy couldn't be sure if any of it was hers or not. Her hands were bound behind her back and she was whimpering. Crazy dude had a small pistol pointed at her forehead and she was crying. Troy couldn't see the man's face, but he immediately recognized his voice and his ... injuries. He was the guy from the hospital. This was the guy who'd kidnapped Karah, attacked Laura, shot Victor, and from the looks of it, his partner, all for the check in Troy's hand. He had to play this just right, or this guy was just going to shoot them both.

He grasped the edges of the check, one side in each hand, and coughed.

The guy jerked his head around and raised his

pistol at Troy.

"Whoa, whoa, whoa, there pardner," Troy said, calmly but quickly, "I know who you are and I know what you want. I got it right here." He nodded his head up toward the check. Tears started to form in the guy's eyes.

"Is that ... " he croaked, "is that what ah think it is?"

"Yup."

The guy raised the pistol like he was going to shoot Troy.

Troy pulled his hands apart slightly and a small rip started in the middle of the check.

"Hold on just a second now," he said quickly. "If ya shoot me, I'm gonna tear it up."

The guy froze. "No, please, no."

"It's alright, now." Troy eased the check down so that it was in front of his chest. "I'm gonna give it to you, but it's gotta be a fair trade."

"Yeah, yeah," the man shook his head, "anything ya want."

"The girl," —Troy motioned toward Karah— "let her go. When she's out the door and gone, I'll hand you the check. Then you can shoot me if you feel it's necessary."

"Please, Darren," Karah whimpered.

He looked down at her. "Shut tha fook up, ya wenc—"

"Darren, look at me," Troy interrupted him.

He made another small movement and the rip in the middle of the check got a tiny bit longer.

"Don't be stupid." Troy shrugged his shoulders. "You give me the girl, I give you seven ... million ... dollars." He paused in between each word for emphasis.

Darren clearly struggled with his choice. Troy had seen this before; the man had been on a mission to kill them all, but now there was no way to accomplish that and still get the check. He finally grunted in agreement. His hand loosened on Karah's hair. She scooted toward Troy, blood pooling up and around her legs.

Darren raised the pistol and pointed it at her as she inched away from him. "No funny business or I'll put a bullet in her head."

"Ain't no funny business goin' on here," Troy reassured him.

He looked into Karah's eyes and mouthed, *RUN*. She squirmed up to her knees, leaning against Troy, and was finally able to get to her feet. She stared into his eyes, and he winked at her. She backed out of the storage unit and Troy could hear her feet padding quickly away. He hoped she'd call the police ... or at least an ambulance, because he was sure this Darren guy was going to shoot him.

"Help me up, mate," —Darren wagged the gun at Troy, motioning him closer— "got a slight problem with me foot."

Troy looked at the guy's leg. The urge to vomit was strong as he realized his foot was almost completely separated from his leg, apparently just hanging by the skin and the disgusting bandages wrapped around it. He had a thought. He wondered if he could just run from the guy. No way he could catch him on that foot. As if he could read his mind, Darren shook his head.

"Nah, mate." He held up a splintered cell phone. "Ya leave me here, ah'll get this phone fixed. Ah got addresses and numbahs. Ah'll find 'em, and ah'll kill 'em all."

Dangit. Troy put the check in his mouth, pressing lightly with his lips to hold it firmly, and leaned down to hook his hands under the man's arms. God, the dude smelled rancid, like a trash can full of rotten meat. He propped the guy up and he hopped to the side wall of the storage unit. Darren seemed to see the hissing engine of the Toyota for the first time.

"Shit," he said as his shoulders dropped, "me

fookin' car's toast."

He looked at Troy and pointed the gun at him. "Wheyah's your car?"

Troy wagged his head back and forth.

"S'in the lot," he said between his pursed lips, "outta gas."

"Fook me."

"But there was a Jeep in the parking lot of that store up there." Troy took the check from his lips, careful to hold it in between his hands. "She's empty and running."

"Right," Darren said, waving the gun, "me and you, let's go."

"Hey, I'm done with my part of the trade."

"Don't look like ya in much of a position ta do any quittin' now, mate. Now gimme my fookin' check, and let's go."

Troy inhaled deeply. He handed the check to Darren and shouldered up under the man's arm. Talk about flashbacks to Afghanistan. He'd carried what was left of Harry Nedman back to the chopper in a very similar way. *Yeah, I'm gettin' outta Pawleys if I make it outta this alive*, he thought to himself again.

It was a long, slow walk, with Darren wincing all along the way. They had to stop a few times to let the man catch his wheezing breath, and Troy wondered what the hell was taking the cops so long to get there. Surely Karah had called them by now.

As they turned the corner from behind the Balls store, the sirens finally started to blare in the distance.

"Ha ha!" Darren cackled upon seeing that the huge red Jeep was still sitting there with its engine running. He untangled himself from Troy's grasp and swung the pistol hard at his head. It didn't have much force behind it, but it caught him by surprise. He lost his balance momentarily, and fell to the curb.

"Dangit, man!" He looked up to see Darren jumping on his one good foot toward the Jeep.

He got to the driver's side and pulled the door open, then lurched into the seat slammed the car into reverse. Troy watched as he held up his hand in an upside-down fist. He realized the man was trying to flip him off ... but his middle finger wasn't there. The words *fook you* were on Darren's lips as the Jeep squealed to the edge of the parking lot toward Ocean Drive. Troy stood up and looked around. No sign of Karah. He jogged to the front entrance of the store and jerked the door open.

The cool rush of air conditioning was the second thing to hit his face. The first was Ellie Mae Gallup.

36

Kid Napping

THE JEEP'S engine roared in a satisfying low growl as Darren figured out how to work the gas pedal with his left foot. His right foot still ached, but the sharp pain of the initial break was dulling with shock. As the giant, knobby tires rumbled to the edge of the parking lot, Darren caught a glimpse of something moving in the back seat.

He craned his neck around to see a girl breastfeeding a baby.

"Howdy, Darren," Daisy Mae Gallup said quietly.

Darren looked forward again at the cashier's check sitting in the passenger seat. That wench was still trying to steal his money. He slammed on the brake and turned around, pointing his pistol at the blonde girl.

"Get the fook outta mah car," he said and wagged the gun toward the door.

"It ain't a car, it's a Jeep," she said, "and if you wake my nappin' kid, I'm gon' bust yer face."

Darren saw red. His breath grew ragged.

"Ah'll say it one more time." He pulled the hammer back, cocking the gun. "Get ... out."

Daisy Mae sniffed. "Jus' like a man ta run out on me and the baby."

Darren said nothing, and just wagged the gun again.

Daisy Mae pulled the baby off her breast and buttoned up her shirt. The angry newborn started to wail. She hopped down out of the Jeep and slammed the door. Tears formed in her eyes as she stood by his window.

Well, fook. She *was* actually kind of pretty. And he had always wanted a baby. Hell, he had plenty of money now, and in his condition, he might like to have someone to take care of him.

He reached down for the window control ... shit ... manual. Of all the bells and whistles on this Jeep, it had a damn handle to roll the window down. He switched the gun to his right hand and started to roll it down with his left. With the missing fingers and the messy ooze coming from the bandages, it was slow going. He cursed and swore he'd run it off a cliff and buy a new one. When the window was finally down, he spoke, the red haze lifting from his eyes for a second.

"Ya don't have ta leave," he said, "if ya don't wanna."

Her lip was quivering, but he didn't see sadness in her eyes. The baby screamed in her arms. No, she didn't look sad ... it was something completely different. Anger. *Shit*, he thought.

"I wouldn't wanna be with a no-good, no 'count, finger-missin', leg-broken criminal like you," she scowled, "and ah'm gon' call the damn po-leese and tell 'em zactly what you done to us."

She reached up and smacked him hard across the cheek. His first reaction was shock, but then as that faded, the anger returned.

"Why, you fookin' whore," he said and raised the pistol up to point out the window, "ah'm gonna murdah ya ass. How 'bout that?"

The gun squirmed in his grip. His right hand was missing the very digits that he needed to operate the gun as Man'ti had ripped them off when he grabbed it from his hand before. His ring finger was on the trigger, and he squeezed. The gun did not fire. In fact, like a bar of soap, it popped up out of his hand and clattered to the ground at Daisy Mae's feet.

"Shit!" Darren screamed. "Gimme that fookin' gun!"

Daisy Mae leaned down and picked up the pistol. She held it in her right hand and worked her finger into place on the trigger.

"Ah'm gon' give it to ya, a'raight."

Darren froze. His eyes widened as he realized what was about to happen. He reached down with his left hand and started working the window's handle furiously. The glass slid up an inch.

Daisy Mae Gallup raised the pistol and pointed it at his head.

"Gimme 'at check," she said, her eyes flicking toward the passenger's seat, "I seen you had it."

Darren continued to work the window. It raised another inch. *Fookin' manual windows!* "Ah'm not givin' you shit, wench," he growled.

She glared at him. The baby wailed again, and she looked down at him.

"It's okay, baby T.C.," she cooed.

The angry red haze filled Darren's eyes again. She'd called him baby T.C., not baby Darren. He was furious. He jerked the Jeep into reverse, backing up twenty feet. He saw the girl and the baby standing in front of him and turned the wheel toward them.

"Eat mah bumpa, bitch!" he yelled, and slammed his left foot down on the accelerator.

37

I'm Your Ice Cream Man

TROY CLINT BODEAN and Ellie Mae Gallup were standing in the doorway to the Balls beach store when they heard a high-pitched voice yell something about a bumper. Ellie Mae had just slapped the crap out of Troy before she realized that he wasn't a random dude rushing her at the door and trying to steal her stuff. She'd apologized and gathered up her shopping bounty when the shouting began.

From the back of the store, Karah ran toward them. She was wrapped in a towel she'd apparently grabbed from the store. It said, Dry Your Balls, and had a picture of the store's garish logo on it.

"Called the cops," she said, rushing toward Troy. "On the way."

They turned in unison to see a red Jeep squeal toward Daisy Mae Gallup and her baby in a haze of burned tire rubber smoke.

"No!!!" screamed Ellie Mae as she started running toward the scene.

Unfortunately, Ellie Mae's arms were now holding a flamingo shaped pool float, a folding beach chair that read: *it's five o'clock somewhere*, two complete sets of snorkel gear, a collection of black and red shot glasses on a tic-tac-toe style tray, and two pairs of sunglasses.

The scene flickered in front of Troy. It was strange to see. It went from being the beach store parking lot to Afghanistan ... and back again. One second it was Daisy Mae Gallup and the baby, the next it was Harry Nedman. In both scenes, Troy was about to watch someone die.

Too far away ... he was too far away and Harry's bottom half had been blown off by an I.E.D. just lying in the road. He'd tried desperately to drag him back to the chopper and get his friend to the hospital. No such luck, he was dead before Troy had gotten to him. He'd wanted to shoot somebody, to avenge Harry, but there wasn't anyone to shoot ... just the charred, black starburst on the ground where the bomb had gone off.

The scene flickered. Daisy Mae was paralyzed like a deer in the angry red Jeep's headlights. The scenario was the same; Troy was too far away to help. Everything slowed down. He ran toward them, yelling and waving his arms, but she didn't seem to notice. The Jeep leaped forward. The baby screamed.

From behind him, Ellie Mae yelled at her. "Daisy Mae, git on outta thar! We gotta git 'at baby home!"

Daisy Mae's head snapped toward her sister and then back toward the Jeep. She had woken up. The Jeep was too close.

Troy's foot thunked against something laying in the parking lot. He looked down. A small .38 caliber revolver with dark smudges all over it lay at his feet. Without thinking, he crouched down on one knee, grabbed the pistol, and raised it up to aim at the Jeep. He rolled his head around once to crack the tight joints in his neck.

He was never sure after that if he'd said it out loud, or in his mind, or if his imagination had just added it to the scene later.

"Check out time, Darren," Troy said as he pulled the trigger.

The bullet pierced the front driver's side tire and it blew out immediately. The brand new, fire engine red, jacked up, decked out Jeep Wrangler Unlimited jerked hard to the left and veered safely past Daisy Mae and her baby, narrowly missing them. The out of control Jeep jumped the parking lot curb and raced across the street perpendicular to the flow of traffic. Unbelievably, no other car happened to be in its path at that exact moment.

Troy could see Darren's shocked face turn to stare back at him. His mouth was open and he was screaming something that he guessed was very angry.

Troy raised the pistol again and pulled the trigger. It clicked. He pulled it again. Click. He'd only had one shot left. *Dangit.*

He dropped the pistol and ran toward the fleeing Jeep. He wasn't sure why, but it just seemed like the thing to do. As he ran, he looked out in front of the Jeep. It was headed straight into the next parking lot, a hardware and convenience store simply called, The Hardware Store. Troy stopped short.

Directly in the path of the runaway Jeep was a bank of gas pumps. There was only one vehicle sitting at the pumps, a beautiful, fully restored, nineteen-fifties, Merry Mobile ice cream truck. *Oh God ... it's Willie.*

He'd said something about his truck being

wrecked and that he had a new one coming up from the Keys to replace it temporarily. And now it sat directly in the path of certain destruction.

It was only thirty feet away and Troy had no time and no way to stop the inevitable. Harry Nedman flashed into his mind again. Someone was about to die. Troy ran. He couldn't stop it, but he would be there to drag someone away from the carnage.

There must've been a spark from the metal grinding against metal when the Jeep smashed t-bone style into the beautiful ice cream truck, because it went up like a small nuclear bomb going off. The fireball stopped Troy in his tracks, and the heat singed his beard. He skidded to a stop as the blaze raged higher. People began running out of The Hardware Store with their hands shielding their faces. No one seemed to be hurt, thank God. Troy watched the fire completely engulf the two vehicles and took a deep breath. He'd let Harry down all those years ago and now he'd let Willie down.

A crowd of people was beginning to gather a safe distance away from the fire. Karah, Daisy Mae and Ellie Mae all rushed over from the store. Ellie Mae had the baby in her arms. Karah nuzzled up to Troy and wrapped her arm around his waist. He put his arm around her shoulder.

"You okay?" he asked her.

"Yeah," she said, and smiled a little, but he could see the shock of all that had happened lingering in her eyes.

She'd be okay, but it would take a while.

He looked over at the Gallup girls and their baby. He was a cute little thing and had finally fallen asleep.

"How 'bout y'all?" he asked them.

"Doin' fine," Ellie Mae nodded. "Thank'ee, Troy. Ya saved ma sister's life ... and the baiby ... " Her voice choked.

"We cain't never repay you," Daisy Mae added.

He returned the nod and touched the brim of his Outback tea stained straw cowboy hat. "No need."

The attendant from the store was nearby and Troy overheard him say that he'd pushed the emergency stop button and that the remaining gas in the pump would burn off soon.

Troy saw a man come trotting around the building, zipping up his pants and carrying a key attached to a tire iron. A black man, wearing a supremely white, freshly starched jumpsuit and a sailor's cap that looked like the one the skipper had worn on Gilligan's Island. The cap had a picture of an ice cream cone and an orange creamsicle on the front. The man had a patch over one eye that had been painted to look like the eye of a clown. Troy laughed the laugh of supreme relief when he heard Willie's voice.

"Ya got ta be gall-dang kiddin' me!" he said, still fussing with his zipper, "three times? Dat ain't right!"

He dropped the key with its steal-proof tire iron and jogged toward the crowd.

"Ken you believe dat, Mista Troy?" he asked.

"Beats all I ever saw, Willie," Troy said, and slapped the man on the back.

"I'm gettin' da hail outta Pawleys, I tell ya dat right now," the one-eyed man said, then shook his head.

"I hear ya." Troy took in a deep breath. "Might be time for me to move on too."

And that's when the swarm of police cars finally arrived.

"Not once in this whole, dang mess have they showed up on time." Troy raised his hands, palms to the sky. "Dangit, y'all need to work on your response time!"

38

I'll Take It

CHESNEY RICHARD BIGGINS watched as the black '89 Lincoln Towncar eased into the parking lot in front of the Balls beach store. He inhaled deeply as Winchester Boonesborough rolled his window down. In typical fashion, he refused to get out of his car. He motioned Chesney toward the car with an impatient wave. Nodding toward his friend from the F.B.I., John Dodd Welford, Chesney hooked his thumbs in his belt and walked toward the car.

"Really screwed the pooch on this one, didn't we, Deputy Biggins?" Winchester said, his meaty jowls bouncing up and down. "You can damn well bet there'll be hell to pay for this!"

Chesney sucked his breath through his teeth.

With deliberate slowness, he pulled his badge off his shirt. He laid it on the hood of the Towncar.

"What's this?" Winchester was dumbfounded.

Chesney ignored him. He slid his police issue pistol from its holster and laid it next to the badge. "I quit," he said to the puffing District Attorney.

"Oh, no you don't," said the fat man, making like he was going to get out of his car.

"Mr. Boonesborough," a voice interrupted him, "we'll take this from here."

John walked up to the car and placed a hand on the door as if to block it from being opened.

"And just who the hell do you think—"

John flashed a badge and I.D. card from his back pocket. "John Dodd Welford, Federal Bureau of Investigation. Perhaps you've heard of it?"

Winchester huffed. "But this is in my jurisdiction!"

"Not since it became a conspiracy to commit fraud and homicide," John said, winking at him. "It's ours now. Why don't you just go on home now?"

Winchester glared at him. John picked up the badge and the gun from the hood and handed them to him.

"Looks like you've got some H.R. problems to attend to anyway," he said.

Without taking them from him, Winchester Boonesborough pursed his lips and pushed the button to roll up his electric window. It moved up comically slow and the three of them just stared at each other in the slow buzz of it rising. The car eased out of the lot, then bumped onto the highway and disappeared down the road.

John shrugged, handing the items back to Chesney. "Guess he isn't accepting your resignation."

"I'll have to file it officially back at the station, anyway."

"What will you do now?" John asked. "I can put in a good word with the bureau if you want."

Chesney shook his head. "No thanks. It's time for a change, just not sure what it is yet."

As if on cue, a maroon Bentley pulled into the lot. Laura jumped out of the back seat as soon as it came to rest and ran toward them. Seeing her, Karah let go of Troy and ran toward her too. They broke into sobs, hugging each other tightly. An older couple stepped out of the car. The man was pale and his eyes were wide. The woman had warm, auburn hair that reminded Troy of Karah's. *Ahhh, mom and dad.*

The woman broke into tears as she ran toward

Karah. Karah released her hug on Laura and wrapped her arms around her mother.

"My baby!" she cried.

They held each other for a long while.

————

NOT FAR AWAY AND standing near Troy, Laura was watching the fire crew controlling the dwindling blaze coming from the gas pumps.

"What happened?" she asked Troy.

He relayed the crazy story in short form, leaving out a few details. Chesney walked up to them and stretched out a hand to Troy.

"Glad to see you're okay, Troy," he said with a smile.

"Thanks, partner," Troy said.

Chesney pointed to his hat. "You get rid of that check?"

Troy inclined his head toward the smoldering mess in front of The Hardware Store. "In a blaze of glory."

"Glad to see the hat survived though."

"Sure enough." Troy pulled the hat off his head and held it out toward Laura. "I guess it belongs to you now."

Laura smiled. "No, Troy. You've made it yours. And I think Rick would be proud of the man who's taken over the hat."

"Are you sure?" he asked.

"I'm sure," she said, reaching up to kiss him on the cheek. "What would I do with it, anyway?"

"Well, dang," he said looking down at it, "that's about the nicest thing anyone has ever given me. If you're really sure, I'll take it."

"Totally sure," she said, and smiled wide.

He put the hat back on its rightful place on his head. Karah's father moved up to the group and extended his hand.

"I hear that I owe you for saving my baby girl's life?" he said, shaking Troy's hand. "I'm Roger Campobello, and I am very grateful to you, sir."

Troy felt a little shame edge onto his face ... seeing as how he had been considering dating this man's daughter. He realized that he was almost the same age as Mr. Campobello. He looked over to where Karah was standing, embraced in her mother's arms. She looked like a little girl. Troy knew the relationship that had started to blossom between them was at an end.

"Listen," Mr. Campobello addressed the group, "Karah is starving. We're going to get her cleaned up and get something to eat. Why don't you all come along?"

Troy looked at Laura and Chesney. "Ummmm ... "

Laura nudged him. "Sure thing, Uncle Roger. I know the perfect place."

Jumping into Troy's awkward silence, Chesney slapped him on the back of his shoulder and smiled. "Why don't you ride with me?"

"Perfect," Troy said, sighing with relief.

"You ride with us, Laura." Mr. Campobello put his arm around her shoulder. "Where shall we go?"

"Lee's Inlet Kitchen, of course," she said, beaming.

"I know the way," Chesney said.

39

Sweet Sorrow

LAURA KATE STARLINGTON and Chesney Richard Biggins sat in a booth alone at Lee's Inlet Kitchen. The group had split up, since the booths only held four people, so Laura had deferred to letting Karah sit with her parents and, awkwardly, Troy.

The whole story had come full circle. This was where they had met and where Laura had found out her stepfather, Rick Hairre, had been murdered in some kind of conspiracy or blackmail plot. Chesney had said that his friend at the F.B.I. was in on the investigation and that the whole mess with some corporate paper mill was going in front of the grand jury or something like that. He assured her that they were most likely out of business, and that someone would probably go to jail for the whole thing. Rick's killers were all dead, so at least that gave her some sense of closure on it all.

"So ... " Chesney swirled a salty fry around in the ketchup on his plate, "what's next for you?"

Laura thought about this for a minute. She opened her mouth, then shut it, then opened it again. Finally, she said, "I hadn't really thought about it. I guess I'll go back to work on Monday."

"Work?" Chesney asked, stuffing the fry in his mouth. "Why would you do that?"

She crinkled her nose. "Um, because that's what people do. They work."

He took a sip of his Coca-Cola. "Not me, actually. I'm pretty sure I just resigned."

Her eyes widened. "Wow," she said, "bold move. So, I guess I should be the one asking what's next for you."

"Yeah, I guess I hadn't really thought about it either."

A long moment of silence passed between them, the only sounds the clinking of glasses and plates and the muted conversation going on between the Campobellos and Troy.

"You know what I really should do," Laura

suddenly said, "I should use the money to start a foundation. I think it's pretty clear that the environment gets a pretty crappy shake around here."

"Mmhmm," Chesney said between bites, "would be a nice legacy for Rick. It looks like that's what he was going to do with the check ... the big check, anyway."

She thought about it for a second. "Hey, won't the F.B.I. be able to trace the second deposit back to me?"

"I doubt it," —Chesney glanced sideways for a second— "I deleted that file from the zip drive and scrubbed it with a cleaner file from the internet."

"Oh," Laura said, not really understanding what that meant.

"And I'm guessing that someone at the Consolidated Paper Mill is working hard in the shredding room and burying any digital evidence of all those transactions too."

Laura sniffed and wiped her mouth. "So, why don't you help me out?" she asked.

"Huh?" He furrowed his eyebrows.

"Help me out, with starting the foundation," she continued. "I don't know the first thing about it, but I can keep us floating with the money until we get real backers."

Chesney laughed. "I have no clue about any of that. I'm sure I wouldn't be any help at all."

"Yeah, me neither," she grinned.

She caught his eyes. He really was a sweet guy.

"Or we could buy a boat and sail around the Keys for a bit," she said, winking at him.

"Now, that sounds more like it," he said. "I am a pretty good sailor, you know?"

"Really?" She raised her eyebrows.

"No, not really," he said, smiling, "but I think I could figure it out. You want to come to my place tonight and talk about it?"

"Well, well, Mr. Biggins." She took his hand in hers. "I'd like that very much. I think this might be the start of a beautiful friendship."

"Indeed," he said, and nodded.

———

THEY ALL PILED out of the diner, patting their bellies and complaining about how full they were. The night air was cool and heavy with a warm wind blowing in from the ocean. The sky was hazy with the moisture of rain on the way.

Karah Campobello took Troy Clint Bodean's hand and walked out into the parking lot.

"I'm gonna go be with my folks for a bit," she said, kissing him on the cheek, "and then I'll come over and we can talk."

Troy brushed a strand of auburn hair off her forehead. "Sure thing, darlin'."

He let her go and waved to her parents as they hugged again and piled into their car. He wondered why his throat felt so thick and his eyes burned. He thought maybe it was because he knew what they'd be talking about later.

"Hey, Troy," Chesney called to him, "you need a ride back to the island?"

He nodded, afraid to speak for fear he'd let out the emotion his mind was holding back.

Laura patted his shoulder, maybe sensing his struggle. They all piled into Chesney's cruiser and drove in silence back to The Turtle House. They let Troy out and waved their goodbyes.

He walked into the house just as raindrops began pattering on the metal roof. He went to the fridge and cracked open a Corona. After taking a long sip of the beer, he walked to the beachside of the house and slid open the glass door.

He stepped out onto the screened in porch and

plopped himself down into a rocking chair. He'd just about finished his beer when he saw a figure walking up the beach holding a rain jacket above their head.

Karah jogged up the steps and knocked on the screen door playfully.

"Anybody home?" she asked.

"Come on in, darlin'." He motioned her to the chair next to him.

She plopped down and shook off the drops of water clinging to her hair.

"Beer?" He held up his empty bottle and nodded back into the house.

"Definitely," she said.

He returned with two Coronas, a slice of lime in each, and handed her one and slid into the rocking chair next to her.

They sat for a long time, saying nothing and staring out at the ocean. In the distance, lightning flashed, but the storm was far away.

"So," she finally said, "I'm going back to school."

"Good idea," he replied, sipping his beer.

She was quiet again.

"You'll be okay, darlin'," he said softly. "It'll take time, but you'll be okay."

"Troy," she said, tears starting to touch her eyes, "I'm gonna miss you."

He took his hat off his head. "Karah, you're a sweet girl. You belong in college, where the future is bright and you got things to look forward to ... "

She reached out and took his hand. "I know, really I do."

"And I belong on a dock with a fishin' pole in my hand," he said, smiling, "but next time I'm wearin' a helmet."

She sniffed out a laugh and wiped her eyes, remembering the first time she'd seen him, getting wacked by the fishing boat.

"And, I'll probably come back to visit Laura during summer breaks and all," she said. "I'm sure I'll see you then."

He nodded and took a swig of beer. He didn't answer that one. He didn't have the heart to tell her he was leaving soon and wouldn't be back.

"Troy ... " she said quietly.

"Yes?"

"Can we sit on the roof again?"

"In the rain? Not much of a sunset to see tonight."

She nodded.

"Sure thing, little darlin'."

As they climbed up to the roof, the rain stopped and the stars blinked into sight. They said their goodbyes in silence.

Troy woke in the hammock under the house the next morning.

Karah had gone.

40

Check It Out Now

DAISY MAE GALLUP cradled her sleeping baby in her arms as her sister drove. Their stolen Jeep had been burned to bits by that asshat, Darren, back at Pawleys Island, but they'd been lucky enough to find another ride behind the cheesy beach store in the parking lot of a self-storage building. Daisy Mae didn't know much about cars, but she figured this one was pretty nice.

The owner's manual had told her this was a Mercedes Benz AMG G65 SUV. She had absolutely no idea what that meant, and had promptly stuffed the manual back into the glove box.

"I'm gon stop at the next gas station," Ellie Mae suddenly whispered. "I gotta pee somethin' fierce."

"Al-right," said Daisy Mae, "sounds good. I need

ta stretch out mah legs anyhow and git these shoes owff. Mah feet are swelled up like a pig in heat."

The next station turned out to be a little mom and pop place with only one pump and a unisex bathroom that looked like a deer had died in it. But when nature calls, ya gotta answer.

Ellie Mae jogged off to do her business and Daisy Mae gently laid little T.C. down in the back seat to let him nap. He was a beautiful baby, that was for sure. She thought she'd have Ellie Mae pull into the next Baby Gear store she saw and steal him a proper car seat.

She leaned back against the side of the car and pulled one of her shoes off.

"Oh, mah God, that's better'n sex," she said, scratching the bottom of her foot.

She tossed the shoe into the floorboard of the car and pulled the other one off. As she did, a piece of paper that must've been stuck to the bottom of her shoe fluttered away and landed at her feet.

"What's 'is 'en?"

She bent down to pick up the paper and unfolded it to read it. Her eyes went wide and nearly popped out of her head.

Ellie Mae Gallup returned to the car and slumped into the driver's seat.

"Whew, dang," she said and started the car, "that was a close one. I dang near peed on tha flah."

Daisy Mae said nothing. She just let out a squeal and handed a piece of paper to her sister.

Ellie Mae's eyebrows furrowed and her lip curled up. "What's got inta you, sis?" she said, unfolding the paper.

"Just read it."

Ellie Mae read the paper, sounding out each word much like a child pronouncing each letter several times to make sure she got it right.

"Certified C ... Ca ... Cashier's Check ... " Her voice trailed off. She returned Daisy Mae's wide-eyed stare. "Ho-lee sheeee-ittt!"

As the Mercedes Benz AMG G65 SUV squealed back onto the highway, the crotchety old gas station couple could hear shouts of *YEEEEEEHAWWWWW* all the way until the car cleared the horizon.

Epilogue
OCEAN BLUE

Troy Clint Bodean closed and locked the door to The Turtle House for the last time. He slid the key into a drop box and tipped his hat to the old place. It wasn't his home for very long, but it had earned a special place in his heart.

He clomped down to the red and white Chevy S10 pickup truck in the carport and flung his army duffle bag into the passenger's seat. He slid the key into the steering column and stopped.

He had no idea where he was going. Maybe farther south. Florida, or something like that. He hadn't been to Florida.

With three cranks, the S10 finally sputtered to life. He turned the radio on and twisted the dial until he found something suitable by the Eagles.

As he crossed the causeway over to the mainland, his phone chirped to life. He didn't recognize the number, so he let it go to voicemail. It took almost five minutes for the caller to finish the message and the notification to hit the screen.

"Jiminy Cricket," Troy said aloud, punching in his PIN to play back the message.

"Troy Clint Bodean," the caller started, "I hope this is you. It's R.B."

Troy almost dropped the phone.

R.B.

Ryan Bodean.

His brother.

"Hey, bro," he continued, "I know it's been a long time and I know I kinda disappeared without giving you a proper explanation, and one day, I promise I'll tell you that story. But right now, I need a pilot!"

Troy reached the traffic signal at Ocean Highway. It was red. He pulled to a stop.

"I've just bought a seaplane business. It's a tourist-y kind of thing, flying people around the Keys. Look at the seashells, look at the waves, blah, blah, blah. Easy shit like that. And the money's amazing!"

Troy huffed to himself.

"Anyway, I just lost my co-pilot and I've got trips on the schedule for this weekend. So, get your ass down here A.S.A.P.!"

R.B. left the address and hung up.

The light changed to green. Troy didn't move. He just stared out the window. A minivan full of screaming kids honked twice and he startled out of his shock. He put on his blinker and turned left, heading south.

He cranked up the Eagles and rolled his window down.

"Cayo hueso," he said as he turned, "here comes Troy."

THE END

TURN THE PAGE TO CONTINUE THE ADVENTURE

Ocean Blue
A TROY BODEAN TROPICAL THRILLER #2

Deep in the water off the Key West coast...

A submerged shadow catches Troy Bodean's eye.

Treasure? Shipwreck? Government drone shot out of the sky?

Troy Bodean is back and flying a seaplane for his brother's Key West tourist ferry to Fort Jefferson. And then he sees it... a shadow deep in the water. Dreams of treasure, fortune, and fame begin to fill his head. He launches a secret salvage operation to bring up the mysterious find. And that's when everyone started trying to kill him.

In a race against time with a hurricane bearing down on the gulf and all the shadowy forces vying to stop him and take his treasure, Troy Bodean is at it again in Ocean Blue.

Find out what comes up from the deep and if Troy will live to enjoy the bounty.

GET Your Copy of Ocean Blue NOW!

Afterword

I owe a tremendous debt to all the people in my family who kept urging and asking for this completed novel. Some of these characters are based on real people we met while playing cards and watching it rain one fateful vacation on Pawleys Island. If it hadn't been for Tropical Storm Debby giving us a rainy vacation, none of this would've ever happened.

Special thanks to Kelly, Sarah, Robert, Linda, Jay, Debbie, and Laura, who continually helped me create characters out of thin air and give them life on the page. And thank you to my early readers who helped me catch errors of grammar and plot and other things.

Thanks be to God for my ability, judge as you may, to create these stories and record them for your enjoyment. And, if you happen to recognize yourself in one of these characters, enjoy it for what it is ... all good fun.

I sincerely hope you've enjoyed this first installment of the Troy Bodean Tropical Thriller Series. I had an amazing time writing it, and as I typed the last few lines, I knew I'd be back for more.

Please be sure to visit TropicalThrillers.com and join the BeachBum Brigade Reader Group so you'll be among the first to know about my promotions, events and specials!

Thank you,

Also by David Berens

If you'd like to stay up-to-date with all of the latest from David Berens, be sure to join the BeachBum Brigade.

JOIN HERE: www.tropicalthrillers.com/ if you haven't already.

Troy Bodean Tropical Thrillers

- #0 Tidal Wave (available FREE exclusively to the BeachBum Brigade Reader Group)
- #1 Hat Check
- #2 Ocean Blue
- #3 Blight House
- #4 Stealing Savannah
- #5 Skull Island
- #6 Shark Bait
- #7 Dead End (Short Story)
- #8 Gator Bite

Hat Check

A Troy Bodean Tropical Thriller #1
All Rights Reserved © 2017 by David F. Berens

No part of this book may be reproduced or transmitted in any
form or by any means, graphic, electronic, or mechanical,
including photocopying, recording, taping or by any information
storage retrieval system, without the written permission of the
publisher.

Tropical Thrillers Press 2017

Printed in The United States of America

Contact the Author at:
www.TropicalThrillers.com

This book is a work of fiction. Names, characters, businesses,
places, events and incidents are either the products of the author's
imagination or used in a fictitious manner. Any resemblance to
actual persons, living or dead, or actual events is purely
coincidental.

Made in the USA
Monee, IL
25 September 2021

78289499R00236